FUN HOUSE

FUN HOUSE

A JOHN CEEPAK MYSTERY

Chris Grabenstein

PEGASUS CRIME
NEW YORK

FUN HOUSE

Pegasus Books LLC
80 Broad Street, 5th Floor
New York, NY 10004

First Pegasus Books cloth edition 2011

Interior design by Maria Fernandez

Library of Congress Cataloging-in-Publication Data is available.

ISBN: 978-1-60598-336-3

10 9 8 7 6 5 4 3 2 1

Printed in the United States of America
Distributed by W. W. Norton & Company, Inc.

For

Philadelphia Police Officer Daniel R. Boyle (1970–1991)
and all the brave men and women
who daily risk their lives
to keep us safe.

FUN HOUSE

1

HE WASN'T HAPPY ABOUT IT, BUT LAST NIGHT MY PARTNER John Ceepak became a TV star.

Maybe you caught his act on YouTube this morning. The video snip of his guest appearance on the reality TV show *Fun House* already has like two million hits. Ceepak, the one guy in America who could not care less about being famous, now is.

And it's sort of my fault.

Back in June, at the all-new, all-wood Rolling Thunder roller coaster, I met a girl named Layla Shapiro. She's my age, just turned twenty-six. Very sexy, very sassy. Turns out Layla (yes, her parents really dug that old Eric Clapton song) was visiting Sea Haven—our sunny resort town down the Jersey Shore—over Memorial Day weekend because she was scouting locations for Prickly Pear Productions, this Hollywood outfit that shoots crap for television like *Hot Dog* (an animal-talent competition), *Hot Tub* (something to do with blindfolded strangers finding true love), *Hot Mommas* (housewives picking the perfect pool boy), and *Hot Plumbers of Brooklyn*. Okay, I made that last one up.

Fun House is Prickly Pear's newest, most original creation. For one thing, it's their first show without the word "Hot" in the title.

"Think *Jersey Shore* meets *Big Brother* meets *Survivor*," said Layla when she described the show to me on our first date. Ten twenty-somethings (five guys and five girls), who are "totally into" tanning, gym-ing, and boozing get crammed into a cheesy rental house a block from the boardwalk. Fun ensues. They have weekly competitions, hook up with each other, drink booze, hook up some more, drink more booze, and then, at the end of the summer, the last drunk standing wins two hundred and fifty thousand bucks.

Ceepak's star turn came during last night's Skee-Ball competition or, since this is *Fun House*, their *Brew*skee-Ball tournament.

I wasn't there when the cameras were rolling, but Ceepak filled me in over breakfast at the Pancake Palace. Plus I have his YouTube moment on my iPod.

Here's what went down:

Tuesday night is family game night at the Ceepak household. But the first week of August is way too hot to stay inside playing Parcheesi without air-conditioning. So Ceepak and his wife, Rita, head over to the Coin Castle on Pier One to amuse themselves.

Unfortunately, they decide to roll a few frames of Skee-Ball, which is sort of like bowling on a ten-foot-long inclined lane but, instead of knocking down pins, you try to whirl your polished wooden ball up a ramp into a series of scoring holes. You get ten points for the easy hole, twenty for the next easiest, and so on up to the fifty-pointer, which is maybe a millimeter wider than your baseball-sized Skee-Ball. When your turn's up, the machine spits out raffle tickets matching your score, which you can trade in for prizes—once you have like a billion of them.

I say Skee-Ball was an unfortunate choice for the Ceepaks because that same night, the rowdy boozers from *Fun House* stumble into the Coin Castle with their camera crews to play the same game and, being blasted on brewskis, make lame "Hey, check out my balls" jokes to each other.

On lane six, Paulie Braciole, the guy who calls himself "The Thing" and is always pulling up his T-shirt to flash his buff bod (he can make his pecs wiggle), is losing to Mike Tomasino, the one who likes to gel his hair with something stronger than Elmer's Glue so he can blow-dry it up into what looks like a very stiff Burger King birthday crown.

In between frames, Paulie and Mike slam back beers, including several cans funneled directly into their mouths via a beer-bong hose. Two of the girls, short-but-top-heavy Soozy K and the trashy one with all the tattoos who calls herself Jenny Mortadella, are cheering them on. I think Soozy K and The Thing are an item. I know they've been hung over together in the hot tub. That was on Episode One, which ran a month ago, the first Thursday in July.

Anyway, Paulie doesn't think his machine is playing fair because Mike has ten times more tickets than he does.

"It's rigged," Paulie snarls at the camera, veins, tendons, and muscles roping in his neck. "My ball-hop is dented."

The ball-hop is a ski-jump ramp at the end of the lane that launches the Skee-Balls up into the ring zone.

"That's lame," says Mike.

"What's lame?"

"Blaming the ball-hop, dude."

"So? You're lamer."

I don't think they hire real writers for reality TV, so the dialogue is never what you might call snappy or punchy.

"Your balls stink, Paulie," shouts Jenny Mortadella. She and Mike Tomasino have an alliance, another thing that's always good to have on reality TV shows involving competitions. Means you can stab the other contestants in the back until it's time to stab each other.

When Jenny says that, Paulie, of course, gets furious. His face, which is already bright orange from when he passed out in the *Fun House* tanning bed (Episode Two), goes all the way to Oompa-Loompa.

"Shut up, bitch!" On TV, it comes out "Shut up, BLEEP." The *Fun House* kids talk trash all the time, so their show has more beeps than dialing a phone call to China.

"Who you calling a BLEEP, BLEEP?" says Jenny.

"You, you BLEEPING BLEEP." At this point, Paulie Braciole hikes up his muscle-man T-shirt to wiggle his nipples. "You see this bod? I am The Thing you want. The Thing you need."

"I think I'm going to puke," said Jenny. And she means it. Not because her obnoxious housemate is wiggling his tuning knobs at her. No, she's done a few too many Jell-O shots.

She races off camera.

When the camera swings right to follow her, it picks up Ceepak two lanes down, with Rita. He's off-duty, so he's dressed in his civilian clothes, which look an awful lot like his uniform clothes except the cargo pants on his days off are khaki-colored and the polo shirt is white instead of navy blue.

Since I know Ceepak pretty well (he's been my partner on the SHPD for a couple years now), it's easy for me to read the expression on his face when it flashes across the frame: agonized disappointment. His family's old-fashioned game-night fun is being ruined by an unanticipated invasion of reality-show drunks and their ever-present camera crews.

Ceepak, of course, knows a thing or two about invasions. He's a former MP who served in Operation Iraqi Freedom and won just about every medal a soldier can and still come home alive. He moved to Sea Haven when an old Army buddy offered him a break from the mayhem of war with a "quiet, peaceful police job" down the Jersey Shore.

There is no peace or quiet in the Coin Castle.

The loudmouths two lanes down are starting to work Ceepak's last nerve. Since he still keeps his hair high and tight in a military brush cut, it's easy to see his jaw joint popping in and out near his ear.

My partner is a six-two tower of power with more muscles than The Thing, but he very rarely pulls up his T-shirt unless he needs to tear it off to rip it into a tourniquet. One time, over in Iraq, when his convoy stopped in a Sunni neighborhood south of Kirkuk, a roadside bomb went off and all hell broke loose. Ceepak lost his T-shirt and one leg of his pants making improvised bandages for two of his buddies. Ceepak, of course, never told me about his heroic actions; I found the story doing a Google search on him.

The camera swings back to Paulie and Mike.

Mike is hooting and pumping his fist because his Skee-Ball machine just spewed out another long strip of raffle tickets.

"Screw this," says Paulie. He scoops up a bunch of wooden balls and cradles them against his chest. He hops up onto the machine so he can march up the ramp toward the scoring holes.

"Yo," says Mike. "What you doin'?"

"Beating you, bro!" Paulie starts stuffing balls down the 50 hole. The scoreboard dings and dongs. Digital numbers flips like crazy. "Yo, Soozy. Toss me some more balls!"

Soozy K giggles and jiggles. The girl, who probably wore a bikini top to her high school prom, has lots to jiggle. Some of it, I'm sure, is the original equipment; the rest looks like a pair of inflatable water wings sewn in under her skin.

"Who's BLEEPING winning now, BLEEP?" Paulie screams as Soozy tosses balls up to him. He slam-dunks like a maniac.

"Yo," says Mike. "That's cheating!"

"This is Skee-Ball, BLEEP. There are no BLEEPING rules!"

Ceepak is off camera, but I figure he's crinkling his eyes down into narrow slits when Paulie says that, because John Ceepak lives his life in strict compliance with the West Point honor code: he will not lie, cheat, steal, or tolerate those who do.

"BLEEP you," says Mike as he climbs up on *his* machine. Totally wasted, he slips on the slick surface, falls backward, and bangs his head. Hard.

"Omigod," gasps Soozy. "He's BLEEPING bleeding!"

A camera zooms in on Mike as he sits in his Skee-Ball lane, holding the back of his head.

"He's BLEEPING bleeding!" Soozy shouts again. Then she burps.

"Who gives a BLEEP?" says Paulie, who discovers he can just jam his arm in and out of the fifty hole to ring up more points.

That's when Ceepak enters the frame. The camera is behind him, so you can't see his face, just his buzz cut. First, he pulls a sterile gauze pack out of the hip pocket of his cargo pants and tosses it to Mike Tomasino.

"Apply that to your head wound, sir."

Next he whips out his SHPD badge and calls out to Paulie.

"Sir?"

Paulie, who has his back to Ceepak, totally ignores him. Keeps pumping his fist in and out of the fifty hole. Bells ring. Whistles whoop.

"Sir?" Ceepak raises his voice. "Sea Haven Police."

"Where?" Finally, the drunken muscleman swirls around. One last wooden ball is gripped in his right fist.

"Please climb down off the Skee-Ball machine."

"Why?"

"You are drunk, sir."

"So? It's the Jersey Shore. Everybody's BLEEPING drunk."

"I'm not, I assure you," says Ceepak.

"Aw, BLEEP you, you BLEEPING BLEEP wipe."

"Please step down from the Skee-Ball machine, sir."

Believe it or not, instead of doing as officially instructed, Paulie tugs up his T-shirt again. Points at his rippling man breasts. "Yo? You see this? I am The Thing you wish you could be."

"No, sir. You are not. You are drunk and disorderly. You are also in direct violation of several municipal codes, not to mention the rules of fair Skee-Ball competition."

In the background, I hear police sirens racing toward the boardwalk. I'm guessing Rita, Ceepak's wife, had dialed 9-1-1 while Ceepak marched over to deal with The Real Idiots Of New Jersey.

Ceepak turns to Mike Tomasino, who is moaning and groaning, pressing the patch of gauze to the back of his head, trying not to ruin his up-do.

"Keep applying pressure to the wound, sir," says Ceepak. "Paramedics are on the way."

More bells ding and dong. Somebody has hit a jackpot.

Ceepak and the camera swing back to Paulie's lane. He is, once again, jamming his arm in and out of the fifty hole.

"Sir?"

"What?"

"Cease and desist."

Paulie spins around.

"BEEP you, jarhead!"

And he chucks that wooden ball straight at Ceepak's head.

2

REFLEXES?

Ceepak's got 'em.

He makes this incredible Mr. Miyagi, *Karate Kid* move. Up flips his left arm. Fingers splay out. Palm springs open.

Boom!

Without flinching, he snags the hard wooden ball in midair, two inches away from his eye.

Clutching it with a very firm grip, he addresses Paulie Braciole: "Now we need to add assaulting a police officer to your list of infractions."

"BLEEP you, you BLEEPING BLEEP," says Paulie, reciting what I like to call the New Jersey state motto, even though he's from Staten Island, which is in New York even if it wishes it could be in Jersey.

"You're not a police officer!" screams Soozy K, rallying to her muscleman's defense. She plucks at Ceepak's polo shirt. "This isn't a police uniform. My dad's a cop." Only when she says it, it comes out "My dashahop" because she's been mixing her vodka and beer again. She did it on Episode Two, too. Fell face-first into some kid's sand castle. Took out two towers, crushed the moat. Ended up with a bright yellow plastic sand shovel stuck between her boobs.

This is when the cops working the Tuesday night shift show up. Dylan and Jeremy, the Murray brothers, storm into the Coin Castle. Jen Forbus and Nikki Bonanni are right behind them. They all got their pictures in the *New York Post* Wednesday, slapping on the cuffs, stuffing The Thing and Soozy K into the back of police cars.

"Leave me the BLEEP alone, your BLEEPING po-po!" Paulie screamed as he thrashed between the two Murrays. It took both of them to haul his chiseled butt out of the arcade. Dylan told me later that the guy was in such a rage, it felt like they were wrestling with Dr. Bruce Banner in the middle of morphing into the Incredible Hulk.

Jen and Nikki dealt with Suzy K, who went ballistic when one of the female cops dared touch the top of her bullet-shaped hair to help her scrunch down into the back of their cop car. Apparently, her Conehead hair bubble is her trademark.

"You guys make good TV," says Marty Mandrake, head of Prickly Pear Productions and the brains (I use that term loosely) behind *Fun House*.

It's Friday afternoon, August 6. We're in the chief's office at police headquarters, watching the raw footage of The Thing and Soozy K being taken into custody on a TV monitor built into the chief's manly mahogany bookcase.

"We're gonna open next week's episode with this next shot," says Mandrake. "Wait for it."

We see the two Murray brothers hauling a very wiggly, very wired Paulie Braciole out of the Coin Castle. His head looks ready to explode. "Fuck you, you fucking fucks!" he screams at the camera.

They haven't had time to edit in the bleeps.

"Boom!" says Mandrake. "I love that shot. This one, too. This one is gold." Soozy K's official SHPD mug shot fills the screen. "You see that mascara running down her cheeks? The tracks of her tears. We'll slug in the old Motown tune!"

"All right," says Chief Baines. "That's enough."

Mandrake presses a button on a remote. The video stops.

The chief, who looks like a handsome TV anchorman back in the days when they all wore mustaches, plucks at his lip hair. He is not happy to be having this meeting.

"Just wanted to give you a preview of coming attractions," says Mandrake. He's a big, burly bear with a beer gut who wears a baseball cap with a prickly pear cactus stitched where the team logo should be. Sporting a white goatee, a purple velour tracksuit, high-end Nikes, and sproingy black-and-white eyebrows, I'm guessing he's pushing sixty even if he dresses like he's barely twenty.

"By the way," says Mandrake, "have you boys seen the overnights?" He snaps open his sleek Italian leather briefcase to retrieve a sheaf of papers. I know it's Italian leather because he told everybody it was, the last time we had one of these "Production Meetings." I also know it cost eleven hundred bucks because it's a Salvatore Ferragamo, which, I think, is a very rare breed of Italian cow.

"The overnights?" says Ceepak. "What are those?"

"The ratings! From last night's show!" This from our mayor, Hugh Sinclair, who is a big booster of *Fun House* because, according to him and his crack team of economists (three kids from the high school math club interning at Borough Hall for advance placement college credits), having the TV show filming in Sea Haven is pumping bajillions of dollars into the local economy. I know the local liquor distributors are happy. The kids crammed into the rental house on Halibut Street have single-handedly doubled beer sales.

"Our numbers are through the roof!" says Mandrake.

Layla Shapiro, who is an associate producer on *Fun House,* rounds out the meeting. She's sharp, funny, and smart. Back in June, she also helped me take down a nutjob toting a tactical shotgun, so I like her a lot more than anybody else associated with *Fun House,* which even straight-arrow Ceepak calls *Dumb House* when the chief's not around.

"Boys," says Mandrake, "'Skee-Ball' pulled in five point three million viewers last night. That's two hundred percent higher than where we were for Episode Five last Thursday. After *ET, TMZ,* and *Access Hollywood* hyped the episode, everybody in America just had to tune in to see the local cop making his Miyagi moves."

He does a quick "whoosh-whoosh" impersonation of Ceepak catching the flying wooden orb barehanded, adding in a sideways leg kick, because he works in reality TV, so that means he likes to take what really happened and punch it up a bit.

"Hey, Chief," says Mayor Sinclair, "have you seen this?"

He pulls a T-shirt out of a shopping bag. *"Step down from the Skee-Ball machine, sir,"* is printed in neon green letters across the chest.

"It's going to be huge!" says Mandrake. "We have a tie-in with Kmart. Going national this weekend and—you're gonna love this—we're going to donate two percent of the net profits to your Widows and Children Fund. You guys have one of those, right?"

"Sure, we do," says the mayor. "Right, chief? We've got Widows and Children?"

Baines nods grimly. "Yeah." He doesn't add that Ceepak has just started a scholarship fund to help take care of the late Dominic Santucci's family. Santucci died working security at that Rolling Thunder roller coaster. It's a long story. Remind me, I'll tell you sometime.

"Your offer is very generous," says Ceepak, "but, Mr. Mandrake, I am most concerned about making certain that Mr. Braciole and Ms. Kemppainen appear in court to face the charges pending against them."

Soozy K? Her real name is Susan Kemppainen. Figures she'd take the rapper route and go with the initial-for-a-last-name.

"Assault with a deadly weapon is a very serious offense," Ceepak continues.

"It wasn't a weapon, John," says Mayor Sinclair sarcastically. "It was a Skee-Ball."

"Made out of solid wood," I toss in.

"And," adds Chief Baines, "it was thrown at an off-duty police officer who had clearly identified himself."

The chief tugs a few more hairs out of his lip caterpillar. The man is conflicted. His boss, the mayor, wants the SHPD to roll over and play nice with the TV people. But people can't chuck projectiles at police officers and not suffer the consequences, which, in New Jersey, would be a maximum sentence of five years. And our state prisons don't have tanning beds. I think the new governor cut them out of the budget, along with everything else.

"Look," says Layla, calming the whole room with her sparkling brown eyes.

Okay. Maybe I'm exaggerating. We've dated a couple times. I'm biased. Let's just say she's a refreshing change of pace from Mandrake and his Italian leather briefcase.

"Everyone at Prickly Pear Productions wants to see justice done," she continues. When Layla speaks, you can tell she went to college—the real deal with ivy on the walls, not Junior College, like me. "Paul and Susan must answer for their actions."

Heads start nodding around the room.

"We only ask that you hold off a few weeks; delay their indictments until after Labor Day."

Which would be after *Fun House* finishes filming in Sea Haven.

"This show is very good for us," says Mayor Sinclair, using his public-servant-looking-out-for-the-little-people voice. "I don't have to remind anyone in this room that these are tough economic times. Our local merchants are suffering—especially after you two scared away so many potential tourists with your shootout at the O.K. Corral."

He flips a hand toward Ceepak and me. I think the honorable Hugh Sinclair is referring to us saving a bunch of lives when things turned ugly at the grand opening of the Rolling Thunder.

"Heck," he continues, shifting into his Ronald Reagan aw-shucks mode, "five point three million Americans seeing these fun-loving college kids having a sunny, funderful day every Thursday night?" Now the mayor is biting his lip like he's choking himself up. "Chief, it's summer in America again."

"Ceepak?" Chief Baines peers at my partner.

Ceepak sighs. "If the county prosecutor agrees to delay processing formal charges until—"

"Excellent!" says Mandrake. "And I agree with Officer Ceepak. We need to keep our cast on a shorter leash."

Um, Ceepak never mentioned leashes, long, short, or in-between.

"Chief Baines, I want to work closer with you guys moving forward. These two officers, Ceepak and Boyle, are already linked to the show. . . ."

Layla shoots me a wink. I think she's the only thing linking me to *Fun House,* even though, for the record, we have not actually "linked up." Not yet, anyway. Our third date is slated for later tonight. After she wraps. That's a movie term. Has nothing to do with sandwiches or flour tortillas.

"How about they head up an SHPD *Fun House* security detail? You have people with us 24/7."

"That's a major manpower commitment," says Chief Baines.

"It's in our budget," says Layla. "We'll pay overtime rates. Officers Ceepak and Boyle set up the security team. Assign officers. The LAPD does this all the time. In fact, they even have a special Film Unit."

"Interesting idea," says Chief Baines, smoothing what's left of his mustache back into place. "We could reach out to some of our retirees. Guys like Gus Davis and Alex Smitten who could use a little extra income."

Mandrake claps his hands. "Bingo. I like it. What size T-shirt do Davis and Smitten wear?"

"I'd, of course, work closely with you guys," says Layla, sweetening the deal for me, if not the happily married Ceepak.

"The show needs you, men," says Mandrake, pacing around the room with his hands clasped behind his back. He'd look like a general in his tent the night before a big battle if he weren't wearing the goofy baseball cap and neon-colored shoestrings on his Nikes. "We're on an extremely tight, almost live, production schedule. Most reality shows shoot for months, edit for months, go on air half a year after they finish filming. Us? We shoot Friday through Tuesday, edit all day Wednesday into Thursday morning, satellite the finished show up to the network on Thursday afternoon, go on air Thursday night at nine. Keeps us fresh. If we can keep the cast out of trouble. . . ."

"And out of jail," jokes Mayor Sinclair, even though, as always, nobody's paying attention to him.

"If we can avoid any future speed bumps, it'll help me guarantee an on-time product."

"I'm not sure," says Ceepak. "As you stated, Chief, this 'security detail' would put quite a strain on the department. It might adversely impact our ability to provide police services during the peak of the township's summer season."

"Not if we deal with it on an overtime-only basis with everybody but you two," suggests the chief.

"But we'd still pay you two the overtime rates," adds Mandrake. "That's part of the deal. Definitely."

"This isn't about the money," says Ceepak.

Mandrake laughs—derisively, I think they call it. "Officer? It's always about the money. Am I right?"

The mayor laughs. Layla chuckles. Hey, the guy's her boss. She has to.

Me, the chief, and Ceepak? Statues on Easter Island smile more.

Ceepak repeats himself. "It is not about the money, Mr. Mandrake."

"Okay. Forget the money," says Mandrake, reaching into his briefcase yet again. "You guys should do it to protect my kids."

Ceepak arches an eyebrow. "Protect them? From what?"

"Drug dealers."

He holds up a tiny glass vial, the kind doctors use when giving you a shot. There's a small sticker glued on the front. Instead of the usual medical mumbo-jumbo, I see a comic-book illustration of a purple muscleman in a hood and loincloth. His head is a skull.

"Might I see that ampule, Mr. Mandrake?" says Ceepak.

Mandrake hands him the small glass container. "The crew found a bunch just like it when they had to move a couple mattresses in the house to set up a shot."

"What is it?" I ask.

"Anabolic steroids," says Mandrake, striking a bodybuilder pose, pumping his chicken wings, pretending he has muscles.

"From Skeletor," adds Ceepak.

3

Last summer, Ceepak and I almost died when this boarded-up ride called the Hell Hole started burning down around us.

Despite the dilapidated old ride's name, the blaze, or, to quote the newspapers, the "roiling inferno," was caused by an arsonist, not Beelzebub pitchforking up brimstone from the basement.

We had crawled into the shuttered ride to rescue a couple of junkies shooting up something called "Hot Stuff Heroin," which was being sold by a homegrown Sea Haven drug dealer who calls himself Skeletor, because, according to our sources, he has a thing for the villain from the 1980s "He-Man: Masters Of The Universe" cartoons.

Skeletor, in the animated episodes—and action figure aisle at Toys "R" Us—was a purple muscleman in a hood and loincloth who had a skull for a head.

The cartoon on the steroid bottle? It's him.

And branding his drugs with cartoons? That's him, too. "Hot Stuff," the little red devil from the old Harvey comic books, was plastered all over Skeletor's white paper heroin bags, the evidence that led us to the Hell Hole ride.

Ceepak and the SHPD, plus a joint federal/state government task force, have been trying to locate and apprehend Skeletor for nearly two years. He and his gang are responsible for most of the drug traffic up and down our eighteen-mile-long barrier island, not to mention the rest of the Jersey Shore.

Needless to say, we haven't caught him.

As soon as we figure out where he's set up shop, he disappears. He's like a ghost or one of those Al Qaeda dudes hiding in their Pakistani caves: always one step ahead of the law and/or the drones.

"Mr. Mandrake, Ms. Shapiro, Mayor Sinclair?" says Ceepak. "Can you please give us the room? Danny and I need to discuss your security detail proposition with Chief Baines."

"Sure, sure," says Mandrake, snapping shut his briefcase.

The mayor sidles over to schmooze the producer. "By the way, Marty, my son, who looks great on video, wanted me to ask you—"

"We can discuss that outside," says Layla, ushering everybody to the door. "You have our phone numbers?"

"Yeah," I say because I do. Well, I have hers, not Mandrake's or the Mayor's. I'm not really into sixty-year-old guys with Billy Goat Gruff beards or anybody who says "Have a sunny, funderful day" on a regular basis.

"Come on," Mandrake says to Layla, fiddling with his iPhone. "We're behind schedule. We need to be shooting the beer pong competition."

Layla smiles at us. "Thank you gentlemen for your time."

"My son is quite good at beer pong," I hear the mayor say as their voices fade away.

"How old is he?" asks Layla.

"Sixteen. . . ."

I close the door and turn around to face Ceepak and the chief.

"What do you think, John?" says Baines.

"I am, of course, conflicted."

"Yeah," I say because I haven't had breakfast and I know there are doughnuts in the break room but an egg, pork roll, and cheese sandwich would stay with me longer.

"Skeletor," says Ceepak.

"Yeah," says the chief.

Ceepak tosses the little steroid vial up and down in his hand like a glass peanut. Normally, he'd be whipping out his stainless steel forceps and tweezering the tiny bottle into an evidence bag so he could have it dusted for prints and scanned for whatever he could scan it for. But since the *Fun House* production crew found this particular piece of evidence under a seedy mattress in a skeevy party house, it's probably way beyond compromised as far as offering us any useable clues.

"This could be the break we've been waiting for," says the chief.

"Indeed," says Ceepak. "However, we may be forced into an ethical compromise."

Oh, boy. Ceepak's not too keen on those.

"We could offer Mr. Braciole and Ms. Kemppainen a deal," suggests the chief. "They help us nab Skeletor, we drop the charges."

Ceepak nods. "It's a possibility."

Wow. He's actually considering it.

"The county prosecutor cuts deals all the time, John," says the chief. "Sometimes, to catch the big fish, you have to let the little ones off the hook."

Ceepak nods some more. Yes, he lives his life in strict compliance with a rigid moral code and people call him an overgrown Eagle Scout. But hey, this isn't his first rodeo, as they say, even though I'm not sure why they say it. Ceepak knows how the game is played: we don't indict Paulie and Soozy on the drunk and disorderly, they give up Skeletor. We let two shrimps skate free to land the big tuna. I'm trying to work with the chief's fish metaphor here.

"I'm not asking you to lie, cheat, or steal, John. Just to take advantage of the first lead we've had on this guy in ages."

Ceepak thinks. Nods. "Talk to the county prosecutor. See how she wants to play it."

"You on board if she says cut the deal?"

"Yes, sir."

"You sure?"

"Roger that."

"What about the other thing?"

"Babysitting *Fun House*?"

"Yeah. What do you think?"

"The more time we spend with the reality show cast and crew, the more information we stand to pick up on Skeletor."

"And," says the chief, "maybe we can stop another one of those yahoos from passing out on top of some poor kid's sand castle."

Chief Baines. Always the dreamer.

"We'll head over to the TV house," Ceepak tells the chief. "Start interviewing the residents."

"I'll contact the county prosecutor. And John?"

"Sir?"

"Try to stay off camera."

Ceepak grins a little. "That'll work."

As we head out the door, I remember what Dylan Murray said about Paulie Braciole when they processed him here at the house. His screaming, his face going bright orange, his neck tendons tightening up like thick cables.

"Roid rage," I mumble.

"Come again?" says Ceepak.

"Paul Braciole. Dylan Murray and his brother were the ones who hauled the guy out of the Coin Castle. Said 'The Thing' was more like 'The Hulk.'"

Ceepak stops in his tracks. Ruminates. "Roid rage. Acting in an overly aggressive, hostile manner after taking large doses of anabolic steroids. Manifesting symptoms of schizophrenia, mania. . . ."

"Tossing Skee-Balls at cops' heads."

"An interesting hypothesis, Danny. As you know, many bodybuilders often turn to the synthetic version of the male hormone testosterone as a shortcut to boost their muscle mass."

Yeah, steroids may make your muscles swell but, from what I hear, they also make other things, such as the family jewels, shrivel down to the size of wrinkled peas. They pump you up, but let you (and your lady friend) down.

"We'll talk to Paul Braciole first," says Ceepak. "Good work, Danny."

"Thanks."

When we hit the lobby, Dorian Rence, our dispatcher, waves Ceepak over to her cubicle.

"Your mother called. From Ohio." Mrs. Rence hands him a pink message slip. "She saw you on TV last night."

"Really? I did not know that she was a fan of the show."

"Her church friends told her you were going to be on."

Ceepak grins. Tucks the message slip into his pocket.

"Oh, and an Officer Vic Daniels from the Elyria Police Department called." She hands Ceepak another piece of pink paper.

"Thank you."

"That's up there in Ohio?"

"Yes, ma'am."

"Officer Daniels, he's the same one who called last week. He need help on a case?"

"Something like that. Anything else?"

"No, you're all clear."

"Anything for me, Mrs. Rence?" I ask. We all call her Mrs. Rence because she looks like your best friend's mom.

"No, Danny, sorry. Oh, that Layla Shapiro who signed in earlier, that's the girl who helped you at the Rolling Thunder, am I right?"

"Yeah. She's with the TV show. *Fun House*."

"She's cute."

"Thanks."

Mrs. Rence gives me a quizzical look.

"Danny and Ms. Shapiro have been dating," says Ceepak to clear up any confusion as to why I would say thank you for a compliment directed at someone else.

"Oh!" says Mrs. Rence. "You're not with Samantha Starky anymore?"

"No."

"Well, what about that other one?"

"No," I say, even though I have no idea what "other one" she's talking about. To be honest, there've been a few.

"Oh," she says. "Well, be careful out there."

"Will do," says Ceepak. "Danny?" He bobs his head toward the door.

We head out the exit, go down the porch steps, and swing around back to the parking lot to pick up our Crown Vic police cruiser.

"You want to drive?" I ask, fishing the keys out of my pocket.

"Negative."

I can tell: Ceepak wants to use the ride over to the rental house on Halibut Street to ruminate some more. Formulate his line of questioning for Paul Braciole.

"So," I say after we slide into the car. "That Officer Daniels up in Ohio—he offering you a job or something?"

I add a "heh-heh-heh" to let him know I'm joking.

Ceepak turns. Looks at me.

"Yes, Danny. Officer Daniels, a high school classmate of mine, is reaching out on behalf of the Lorain County Sheriff's Department. They're interested in me becoming their new chief of detectives."

I nod. Swallow. "Good salary?"

"Yes. With an excellent benefits package. Plus, my mother, as you might recall, lives in Lorain County, Ohio. I'd be moving home."

Ceepak.

The guy will not tell a lie—even when you wish he just would.

4

We're cruising north on Ocean Avenue.

I'm behind the wheel; Ceepak's working the radio. By the time we hit Cap'n Scrubby's Car Wash at Swordfish Street, Ceepak and the desk sergeant have just about worked out a duty roster for *Fun House*'s enhanced security detail.

"We offer shifts to off-duty personnel only," Ceepak reiterates.

"And retirees," Sergeant Pettus crackles back through the radio.

"Roger that. Reach out to Gus Davis. He can help you put together a list of names."

"On it."

"Tell everybody it's an eyes-and-ears assignment only. They see something, sense trouble, they radio it in. On-duty SHPD personnel respond in an appropriate manner."

"It'll take me about an hour to make the calls."

"Appreciate it, Reggie."

"No problem. Hey, this gig will sure beat my side job unloading ice cream pallets at the Acme."

"10-4," says Ceepak.

It's true. Most cops have to work a second job—carpenter, plumber, supermarket loading dock schlub—on their days off to make ends meet. At least half of the SHPD's eighty-some cops will jump at the chance for a ton of easy overtime pay babysitting the TV show. And Prickly Pear Productions is picking up the tab. It's what they call a win-win situation. Unless, of course, The Thing starts chucking Skee-Balls at you or, worse, wiggling his nips in your face.

Ceepak reracks the radio mic.

"Take Kipper," he says when we pass King Putt miniature golf.

I flick on my turn signal.

Even though the Fun House is up on Halibut Street, the production offices are in trailers and Winnebagos lining Kipper and John Dory streets. The streets in this part of the island are all named after fish; farther south, you get trees. After that, the Sea Haven Street Naming Commission just sort of gave up and started going with the alphabet and numbers. There's even a "Street Street" way down near the southern tip. I think the Commission was meeting over at the Frosty Mug during happy hour when they made that particular decision.

A young Class I SHPD officer in a glo-stick green fluorescent vest waves at us. He's a summer cop, like I used to be back when I first met Ceepak. The department already has four "seasonal hires" working traffic control in the blocks surrounding 102 Halibut Street, the rundown rental where the TV kids are spending the summer.

The house on Halibut is one of the butt-uglier ones on the island: a one-story house that looks like a three-story bungalow because it's propped up on top of a two-car garage and has a triangle-roofed bedroom up where the attic used to be. To get to the main floor, you have to hike up a set of rickety wooden steps lined with PVC railings.

First stop is the main party deck, with its hot tub, picnic table, and gas grill (that's where the guy named Vinnie taught the girls how to toast cream-filled cannoli pastries on a stick—like sober people do with marshmallows).

A sliding glass patio door leads you into the living room/kitchen/pigsty. The sides of the house are covered with tobacco-brown shingles, but the garage doors below are painted green, white, and red so they look like two aluminum Italian flags.

Paulie, Mike, and Vinnie, the three guys left in the house (Tony DePalma got the boot in Episode One; Salvatore "Salami" Amelio lost the Skee-Ball competition), are always calling themselves Guidos. Soozy K, Jenny, and Nicole, the three remaining girls, call themselves Guidettes.

Meanwhile, Italian-Americans everywhere call them "*faccia di culos*," which means "faces of a buttocks," or, you know, jerks.

"Parking could prove problematic," says Ceepak as we crawl up the street crowded with trucks, campers, step vans, a diesel-guzzling generator—all sorts of major vehicles corralled behind bright orange parking cones. There's even a pop-up pavilion serving chips and salsa and Oreos and pretzel sticks and M&M's to any crew members who waddle by. The crew guys all have radios jangling off their belts and multi-colored tape rolls bouncing against their thighs.

"Maybe we should swing up Shore Drive, park there," I suggest.

"That'll work."

As we inch along, seashells crunching beneath our tires, I see more crew members, all of them dressed in cargo shorts and sloppy tees. They're rolling carts loaded down with video gear, lighting equipment, electrical cables. They're pushing lights on rolling tripods, carrying stanchions rigged with flags of black cloth, hauling props. They shove dollies, trolleys, and laundry carts with wheels gone wobbly. These are the grips and gaffers and best boys and electricians and all those technicians listed at the end of a movie when they roll the credits. Not that I stick around to watch them—except in movies that give you funny bloopers, too.

With the help of a summer cop who keeps calling us "Sirs," we find the last available parking slot on Beach Lane and walk past a gaggle of "looky-loos"—tourists straining to see one of the reality show stars or have their picture taken in front of The Fun House. I imagine half the guys posing for cell phone pix will tug up their shirts and try to wiggle their nipples.

"Hey, Danny! Ceepak!"

It's Layla. She comes bounding down a set of steel steps attached to a gleaming white mobile home.

"Great to have you guys on board," she says, beaming that smile that got me hooked on a New York City girl in the first place. Layla has changed into a tight gym top that doesn't quite cover her belly button. Cargo shorts hug her hips. All kinds of radios spank her fanny.

Sometimes, a dirty mind is a terrible thing to waste.

"We're rolling live up at the house. There's coffee at craft services. You need to hit the head?"

This is how Layla Shapiro talks. Scattershot. She's what they call a multi-tasker. While she's telling us about the toilets, she's texting on her BlackBerry and futzing with the volume dial on the walkie-talkie clipped to her hip.

"Is there somewhere we can go to discuss the details of our liaison work moving forward?" says Ceepak.

"Sure," says Layla, jabbing a thumb over her shoulder. "This is the production office. Marty's inside. There's bagels. It's air-conditioned."

My turn to smile. Hey, it's August. 98 degrees with 98 percent humidity. My shirt is glued to my back. My sunglasses are fogged up because I had the AC blasting in the Crown Vic. There's only one way to defog them: more AC.

"We should have the full duty roster for the coming week completed within the hour," says Ceepak when we're inside the nice and chilly trailer.

"Excellent," says Layla, clicking her BlackBerry. We've only dated twice, but the girl has lots of lists. And schedules. If we do have sex on our third date, I'm sure she's already blocked out exactly when it needs to happen and what gear and refreshments need to be on location. "Can you put a downloadable PDF in your cloud?"

"Come again?" says Ceepak.

My man doesn't know from Internet file-sharing clouds. Hey, he's thirty-seven. His generation still sends e-mails instead of texting.

"We'll have Mrs. Rence fax it over," I say.

"Awesome," says Layla, her thumbs launching into a fresh text message.

Marty Mandrake is in the truck with us, munching on a bunch of grapes, staring at a bank of monitors. Three of them, the ones directly in front of Mandrake, seem to feature today's big scene: the beer pong tournament being played on and around the picnic table on the Fun House deck. Twelve smaller monitors built into the wall above the "hot" camera feeds remind me of the screens you'd see behind the security desk in a high-rise office building. High-angle, locked-off shots peering down on every room in the house. Very Big Brotherish.

On the three main screens, I can see Paulie and Mike Tomasino. They're tossing ping-pong balls into a triangle of ten red Solo cups set up on opposite ends of the table. The cups are semi-filled with beer. The rules of this extremely popular frat house drinking game are quite simple: you plop your ball into a cup, the other team has to drink it. First team to have the other guys drink all their cups wins.

"Are these organic?" Mandrake snaps, plunking a grape into his pie hole.

"Yes, sir," says Layla. "We had a P.A. pick them up at the Whole Foods up in Red Bank."

I'm impressed. Red Bank is about sixty miles north of Sea Haven.

"Oh!" says Mandrake. "How long was that, Grace?"

Mandrake is sitting in one of those foldout director's chairs with "Mr. Mandrake" stenciled across the back. A middle-aged woman with three different stopwatches dangling around her neck is seated beside him. Her chair doesn't say "Grace."

"From when Paulie ricocheted his ball off the porch railing until it bounced off the wall and plopped into the middle cup?"

"Yeah."

"Five seconds."

"Mark it. It's gold. Pure gold." He presses a button on the side of a handheld radio. "Rutger?"

"Yes, sir?"

"Get me a close-up of that ping-pong ball in Mike's cup when he goes to drink it."

"There's a bug in the cup."

"Beautiful. Shoot it."

"You got it, Chief."

"Rutger Reinhertz is the best director in reality TV," Mandrake announces to the world. "Gets the money shots. Doesn't cost a fortune."

Ceepak clears his throat. "Mr. Mandrake?"

"Yeah?" Mandrake keeps his eyes glued on the three TV screens flickering in front of him.

"We'd like to talk to you about Paul Braciole and the anabolic steroids. If he cooperates with us, the county prosecutor might be interested in discussing a deal wherein no charges are brought against him or Ms. Kemppainen."

"Great. Give me a minute. We need to wrap this sequence."

"Marty has an ambitious day planned," Layla whispers. "Including a company move down to Morgan's Surf and Turf for the etiquette competition later tonight."

Ceepak just nods. His wife, Rita, used to waitress at Morgan's. Me? I'm wondering what the heck goes on in an etiquette contest.

"Come on, Paulie," Jenny Mortadella (the skanky one) shouts as she cozies up to The Thing in a very skimpy bikini that shows off the mermaids tattooed all over her boobs. *"Beat this bitch. Bounce a ball up his ass."*

"Um, we'll, you know, clean that up in edit," says Layla.

"You win this competition, I'll give you a pwize." Jenny's doing drunken baby talk now.

"Oh, yeah? Like what?" says Paulie.

"This." She tugs up her bikini top and flashes "The Thing" her things. She'd probably wiggle them but I don't think that kind of plastic shimmies.

Now Ceepak's closing his eyes, and, if I'm not mistaken, uttering a silent prayer.

"We'll, you know, pixellate over those, block them out," Layla explains.

The middle monitor shows a horrified reaction shot of Soozy K's face when Jenny flashes her tattooed nay-nays. The mermaids look like they are harvesting pistachios for the winter.

"I thought you had an alliance with Mikey?" Paulie says to Jenny. Yep, there are a lot of "ee" names in the house.

"Not after he fell on his ass playing Skee-Ball because he was so drunk—"

"I wasn't drunk, bitch—"

In my head, I start adding in the bleeps.

"Yes, you BLEEPING were."

"So?" says Mike. *"You're a BLEEPING cow! Flashing your BLEEPING BLEEPIES. What kind of pig does that? A cow, that's who."*

"You want to hook up later?" Jenny says to Paulie.

Paulie shrugs. *"Whatever."* He bops a ping-pong ball off the picnic table and into the beer cup Soozy's holding in her hand.

"What the BLEEP!" shouts Soozy when beer sloshes up and splatters all over her chest.

"Maybe you better take off your top too," jokes Paulie. *"Hang it up to dry!"*

Now the guy named Vinnie, another bodybuilder type who spikes his hair up into a waxy Mohawk, comes stomping out of the house.

"Yo, Paulie? What the BLEEP? I found this BLEEP under your bed." Vinnie has something in his hand. We can't tell what it is.

"Get me a close-up!" Marty Mandrake shouts into his radio.

Two of the cameras rush in to see what Vinnie found.

"This is huge!" says Mandrake. "I'm working your drug investigation into my storyline!"

"What the BLEEP," says Jenny Mortadella. *"That BLEEP will shrivel your BLEEP, you stupid BLEEP."*

In the close-up on monitor three, we see what Vinnie found in Paulie's room.

Another little glass vial with a cartoon label.

More Skeletor steroids.

5

"YOU'RE PUTTING ILLEGAL DRUGS ON NATIONAL TELEVISION?" says Ceepak.

"Maybe," says Mandrake. "This is a reality show. We shoot a ton of footage. But we don't know what we'll actually air till we get in the edit suite and start hacking away at it."

Dialogue seeps out of the live monitors.

"That's not my shit," from Paulie.

"I found it under your fucking bed," from Vinnie.

"That's how you fucking beat Tone?" from Mike. *"Dope?"*

Anthony "Tone" DePalma was the first guy kicked out of the house back in July. He lost to Paulie in the Beach Badminton Beer Blast (they played with racquets and wadded-up aluminum beer cans instead of the more traditional shuttlecock).

"Your balls are going to fall off," from Jenny Mortadella.

Ceepak leans forward and snaps off the audio.

"Hey!" protests Mandrake, who was gobbling up the garbage faster than a rat in a Mickey D's dumpster after they clean out the Big Mac bin.

"You realize," Ceepak says to Mandrake, "that since the enactment of the Federal Anabolic Steroid Control Act, steroids are placed in the Schedule III class of illegal drugs, along with barbiturates, veterinary tranquilizers, and narcotic painkillers?"

"No," says Mandrake, somewhat sarcastically, "I did not know this. Now can I go back to doing my job?"

"By simply holding the illegal steroids . . ." Ceepak gestures toward the silent monitor because, I think, all the *Fun House* kids look pretty much the same to him (muscles, olive skin, too much hair gel).

I help out. "Vinnie."

". . . Vinnie is committing a federal offense, punishable by up to one year in prison and/or a minimum fine of one thousand dollars."

Mandrake grabs his walkie-talkie. "Rutger? Cut! Hold the roll!"

The camera crews do as they're told.

"We're cutting," squawks out of the radios attached to Layla, Grace, and Mandrake. Even though they're not spinning digital tape, the cameras are still feeding images to the monitors. The *Fun House* boys stop yelling at each other. The girls adjust their boobs inside their bikini tops. It's kind of funny watching the cast when they think they're not being filmed. It's real reality. It's also boring.

"What if that ampule is empty?" asks Layla.

"Come again?" This from Ceepak.

"What if Vinnie is in possession of nothing more than an empty glass bottle with a Skeletor sticker glued to its front?"

"Then, technically," says Ceepak, "he is not in violation of the State and Federal Steroid Control Acts."

"Exactly," says Mandrake. "You see why I rely on Miss Shapiro here? She's not only got a hot bod, her brain ain't half bad, either."

Layla blushes. Tugs down on that Lycra tank top. It still doesn't cover her belly button.

"Our intention with this subplot—" she says before Ceepak cuts her off.

"Subplot?"

"Sorry. TV talk. Sure, the show's unscripted, but, well, we're always looking for plot points. Conflict. Something to give each episode an arc and narrative drive."

"Ms. Shapiro," says Ceepak, "the criminal distributor of these illegal drugs is a person of great interest to the Sea Haven Police Department."

"So let's use the show to help you catch him!"

"Ma'am, with all due respect, this is a matter for law enforcement professionals."

"So you don't welcome the help of a concerned citizenry?" says Mandrake. "You need to be the Lone Ranger? Hunt the bad guy down all by yourself?"

"I did not mean to imply—"

Layla holds up a hand. "Hear me out, Officer Ceepak. Please?"

Ceepak crosses his arms across his chest to signify that he'll listen. For a minute, anyway.

"We won't run any of this footage from the steroid storyline, not even this confrontation between Paulie and Vinnie, until after you guys apprehend Skeletor."

"We have your word on that?"

"Sure," says Layla. "That's the beauty of reality TV. We create our own timeline and continuity. We can cut out of the beer pong bit before the big Paulie–Vinnie blowup and recycle it back into the show later—after you have Skeletor behind bars and Paulie has redeemed himself on the steroid front. Maybe he goes up to Newark, talks to inner-city kids. . . ."

"Audiences love redemption scenes," says Mandrake. "Even the Schnauzer on *Hot Dog,* the one who bit the Poodle on its pom-pom, even the Schnauzer had a redemption scene. Licked a sick Beagle's ear."

Ceepak sighs.

"Here's what we do," says Layla. "We lean on Paulie. Have him make contact with his drug dealer."

"You're assuming the illegal steroids are his?"

"Hey, that stunt he pulled on the Skee-Ball machine? Come on. That's classic roid rage. Surely you guys figured that one out already."

Ceepak has to nod because, to tell the truth, which he always does, we had.

"Okay. We tell Paulie that the only way out of this jam is for him to set up a meet with his dealer. When he does, I alert you and Danny. Give you the where and when. You take Skeletor off the street. Paulie repents. We fade to black and roll credits."

Ceepak squints. "Would your cameras be filming this hypothetical drug deal?"

"Second unit only. We document the transaction so you can use it in court. Like those stings in airport hotel rooms the FBI is always running."

"But you won't use the footage on your program?"

"Not until Skeletor is safely behind bars, right, Marty?"

"Hmm?" Mandrake was distracted, picking through the grape bowl again.

"We don't run anything on the steroid storyline without clearance from SHPD."

"Definitely," he says. "Of course not. No way."

"You guys will save a ton of time if we play it this way," Layla tells Ceepak. "I'm guessing Skeletor is off the street before we're on the air next Thursday night."

"It is highly doubtful that Skeletor, himself, will take the meet with Mr. Braciole."

"Well, if he sends a flunky," I say, trying to lend Layla a hand, "at least we'll land the next fish up the line. We cut that fish a deal, he leads us up the food chain to an even bigger fish. Sooner or later, we're reeling in Skeletor."

Ceepak turns to Layla. "Encourage Mr. Braciole to contact his supplier."

She smiles. "Come on. Let's do it together!"

We hike out of the production trailer and head around the corner toward 102 Halibut Street.

"So, Danny?" says Layla, "you free between five and eight?"

"Huh?"

"We're wrapping here at five. The crew has three hours to make the move to Morgan's Surf and Turf. I don't have to be on set till eight. Thought we could hang."

One of the things I immediately liked about Layla Shapiro when we met under less-than-ideal conditions was how bold and ballsy she acted in a high-stress situation.

Right now? Not so much.

I mean, Ceepak is walking with us. Ballsy Shapiro? She could care less.

"I'm not sure." I turn to Ceepak. "Boss?"

"I anticipate we'll also stand down when the cast is confined to quarters. I, too, need to attend to a few personal matters on the home front."

I nod. I figure one of the personal matters is calling a certain sheriff's office up in Ohio to see how soon he can take their chief-of-detectives job. I can tell: John Ceepak is not having a very sunny or funderful day in Sea Haven today.

We climb up the world-famous Fun House steps and hit the deck. The beer pong glasses—filled with flat Budweiser, balls, and bugs—sit on the picnic table, fermenting in the sun.

"This way," says Layla, sliding open the patio door.

We wade into the living room. It smells like my dirty clothes-basket during the sweaty months.

"Where's Paulie?" Layla asks Soozy K, who is even shorter than she looks on TV.

"Who the fuck cares?"

I'm thinking these kids need to carry personal bleep boxes.

"The cameras are off, Susan," says Layla.

"So? My heart is breaking here," she says with a tanned hip thrust. "I thought, being on this journey together, me and Paulie had made a connection, you know?"

"Sorry, hon. This ain't *The Bachelorette.* Where is he?"

"Upstairs. With Mike."

"Thanks."

We follow Layla up a hallway littered with empties: beer bottles, vodka bottles, pizza boxes, chicken buckets, hoagie wrappers.

"Guess the maid took the day off," she jokes.

We're not laughing. If we did, we wouldn't be able to breathe through our mouths to fight off the stench of B.O. mixed with Axe body spray.

Now we're ascending a very steep set of steps. Littered with underwear, socks, and clothing items I don't recognize. We can hear Mike and Paulie shouting at each other.

"You're gonna blow it for me, bro," screams Mike. "My dad's setting up this endorsement deal. My own Ab Ball infomercial."

"So?"

"So you do this shit, everybody will think I'm doing it, too, and I can kiss my infomercial deal—"

We enter the cramped attic bedroom.

Conversation ceases. It has a way of doing that whenever two armed cops step into a room.

"Hey, Layla," mumbles Paulie.

"Hey," echoes Mike.

They sound like what they really are: two scared kids barely out of high school.

Layla plants her hands on her hips. “Paulie?”

“Yeah?”

“I need you to call your drug dealer.”

“What are you talking about?”

“The steroids.”

“They’re not mine.”

“Yes, they are.”

“I swear—”

“Look, Paulie. If you help these gentlemen,” she gestures toward Ceepak and me, “they might let you off the hook.”

“What?”

“Did you know that simple possession of anabolic steroids is a federal offense, punishable by up to one year in prison and/or a minimum fine of one thousand dollars?”

I glance over at Ceepak. He can’t help but grin to hear Layla parrot him so perfectly.

“Remember where Marty found you?” she continues.

“Yeah,” mumbles Paulie.

“You want to go back to your mother’s basement when you get out of jail?”

Paulie curls a lip. Shakes his head.

“Okay. Here’s what you’re going to do. You’re going to call your dealer. Set up a meet.”

“I didn’t go lookin’ for the shit,” says Paulie. “Dude hit me up first.”

“How so?” asks Ceepak.

“I was at the local gym. Beach Bods.”

“Go on.”

“He came up to me. Skinny dude. He’s all like ‘I love your show, man,’ and ‘You got a pretty good bod, man, but science could make you buffer.’ Shit like that.”

"Paul?" says Layla.

"Yeah."

"I want you to contact this guy."

"Okay."

"Set up a buy."

"Okay."

"Then tell me where and when."

"These guys gonna be there for the meet?" He gestures toward Ceepak and me.

"Is that a problem, Paulie?"

"Hell, no. This skinny dude? He's trouble, man. Has psycho eyes. Wore one of those floppy camouflage hats."

Ceepak pulls a notepad and pen out of his shirt pocket.

"Can you tell us anything else?"

"You mean like his name?"

"Yeah," I say. "A name would be good."

"It's even freakier than the hat. Dude calls himself 'Skeletor,' like the old cartoon. How whacked is that?"

6

I'M SURE CEEPAK CAN'T BELIEVE OUR GOOD FORTUNE.

By doing like Layla suggested, we're saving all sorts of time.

We kick Mike Tomasino out of the attic bedroom. Boom—Paulie calls his local druggist. Skeletor answers on the second ring. He's happy to hear from The Thing. Caught the show last night.

They chat about that for a minute.

"So, I need a refill," says Paulie.

He nods at us. Gives us a big thumbs up. Skeletor will meet Paulie Braciole in the parking lot of Morgan's Surf and Turf at 8:30 P.M., right before the cameras start rolling inside the restaurant for the etiquette challenge.

Skeletor is such a fan of the show, he wants to visit the set.

The slippery drug dealer, the man who has evaded local, state, and federal authorities for at least two years, will be bringing Paulie some fresh steroids and a "This Is The Thing You Want" T-shirt so Paulie can autograph it for him.

"You handled that quite well," Ceepak says to Paulie when the phone call ends.

"Thanks, man. Can I go downstairs now?" he asks Layla. "I need to hit the tanning bed."

"Go," she says. Paulie hurries down the steps. I think the tanning beds are parked down in the garage since none of the kids in the house is allowed to have a car. Drunks stumbling up and down the beach and boardwalk make for funny TV; drunks driving cars, not so much.

"Danny?" says Ceepak when Paulie is out of the room.

"Yeah?"

"Meet me at Morgan's at twenty-hundred hours."

That would be 8 P.M. Thirty minutes before the "buy-and-bust."

"Wear street clothes. Conceal your sidearm."

"We're working this thing undercover?"

"Roger that."

"Do you think 'sidearms' are really necessary?" asks Layla.

"Yes, ma'am. The last time Officer Boyle and I were close to Skeletor, we were almost cremated while still alive."

Layla nods. I think she gets it. She may work in reality TV. But Ceepak and I have to work in the real world, where really bad people have all sorts of real weapons.

Before leaving the Fun House, Ceepak radios the desk sergeant to finalize the "enhanced security" detail schedule. Mrs. Rence will fax it over to Layla in the production office.

Everybody's happy, including Gus Davis, who'll be working the first shift with Alex Smitten, covering the kids while they're inside Morgan's Surf & Turf, one of the classiest restaurants on the island. Gus loves Morgan's World Famous Crab Pie—a melted cheese-covered concoction of lumpy crabmeat congealed in a cream sauce the consistency of half-melted butter. I figure, at age 66, Gus still has one artery left to clog.

Ceepak has also arranged additional armed backup for when the Skeletor deal goes down at twenty-thirty hours (that's 8:30, outside the military time zone). Unmarked SHPD patrol cars, two of them, will be parked on the side streets near the restaurant. Ceepak and I, wearing our best beach-bum gear, will be stationed in my Jeep, a few feet away from the spot in the parking lot that Paulie set up as the rendezvous point for his drug transaction/T-shirt signing.

Ceepak and I will both be packing Glock 31.357's, our brand new, official SHPD service weapons. According to the catalog, these semi-automatics are "characterized by extremely high muzzle velocity and superior precision even at medium range." I like the Glock because it's light and because I've already won a few ribbons (not to mention a couple friendly wagers) with it down at the firing range.

We can only assume that Skeletor will be packing whatever lethal sidearms have made the New Jersey Skeevy Drug Dealer Association's approved weapons list this year.

To kill time between 5:30 and 8, Layla and I go on our third date.

Given the tight time parameters, I don't think it's going to be, you know, real "third date" material. I'm not sure where the rule about sex being a semi-given on date number three came from, but no way are Layla Shapiro and I going to get intimate during the two and half hours between the Fun House and the crab pie—not that I typically need that much time to, you know, express my intimacy.

Besides, at the risk of sounding girly, I'm not really ready. I like to know someone before I *know* them in the biblical sense. (Learning that "know" was code for "have sex with" may have been the highpoint of my Catholic education.)

Instead, we head over to the boardwalk.

Turns out Ms. Shapiro has always wanted to see a real Fun House, and we have one on Pier Two. In fact, it's one of the oldest attractions in Sea Haven. The Fun House isn't a thrill ride, because you don't ride: you have to walk through it on foot to experience it. It's what they call a participatory amusement. It's also why nobody's building the rickety things any more. People today, they like to sit in cars after they've driven their cars to where they're going.

We stroll up the boardwalk. Soak in the blinking lights, gaudy sights, and greasy smells. Layla is nibbling on a cyclone of cotton candy. I'm not. I'm still in uniform and nobody wants to see an armed cop looking like a two-year-old with a gob of pink gunk stuck to his nose.

"Thanks for hanging with me, Danny," says Layla. "I just needed to get away from the Nut House. Take a break."

"No problem."

"Marty's been driving me crazy."

"How so?"

"The ratings."

"They're good, right?"

"Yeah. This week. Next week, who knows? It's like they say on *Project Runway:* 'One day you're in, the next day you're out.'"

I'll take her word for it. I've never watched *Project Runway.* Don't think it's about airplanes.

"So where's this real, live fun house?"

I point to a brightly colored building dead ahead.

"Those big red lips?" says Layla.

"Yeah. The clown's mouth is the entrance."

The front of the Sea Haven Fun House is basically a two-story-tall clown face with a huge gaping mouth under demented eyes, because the Fun House clown has the same psychological profile as the one in Stephen King's *It.* The red carpet you walk down after giving the ticket-taker five coupons is the big monster's tongue.

"Do they have those mirrors in there?" asks Layla. "The ones that make you look fat and skinny?"

"Definitely. Two sets of 'em. Wouldn't be a Fun House without funhouse mirrors. There's also a barrel of fun—a rolling hallway you have to walk through. And, my favorite, the Turkey Trot."

Layla laughs. "What's that?"

"This long corridor with an oscillating floor. Three planks sliding back and forth. I set the indoor world record. Trotted the whole thing in under twenty seconds."

"Danny, tell me: Exactly how much of your misspent youth was misspent in the Fun House?"

"One whole summer. Right after my second year of high school. My buddy Jess's dad used to run it. Gave us both summer jobs as 'custodial engineers.'"

"You were a janitor?"

"No. I think the janitors made more than us."

"I see."

"It was a blast," I say, remembering how the guy in the control booth would blast air up unsuspecting girls' skirts, giving them their very own Marilyn Monroe moment.

Every once in a while, Jess and I would sneak behind the body-warping mirrors and say funny stuff to the girls checking themselves out, especially if they were girls we knew from school.

Well, *we* thought it was funny stuff. The girls didn't always agree. Especially since most of our mirror material included the words "big," "boobs," and "butt." Fortunately, Jess and I knew every nook, cranny, and secret passageway; knew how to get to the exit slide faster than any of the girls chasing us.

"Hey, Danny," says Layla, "is it too early for a cold one?"

She's eyeballing this pizza stand tucked in next to the Fun House entrance. It squats underneath a "Draft Beer" sign shaped like a frosty, overflowing mug. A strobing red arrow full of chaser lights points down to the promised land of liquid refreshment.

"Well, I'm still in uniform," I say.

"I'll drink. You can observe. Slap the cuffs on me if I get out of line."

"That'll work," I say.

We head into the pizza joint, find a couple swivel stools at the counter. Layla has a beer, almost as tall and frosty as the one on the neon sign. I order a Coke so everybody can see that their public servant is not drinking a beer. Unless they think it's a Guinness or something. Darn. Didn't think of that.

"Marty's a snake and a hack," says Layla after her third sip of beer, which, I guess, has completely washed away the lingering sweetness of the cotton candy.

"Really?" I'm sipping my soda through a straw now. Nobody drinks Guinness with a straw.

"He's a backstabber and a hack. All he knows are crappy cliches, because that's all he's ever done. His last three shows totally tanked. That one about the oversexed cougars looking for love with pizza delivery boys? *Hot To Trot?* Nobody watched it. And the only reason he wanted to do *Fun House* was so he could be closer to Atlantic City. He didn't have any ideas on what to do with the kids in the house; he just wanted to hit the casinos on his nights off. That's why he needs me. To do his thinking for him, because I have ideas like some people have pimples. They just pop up."

"Like putting steroids in the show?"

"It's reality, Danny. Steroid use to keep your body buff is a very real, very contemporary issue. When drugs turn up, like they did today, we shoot it. It's a conflict that hits home with males 18 to 24, the sweet spot of our target audience demographics. You live around here?"

Okay. That was rather random.

"Excuse me?"

"Your apartment. Is it close?"

"Not really. I'm about thirty minutes south."

Down where the rents are cheaper.

Layla whips out her iPhone. Swipes her fingers across the face. "It's six-fifteen. Maybe we should skip the Fun House."

"Huh?"

"You need to change into your undercover clothes, right?"

"Yeah."

"And get to the restaurant to meet Ceepak by eight."

"Right. Twenty hundred hours."

"Six-fifteen to six-forty-five, six-forty-five to seven-fifteen. That's just the travel time."

She's right. I need to boogie.

Layla gulps down the foamy dregs at the bottom of her plastic beer glass. Slams it on the counter. "How long will it take you to change?"

I shrug. "Not long."

"Five, ten minutes?"

"Yeah. I guess."

"Seven-fifteen to seven twenty-five. We've still got thirty-five minutes."

"Oh. Okay. You want to grab a slice or something?"

Layla smiles at me.

"What?"

"Danny, how long do you need to take a shower before you change clothes?"

"Don't worry about it. I took one this morning."

"How long?"

"Another five minutes."

"Good. That gives us thirty minutes."

Now I'm confused.

Layla reaches over, puts one hand on each of my thighs.

"Danny? It's our third date."

Oh.

I think I know how she wants to spend those thirty minutes.

And it's not eating pizza.

7

My hair's still damp when I whip my Jeep into the parking lot of Morgan's Surf & Turf.

Yes, I grabbed a shower.

No, Layla and I did not hook up, get busy, or "know" each other.

She offered. I turned her down.

Fine. Go ahead. Kick me out of the red-blooded-American-male club.

"Drop me off at the front door, okay?" she says. "Pull into the handicap parking slot."

It's empty. I'm not parking. Technically. I pull in.

In the rearview mirror, I can see Ceepak standing with a short woman in the only other empty parking spot in Morgan's gigantic lot.

The woman is leaning on the handle of a rolling case of some sort. Ceepak, on the other hand, is glaring at me. He would never,

ever pull in to a designated handicapped-drivers-only spot. To do so would be considered cheating.

"Good luck," says Layla as she blows me one of those Hollywood style "m'waw" air kisses and hops out of the Jeep. "I need to check inside. See if the watermelons arrived. Catch you later, Danny."

She bops up the walkway to the restaurant's front doors.

Tons of people are streaming in and out of the restaurant. The Early Bird specials leaving; the 8 o'clock reservations arriving.

Layla shoves open the front door.

"Hey, Danny!"

Before the front door glides shut, I see Ceepak's wife, Rita. She's right where we first met her a couple summers ago: near the hostess stand.

She waves. I wave. The door whooshes shut.

I'm figuring Rita, who used to waitress at Morgan's, came down to see some of her friends become TV stars, serving dinner to the famous kids in what Morgan's calls their Party Room. It's a couple long tables that can be sealed off from the rest of the dining room with an accordion wall. It's where the Kiwanis and Rotary clubs hold their monthly meetings. Tonight, *Fun House* has it closed off for their etiquette contest. Layla tells me that the winner of the competition gets "immunity," which is a very good thing to have in reality TV shows because that means you can't be booted out of the house that week.

"Danny?"

This from the other Ceepak.

The one waiting—somewhat impatiently—for me to drive our surveillance vehicle (my Jeep) into position for the sting, which is, geeze-o, man, supposed to take place in like twenty minutes!

I slam my ride into reverse, peel wheels backward, cut a fishhook swerve to the right, jam the transmission into drive, and blast-off for Ceepak and the empty parking spot, twenty feet away.

Ceepak and the short lady have to dodge my front bumper when I screech to a stop.

"Hey," I say as nonchalantly as possible when I climb out the Jeep. The engine is ticking, trying to cool down. My tires smell like it's rubber-burning day down at the town dump.

I notice Ceepak stealing a glance at his personal time control unit, what other people might call their wristwatch. His jawbone is popping and out near his ear again. I think he's ticking and trying to cool down, too.

"Danny?"

"Yes, sir?"

"When I was a Boy Scout, our troop leader encouraged us to operate on what he called White House time."

My face must say "Huh?" because Ceepak clarifies.

"When invited to the White House, if you are not five minutes early, you are considered ten minutes late."

"Sorry," I say.

"This our rig?" says the lady with the rolling luggage.

"Roger that," says Ceepak. "Danny, this is Ms. Tory Wood. She is a sound technician, working for Prickly Pear Productions."

"Gimme a hand with this stuff, kid." She pops open the rolling case. I see all sorts of electronic gear stowed in custom-cut foam slots. She pulls out a suction-cupped antenna, slaps it to the hood of my Jeep. "Put the recorder in your cargo hold. But be careful. That's a Nagra Six."

"Okay," I say, placing what looks like the high-tech gizmo into the back of my Jeep.

"Ms. Wood will be recording Paul Braciole's conversation with Skeletor," says Ceepak.

"Just the audio," she says as she runs the antenna wire through the passenger-side window, heaves it behind the seats to where I just stashed her knob-covered recorder. "Paulie's wearing a wireless mic. They all do, all the time. Stupid kids forget to turn them off when they hit the head, which they do an awful lot, seeing how they guzzle beer 24/7. I should mix together a bootleg compilation of their longest farts and pisses. 'Scuse me."

She says this, not because she's "crude as oil," as my Irish grandmother used to say, but because she's crawling into the Jeep to go fiddle with her dials and slap on her headphones.

"Are we getting video too?" I ask.

"Roger that," says Ceepak, gesturing toward a van parked three spaces away. Its running lights flicker. I wave to whoever's behind the tinted windows.

"That's the 'A' camera," says Ms. Wood, crouched in the back where I usually toss crap. Like the Styrofoam ice chest she's using as a seat cushion. "I'm not sure where Rutger put 'B' and 'C.'"

Up arches Ceepak's eyebrow. "B and C?"

"Yeah. He likes to roll three cameras at all times, catch the action from three different angles. And since we can't use the steadicam rig on this setup without blowing the shot. . . ." Now she holds up two small boxes with earbuds attached. "You guys want headsets?"

"Come again?" says Ceepak, taking the audio unit and staring at it confusedly.

"They're wireless. You can hear what I hear."

Ceepak nods. We both jam foam buds into our ears.

"You gentlemen are good to go. You better climb in. Here comes Paulie."

Ceepak takes the passenger seat. I slip in behind the wheel. Layla escorts The Thing out of the restaurant, into the parking lot.

Back in the cargo hold, Tory Wood flips a switch and we hear Paul Braciole saying, *"I need more fucking money. Juice is expensive."*

"Here." Layla's voice. *"But return whatever's left to the prop department when we wrap the drug dealer scene."*

Ceepak's eyebrow inches up.

I try to explain: "I think, you know, everything's a scene from a TV show to Layla."

"I get to fucking eat later, right?" Paulie whines. *"I want some of that fucking crab pie. . . ."*

"Ms. Wood?" says Ceepak.

"Yeah?"

"Have you set your recording levels?"

"Yeah."

"Would you mind muting Mr. Braciole until our suspect arrives?"

"Officer, it would be my pleasure."

She flips a switch and cuts The Thing off in mid F-bomb.

Ceepak checks his watch again. Reaches for the walkie-talkie hidden under the tails of his untucked Tommy Bahama Hawaiian shirt, which I think he raced out and bought special for tonight's undercover drug bust operation. No way he wears green and yellow hibiscus-covered tops on a regular basis.

"Reed? Malloy? This is Ceepak. Radio check."

"Standing by," says Reed.

"Locked and loaded," says Malloy, who watches way too many cop shows on TV.

I'm assuming Reed and Malloy are commanding our two backup vehicles.

"Where are they?" I ask.

Ceepak gestures right, then left. We have the parking-lot exits covered.

Ceepak's eyes narrow. "Now we just wait."

I nod. It's deathly quiet in my Jeep.

"Sorry I was late," I finally say.

"Danny?"

"Yeah?"

"We both need to focus on the task at hand."

"Right."

"Avoid distractions."

"Gotcha."

"I know you recently lost a girlfriend. . . ."

"Katie really wasn't my girlfriend anymore."

"You recently broke up with Ms. Starkey."

"Actually, she kind of broke up with me first."

Ceepak sighs. "Never mind."

"What?"

"'Nothing we can say can change anything now.'"

Oh. Great. He's quoting Springsteen at me. Lyrics from "Independence Day." We used to swap Springsteen's words to fill in the gaps when we didn't know how to express what we were feeling, which, come to think of it, maybe Ceepak's doing now, because he feels I've been letting down the team because I've been a bit distracted by the lovely Layla.

Which would be correct.

"You're right," I say.

"What are you two talking about?" This from Ms. Wood in the back seat.

"Nothing," I say. "Just that, maybe, I've been blinded by the light."

"What?" Ms. Wood, it seems, doesn't know from Springsteen.

So I keep mangling lyrics: "Some fleshpot mascot may have tied me into a lover's knot with a whatnot in her hand."

Ceepak grins.

"What?"

"It's all good, Ms. Wood," says Ceepak. And then, unexpectedly, he reaches over and gives me a man-sized pat on my knee, the way your dad would when you finally admitted you'd made a huge mistake and promised not to be so stupid in the future.

The police radio crackles again. "Yo? Ceepak?"

It's Gus Davis from inside the restaurant. When he worked the desk at the SHPD, everybody called him Grumpy Gus. Retirement, it seems, has not mellowed him. With just two words, I can tell: Gus still has his grouch on.

Ceepak brings the radio mic up to his mouth. "This is Ceepak. Go."

"Yeah, these freaking TV people—they're putting plastic sheets all over the floor. They're loosening the tops on all the saltshakers. They've got one of those cardboard bins from the supermarket filled with freaking watermelons."

"Gus?"

"Yeah?"

"Has anyone broken the law?"

"No. Not yet, anyways. But I gotta tell you: something doesn't smell right about this setup in here."

"Stand by, Gus," says Ceepak. "Hold down the fort. We have company."

He nods his head at a guy cruising into the parking lot on a rumbling Harley-Davidson motorcycle.

A guy wearing an Army-surplus Boonie hat.

His chopper scoots between a couple cars, heads straight for the lamp pole where Paulie Braciole, hands stuffed into his baggy shorts, stands waiting.

"You guys want wedding mints?" Gus suddenly asks over the walkie. "Smitten and me both snagged a pocketful from the bowl up front. They got jelly in the middle. Mint jelly, like with lamb."

"Sure, Gus," says Ceepak, distractedly. His eyes are glued on Skeletor as the drug dealer dismounts. "We'll be inside, ASAP."

"Yeah, yeah. Whatever. Roger, wilco."

Ceepak buries the radio under his flowered shirttails.

"He is once again wearing the Boonie hat," Ceepak mumbles, totally focused on his prey. "No helmet."

And Skeletor definitely needs one. His emaciated head looks as brittle as an empty eggshell. The guy is maybe six-six, all jangling bones and knobby joints. He looks like a cadaver who just slinked out of his tomb.

I stare at his hat—a floppy, stiff-brimmed, camouflaged number that a lot of vets still wore after they came home from the jungles of Vietnam.

Believe it or not, I recognize it. *The hat!*

Two summers ago, we were patrolling the boardwalk, looking for a paintball prankster who had been splotching up billboards and people all over town. This creepy guy came up to us while we were conducting an interview. Super skinny. Dressed in chocolate-chip camo shorts, a matching T-shirt, and a Boonie hat. Challenged Ceepak to a shooting match. Called him an Army asshole when Ceepak refused.

Back then, I called him Bones.

But it was Skeletor.

And he's been more or less challenging us ever since.

8

"Ms. Wood?" says Ceepak. "Audio?"

"Roger that." She learns quickly.

"You lookin' good, man." This from Skeletor. His voice wispy and thin, like even his voice box is bony.

"Thanks, bro," says Paulie, sounding nervous.

"Where's Soozy K?" I see Skeletor go up on tippy-toe, peer over Paulie's shoulder.

"Inside."

"For real?"

"Yeah."

"Cool, cool. You tap that stuff?"

"Soozy?"

"Yeah."

"Maybe."

Skeletor makes basketball palms over his chest. *"Those tig ol' bitties. Those real, man?"*

"Nah," says Paulie.

"For real? They're fake?"

"Inflatable airbags, man." Paulie. Such a gentlemen. He touches and tells.

"What about the skanky one? Jenny?"

"She's the real deal."

"Yeah?"

"You see the hula hoop dealio?"

"Sure. Episode Three."

"They bounce and swing like that, bro, those biznoobies be real."

"All right," says Skeletor, wiping a bony elbow under his bony nose. *"That's what I'm talkin' about."*

"So, you bring the juice?"

Skeletor twitches some. Adjusts his hat. *"Am I on TV?"*

"No, man."

"Why you wearing that microphone?"

"This?" We hear a "fwump" as Paulie taps his chest. *"I always got to wear this fucking thing."*

"Even when you take a dump?"

"Yeah. But there's a switch to, you know, turn it off."

"Which he never uses," mumbles Ms. Wood in the back.

"So," says Paulie, sounding antsy, *"I need to get back to work."*

"Work? Shit, man, all you people do is get drunk, play Skee-Ball, and bang each other. You call that fuckin' work, bro?"

Paulie laughs. *"Not really, man. But you know, I want to make the finals; win the fuckin' money."*

"I'm pulling for you, bro. Big fan of The Thing. Want The Thing to take the whole thing, know what I mean?"

"Yeah. Thanks." Now Paulie pulls a crumpled wad of cash out of his baggy shorts.

Skeletor doesn't take it. He has this crackbrained gleam in his eye. In a flash, his hand reaches for his belt.

Mine goes to my Glock.

Has Skeletor figured out this is a buy-and-bust?

No.

He yanks up his T-shirt. Flashes Paulie his bony ribcage. *"Check it out. This is The Thing you wish you had. The Thing you wish you could be."*

He starts cackling like a crazy person.

I start breathing again.

"Cute," says Paulie. *"Cute."*

Now Skeletor drops his shirt. Turns around and pops open the hardcase trunk on the back of his motorbike. Palms something we can't see, but maybe the cameras do. He swivels in a blur back to Paulie. Looks left, right, left again. Shakes Paulie's hand.

"No charge, bro," he says.

"Huh?" says Paulie.

"You're a celeb, man. People see you on TV, looking all chiseled, I tell them how they can look the same way." He turns his thumb and pinky finger into a jiggling telephone. *"One call scores it all!"*

"I'd rather pay," says Paulie. *"I got the money."*

"Sorry, bro. Your green is no good. That Red Power Ranger Go-Go Juice is on the house. Compliments of me and my crew."

I glance over at Ceepak.

Technically, there's been no buy; so can there be a bust?

And, so far, we have no proof Skeletor was ever actually in possession of steroids, so we can't bust him on that.

I raise my eyebrows to ask Ceepak, *"What now?"*

"Thirty-nine, three dash seventy-six dot seven," mumbles Ceepak.

My eyebrows go higher.

"The State of New Jersey's Mandatory Helmet Law."

Oh. Right. *That* thirty-nine dash-dot-whozeewhatzit.

Ceepak works the listening buds out of both ears and mutters the memorized ordinance: "No person shall operate or ride upon a motorcycle unless he or she wears a securely fitted protective helmet."

Great. Instead of a drug bust, we'll slap Skeletor with a twenty-five-dollar fine for wearing a floppy Army surplus hat.

Earphones out, Ceepak yanks up on his door handle. I'm a split second behind him. Go for my weapon.

"Keep it holstered," says Ceepak through a tight smile without even looking over to see what I'm doing. "Too many innocent civilians."

Yeah. The prospect for collateral damage is extremely high right now. Folks are piling out of cars. Moms, dads. Couple kids. Granny with her walker.

We stroll casually across the parking lot. Ceepak even whistles a little. "Waitin' on a Sunny Day." More Springsteen.

Paulie Braciole looks over. Sees us.

Skeletor's bony head bobs sideways. He sees Paulie seeing something. Twirls around.

He sneers. His teeth are spiky. The guy has no gums.

"Hello, Army asshole."

That's what he called Ceepak that day at Paintball Blasters. I was right. It's the same walking bone bag.

"Sir?" Ceepak flashes his badge. "We're with the Sea Haven Police Department."

Skeletor retreats a step. "So?"

"Is that your motorcycle?"

"Yeah. So?" Cocky as hell, Skeletor straddles his motorbike. Plops his bony butt down on the seat.

"Where is your helmet, sir?"

Skeletor kick-starts the bike. The engine varoom-pop-pops to life. He puts a hand to his ear. "What?"

"Where is your helmet?" Ceepak shouts as we move closer. Paulie, The Thing, moves backward, his hands trembling.

Skeletor tugs down on the Boonie hat's leather straps.

"I don't need a fucking helmet."

"Yes, sir. You do. In New Jersey, all motorcyclists are required to wear DOT-approved headgear."

"Not me. I got other protection."

"Sir, you need the full gear," says Ceepak. He gestures at Skeletor's hat. "Not the fool's gear."

I think Ceepak's cribbing that corny line off a motorcycle safety poster he hung up in the SHPD locker room a few months ago.

Skeletor responds by flicking his wrist on the twist grip throttle to rev his engine, make it go chug-pop-pop.

"Sir? Kindly shut down your engine and dismount."

Skeletor snaps his bony teeth shark style at Ceepak. "Bite me."

Ceepak doesn't flinch. "Dismount, sir. Now!"

"Shit," gasps Paulie. "I'm out of here!"

I hear glass shatter. Reflexively, Ceepak and I both glance behind us. We see Paulie turning tail to run, crunching across the shattered steroid bottles he just dropped on the blacktop.

That's when Skeletor gooses his throttle to the max, lets go of the clutch lever, and pops a wheelie that sends the front tire spinning like a studded chainsaw at Ceepak's head.

And Ceepak isn't wearing a helmet either.

9

Ceepak ducks left.

The whirring motorcycle tire grazes the shoulder of his shirt on the downswing, chews into the Tommy Bahama gardenias like a hedge trimmer. Ceepak rolls right. I go for my gun.

"No weapons!" shouts Ceepak, gritting through the pain that comes when your collarbone gets clipped.

Skeletor lands hard and rips up a lane between parked cars.

Okay. Now he gets more than a twenty-five-dollar fine; he goes to jail for resisting arrest.

Ceepak grabs his radio mic. "All units," he shouts, "suspect is fleeing the scene on motor—"

Before he finishes, the throaty roar of rolling thunder shatters the air around us. Not the roller coaster—fifteen more choppers or hogs or whatever the hell Hell's Angels geezers call their rides these days. Only these aren't fat old guys with black leather vests, David Crosby hair, and too much facial hair.

This looks like The Creed. Tattoo sleeves. Wallets on silver chains. I see pirate skulls with devil horns, the Creed logo. They're a gang of outlaw bikers that runs drugs in South Jersey. These guys are the mafia on motorcycles.

The Creed, like Ceepak, live their life in strict accordance to a code. Theirs includes stuff about brotherhood and loyalty, like "If a citizen hits your brother, you will be on that citizen without asking why. There is no why."

I'm figuring Skeletor is a brother. The gang has probably been protecting him for years.

Ceepak and me? We're lousy stinking citizens.

Up near the Spruce Street exit, Skeletor slams into a swerving fish-tail turn, falls in behind three other Creed riders. They do this Shriner Circus move, cutting tire-smokin' doughnuts around a terrified couple who had been toothpicking their way to their Volvo when the wild bunch rolled into the parking lot. The four thrumming motorbikes circle the trembling tourists and then split off in different directions.

When they make their big finish and peel apart, I can't tell which one is Skeletor any more.

Ceepak, however, can.

"Reed? Malloy?" he barks into his radio mic, which he holds with one hand while the other one massages that tire gash on his shoulder. "Suspect is headed west on Tangerine."

"Which one?" shouts Malloy. *"There's a whole pack of 'em!"* I can tell by Malloy's choppy voice that he is in hot pursuit of something or somebody.

That's when I hear another blast of gear-ripping engines scream into a turn off Tangerine Street to tear up Ocean Avenue. Meanwhile, the first battalion of bikes is still zipping around the restaurant parking lot, hard-cranking through gearshifts, stuttering up the musical scale, straining to hit the high notes.

"Boonie hat!" says Ceepak. "Look for the rider without a helmet. He's wearing a green tiger-stripe camouflage hat."

"They all are!" says Malloy. *"All of them are wearing the same stupid hat."*

Ceepak brings down the mic. "Damn," he mutters—a word he very rarely uses.

That's when I know we're toast.

One of the parking-lot invaders screams up the lane where we're standing. Bops me on the head as he passes. He's laughing so hard as he speeds away, I can hear him over the whine of his tweaked-out engine.

Now the first wave of motorcycles swarms into a pack and streams out of the parking lot, heading north after their brothers in the Boonie hats.

"Lock down the causeway!" Ceepak shouts into the mic. "Lock it down!"

Malloy and Reed both start calling in the disaster to the dispatcher. The causeway, about thirty blocks north of where we are, is the only bridge connecting our island with the mainland; it's their only escape route. I don't hear much more of the radio transmission; just the dispatcher frantically searching for any available units—enough to throw up a roadblock.

But motorcycles? Unless we can immediately pull together enough cop cars to line them up bumper to bumper across both sides of the span, they'll slip through. On the shoulder. Between vehicles.

Ceepak and I stand stranded in the parking lot.

The last of the motorcycles squirts out of view.

We can hear the throaty roar as the motorcycle gang, all two dozen of them, flees the scene.

They'll be at the causeway in no time.

They'll get away. Maybe the highway patrol will grab them. Or maybe they'll hide their bikes in the back of a tractor-trailer when they hit the mainland. Ride up a ramp, roll down the door.

Hey, they planned this thing.

They knew the drug buy might be a setup.

Because, to tell the truth, I don't think The Creed rolls around in Boonie hats on a regular basis.

This is bad. Very bad.

A door slides open on a nearby van. Out steps this dude in khaki shorts and a safari vest. I can see a couple guys huddled around a video camera set up on a tripod behind him.

"And we're clear!" the dude shouts into his handheld walkie-talkie. "You get that, Jimbo?"

"Got it, Rutger."

The dude in the safari clothes, whom I guess is Rutger Reinhertz, the *Fun House* director, practically dances a jig. "I smell Emmy Awards!"

Geeze-o, man. The reality show cameras. They saw and recorded everything.

And then things get worse.

"Ceepak? Boyle?"

Gus Davis's voice crackling out of our radios.

"You better get in here!" Gus shouts. *"These freaking punks are tearing the place apart!"*

10

And then things went from worse to horrible.

Since we couldn't do much with my Jeep to aid in the pursuit of Skeletor and his biker brethren, we hotfooted it into the restaurant to answer Gus Davis's security-detail distress call.

The Etiquette Competition was actually a very messy food fight.

You see, in the twisted world of *Fun House,* the winners would be whoever had the *worst* table manners, as determined by this week's celebrity judges, the surviving members of a 1980s hair band famous for trashing hotel rooms.

If you've ever seen bratty kids running around a restaurant while their parents sip their third umbrella drink, you have a pretty good idea of what awaited Ceepak and me when we made it into the back room of Morgan's Surf & Turf. Every sugar packet had been torn open and emptied. Dinner rolls were flying. Globs of world famous crab pie were being spoon-catapulted.

And then there were the watermelons.

Like I said, I've never been to a real college, but I'm told, in certain circles, the ceremonial smashing of a watermelon is considered the traditional way to open a frat house barbecue bash. Mike Tomasino had a ball-peen hammer and was making a squishy mess in the middle of his table. Morgan's nice white tablecloths were turning pink.

"Taser 'em!" shouted Gus Davis, who was in a corner, pawing mashed potatoes out of his eyes. "Taser 'em all!"

"Cease and desist," Ceepak said to the rowdy drunks. "Cease and desist!"

They weren't listening.

Paulie had quickly caught up with his inebriated housemates. He was swilling vodka straight from a gallon jug he must've snatched from behind the bar. It still had the silver shot spout in its neck.

I saw Layla. Huddled behind one of the roving camera crews capturing all the action.

She, like everybody else working behind the scenes, was wearing a bright yellow rain poncho so her clothes wouldn't get splattered. She was also laughing her ass off.

Probably at me.

I was wrestling with tattooed Jenny Mortadella, trying to persuade her not to smash Morgan's lobster tank with *her* ball-peen hammer.

Ceepak's wife, Rita, the former Morgan's waitress who had come down to catch a whiff of Hollywood glamour, was in the kitchen. Weeping.

We didn't Taser anybody, but we did shout a lot.

"Put down the corncob. Step away from the clam chowder. Leave those lobsters alone!"

Maybe you've seen the T-shirts.

Because now I'm a TV star too.

Here's how *that* happened:

The parking lot buy-and-bust went bust on Friday night.

Our SHPD mobile units and the New Jersey State Police didn't catch Skeletor or a single member of his motorcycle gang. Once they roared across the causeway bridge (six abreast, we were told by startled eyewitnesses), they apparently split up and headed for what the guys in the state's Narcotics and Organized Crime Bureau call "safe garages." They're like safe houses for motorcycles. Places where a badass biker and his hog can lie low until the heat blows over.

Friday night and all day Saturday, Ceepak and I worked the obvious Sea Haven leads. Paulie gave us the number he had used to contact Skeletor.

Disposable cell phone. They sell them at Wal-Mart, Rite Aid, Target.

We interviewed Mike Charzuk, this trainer at Beach Bods, the local gym where the *Fun House* cast works out. That's where Paulie said he'd first bumped into Skeletor. Charzuk remembers seeing the walking cadaver but can't give us anything we don't know, like Skeletor's real name or his address. Apparently he isn't a dues-paying member. He just scares the girl at the front desk so creepily, she never asks for his I.D. tag.

Sunday, we more or less took the day off, stayed home and licked our wounds. I did not respond when Layla texted me. Six different times. She had Sunday off, too. Wanted to hook up.

Not gonna happen anytime soon.

In fact, the one time it had almost happened, I think there had been what they call an ulterior motive. Ms. Shapiro wanted me and Ceepak nowhere near Morgan's Surf & Turf during that early-evening break so her prop crew could set the stage to transform the restaurant's party room into the cafeteria scene from *Animal House.* She knew Ceepak would be busy organizing the buy-and-bust. Me? Let's just say she tried her best to keep me distracted.

Anyway, let me cut to the chase, as they say in Hollywood. All week, we get nowhere on the Skeletor case. Then Thursday night, at ten, nine Central, I see him again.

On TV.

I'm watching *Fun House.*

"America, you've heard about it all day," says Chip Dale, the wannabe Ryan Seacrest who hosts the show.

He has very bright chompers.

His dentist must be proud.

"Well, tonight you'll meet the crazed stalker who threatened to take the fun *out of the* house."

Okay. I didn't have time today to watch *Access Hollywood, E.T., Extra,* or any of those other shows where they plug the shows their networks need plugged that day, so I had no idea what America had heard all day.

They cut to Soozy K sitting somewhere, doing an interview. She doesn't look directly at the camera, they never do. Cheesily dramatic reality show music, the same soundtrack they use in all these shows, makes what she's saying sound important.

"We were all like, you know, freaked out. That skinny dude was BLEEPING scar-ee. I'm glad the undercover cops were there to protect Paulie, even if we're not, you know, on this journey together anymore."

Next, they went to some of the footage they shot last Friday. In the parking lot. The buy-and-bust.

Yep. They're showing everything they promised they wouldn't.

"Welcome to Morgan's Surf and Turf," Chip the deejay continues in a voice-over as we watch Paulie Braciole strut out the front door and into the parking lot. *"Home of the world's best crab pie and creepiest parking-lot stalkers."*

They cut to Skeletor in his Boonie hat, talking to Paulie. His Harley gleams in the background.

"I'm pulling' for you, bro," says Skeletor, who looks even skinnier on TV. *"Big fan of The Thing. Want The Thing to take the whole thing, know what I mean?"*

"Yeah. Thanks." Paulie actually sounds humble. I think they looped the line. That means they recorded it later, when he could be coached, matched it with the picture.

They cut from modest Paulie to Skeletor yanking up his T-shirt to flash his bony ribcage.

"Check it out. This is The Thing you wish you had. The Thing you wish you could be."

Quick reaction shot from Paulie looking disgusted. The light seems different. Like maybe they shot this last *Saturday*—right before we had all those nasty thunderstorms.

The sequence of events? It isn't the order it actually happened in.

"Where's Soozy K?" asks Skeletor, going on tippy-toe. Behind him, in this shot, the sky is clear again.

"I need to get back to work," says Paulie, sounding like an honest day laborer unpacking fruit trucks somewhere.

"Work?" scoffs Skeletor. *"BLEEP, man, all you people do is get drunk, play Skee-Ball, and BLEEP each other. You call that BLEEPING work, bro?"*

Paulie shakes his head and laughs good-naturedly. The sky is, once again, partly cloudy.

"Fortunately," said Chip the narrator, *"some undercover law enforcement officers had been trailing the psycho known to local authorities only as Skeletor."*

Ceepak and I make our big entrance.

Ceepak flashes his badge. *"We're with the Sea Haven Police Department."*

And they cut to a grateful Paulie throwing up his hands. *"I am so out of here. Thanks, guys."* He heads toward the restaurant—before all those dark clouds in his Saturday sky can open up and drench him.

Back to Ceepak, Skeletor, and me. Three different angles. None of them very flattering. Except for the sky. It looks clear again.

"Where is your helmet, sir?" says Ceepak.

Skeletor kick-starts the bike and, in what they call a jump cut (because they chop out a whole chunk of action, which makes the film look jumpy) immediately tugs down on the Boonie hat's leather straps.

"I don't need a BLEEPING helmet."

"Yes, you do."

They've eighty-sixed all of Ceepak's polite "sirs" to make him sound more like a hardcase cop.

"You need the full gear," says Ceepak. He gestures at Skeletor's hat. *"Not the fool's gear."*

Friday, August 13, the day after our chase scene in the parking lot airs on *Fun House,* we're back at the mobile production office.

Ceepak and I are about to storm up the steps when out waltzes the mayor.

Hugh Sinclair looks extremely happy. He is wearing his standard sunglasses on a red Croakie string and a brand new item: a T-shirt that says "Put Down The Corn Cob!"

See? I told you I'm famous.

"Officers! Awesome work last night!" He gives Ceepak a finger pistol. "Picked up one of yours, too!"

"Pardon?" says Ceepak.

"Your shirt. The one that says 'Give Me The Fool's Gear!'"

Geeze-o, man.

"Hey, how come nobody told me last night's show was going to be all about the SHPD and that awesome chase scene?"

Yeah. In case you missed the episode, Ceepak, Skeletor, the motorcycles, and me got almost as much airtime as the food fight and celebrity guest judges. And, if you care, which I don't anymore, Nicole Stanziale got the boot at the end of the show. The "Fun House" ten is down to five.

"But hey," the mayor continues, "I talked to Chief Baines first thing this morning. Guess you guys didn't know you were about to become movie stars either, huh?"

"No, sir," says Ceepak, that popping jawbone joint about to shoot sideways out of his skull. "We did not."

The mayor scampers down the short set of steel steps. Gives Ceepak a hearty handshake.

"We're booked up for the season!"

"What?" I say, because Ceepak is too busy trying to shake free from the mayor's smarmy grip.

"Every hotel, motel, guest house, and B&B on the island is completely sold out. Reservations came pouring in over the Internet last night and early this morning. Morgan's? You can't eat dinner there until sometime in early December. Everybody wants to try their crab pie and see that lobster tank the drunk girl tried to smash with her hammer. So, you guys catch that psycho stalker yet?"

"He is a not a stalker, sir," says Ceepak. "He is a drug dealer."

The mayor crinkles his nose. "Nah. I like the stalker angle better. But hey, talk to Marty." He thumb-gestures over his shoulder. "Maybe he'll go with your idea. Well, I gotta run. TMZ wants to do a satellite interview!"

He bops into his BMW. Ceepak and I storm up the staircase, shove open the trailer door.

We see Marty Mandrake, Rutger the director, Grace the stop-watch lady, and Layla. The TV team is huddled around a table loaded down with trays of doughnuts—the kind they probably have to fly in from a gourmet bakery in Brooklyn.

"Ladies and gentlemen, we are now the top-rated show on television!" says Mandrake proudly.

"Excuse me," says Ceepak as we impolitely barge in.

The production team looks up. Some are in mid-doughnut chomp.

"All *right*!" says Rutger the director. "My two stars! Give me the full gear, baby, not the fool's gear!"

Marty Mandrake swaggers over. His face is puckered up in what he probably thinks is an expression of earnest sincerity. To me, it looks like he has gas.

"Gentlemen, glad you could join us. We need to talk about working you two into next week's scenario."

"You lied to us," says Ceepak.

Mandrake looks shocked. Insulted. "Lied?"

"Yeah," I butt in. "You told us you wouldn't use any of the footage from the drug bust until *after* we arrested Skeletor."

"We *had* to use it, Danny," says Layla.

"Had to?" says Ceepak before I can.

"To protect the kids," says Mandrake. "We can't have these kinds of crazies stalking our stars."

"Mr. Mandrake, the man known as Skeletor is a dealer of illegal drugs. He was not stalking—"

"Did you see the way he tugged up his T-shirt, did that whole Thing thing? He's clearly obsessed with Paulie."

"I don't see how that changes anything."

"Of course not. You're not in show business. Don't know what kind of crazies we have to deal with on a daily basis. So, I'm sorry if we hurt your feelings, if you think we 'lied.'"

"I don't think it; I *know* it."

"Fine. Good for you. Now we have to deal with what comes next. Layla?"

She shoves a folder across the table.

"Paulie Braciole received a very upsetting text message," she says. "A death threat."

"Oh, really?" I say, because I'm guessing they cut together some kind of fake text message the same way they messed with reality in their edit of the parking lot footage. "When'd he get this threat?"

"Wednesday," says Mandrake. "While we were in the editing room. It's what made us scrap our original cut and go with a lot more of the action with Skeletor and the motorcycles."

Yeah. Including the scene where the biker bopped me on the head.

"We needed to let this creep know we've got the goods on him," says Mandrake.

"Might we see this threatening message?" says Ceepak, sounding like he doesn't believe it's any more real than Paulie's humble-pie act under the stormy summer skies.

"Of course," says Ms. Shapiro, flipping open the folder.

Ceepak and I move to the table. Read what's printed on the paper.

"U ratted me out? U R The Dead Thing."

And, as it turns out, that death threat is the one thing from this reality TV show that's really real.

11

THE NEXT MORNING, I GET A CALL FROM CEEPAK.

"It's Paul Braciole," he says, sounding grim.

"What's up?"

"He has been murdered."

I have the phone tucked under my chin so I can pull on my shorts. I glance at the clock. It's eleven thirty. Saturday is my day off. Guess I slept in. I also guess I won't be doing that again until Ceepak and I figure out who murdered Paulie Braciole.

"How?" I ask.

"Single gunshot to the brain. Powder burn on the left temple, exit wound on the right—slightly lower, suggesting that the bullet traversed straight through both hemispheres of the brain, making death instantaneous. We'll know more after Dr. Kurth runs her post-mortem."

Dr. Rebecca Kurth is the county medical examiner. We've been keeping her kind of busy this summer.

I tug on my sneakers.

"Where are you?" I ask, sniffing my uniform polo shirts to find the cleanest one.

"Boardwalk. Pier Four. A booth called the Knock 'Em Down."

Ceepak can't see me, but I'm nodding.

The Knock 'Em Down is one of several "games of chance" tucked into a side alley off the main path to the Giant Ferris Wheel at the end of Pier Four. If I remember correctly, the Knock 'Em Down is done up with a Farmer-In-The-Dell look: a mural with a cartoon horse and cow making goofy faces at you; three wooden barrels with a pyramid of six white milk bottles stacked on top.

You pay a buck and hurl a baseball at the bottles, half of which, I swear, are filled with lead. The only guys knocking them down are friends of the booth operator, who probably has a button he pushes to make the stack topple every once in a while so he can keep reeling in suckers like me.

But I digress.

"Was Paulie shot inside the booth?" I ask.

"Highly doubtful," says Ceepak. "The game operator, a young man named Hugh Williams, discovered Mr. Braciole's body when he rolled up the security gate at eleven hundred hours."

In Sea Haven, our boardwalk amusements don't open till noon, because everybody spends the morning on the beach. Opening at noon also gives the vendors time to fill the bottom of those milk bottles with wet cement.

"Danny?"

I have one arm inside my shirt, but I freeze: I can tell from Ceepak's voice that whatever he's going to say next isn't going to be pretty.

"Yeah?"

"Mr. Williams discovered the body on a side wall of the booth. It was hanging in the middle of the stuffed animals they award as prizes."

I hop in my Jeep and race up to the boardwalk, a good thirty minutes north of my apartment.

Ceepak and the other first responders have sealed off the crime scene with rolled-out POLICE LINE, DO NOT CROSS tape. The taut yellow plastic snaps in the gusts blowing up from the ocean. It looks like we've locked down the whole block of games, even though blinking bulbs are still throbbing in signs outside the unmanned booths: Water Gun Fun, Whack A Mole, Duck Pond, Frog Bog, Clown Bop, Balloon Pop, and Bucket Drop.

Most of the brightly colored booths have their fronts open, and I can see all sorts of stuffed animals hanging off hooks. Giant Teddy Bears wearing New York Mets, Yankees, Jets, and Giants uniforms. SpongeBob SquarePants flashing his two-toothed smile. Giant yellow banana people with pudgy cheeks. Long-limbed fleecy things that look like an octopus crossed with a rhesus monkey.

One or two booths are even offering "Official Fun House" prizes. I see a towering display of boxed-up bobblehead dolls. Paulie "The Thing" molded in mid T-shirt tug, his incredibly ripped chest immortalized in tan plastic.

"Danny?"

It's Ceepak, waving at me from up at the Knock 'Em Down booth. One of our SHPD cruisers is parked thirty feet beyond the booth, its roofbar lights swirling, blocking off the mob of onlookers licking their orange-and-white swirl cones, trying to see what the heck is going on.

Officers Nikki Bonanni and Jen Forbus are working crowd control at the far end. The two Murray brothers have caught the duty at the end where I entered.

"Put down the corncob," yells some young wiseass in the crowd.

"Give me the full gear!" shouts another.

I shake my head. Six years ago? Both those guys would've been me.

"Detective Botzong is on his way," says Ceepak when I reach the Knock 'Em Down.

William Botzong heads up the State Police Major Crimes Unit. They always get called in to do all the stuff they do on those CSI TV shows when a murder takes place in, oh, say a Jersey Shore resort town where the police department isn't geared up to handle all the forensic work needed to mount a modern-day murder investigation, even though Ceepak has his own mini-crime lab on the second floor of police headquarters and watches every episode of *Forensic Files*. I think he has them on DVD too.

We had worked with Botzong back in June. He's good people. In his spare time, he likes to sing in community theatre productions. Ceepak and I caught him in *Jesus Christ Superstar.* He'd had to wear a wig to hide his cop crew cut.

"We can assume that the killer placed the body in this very public location to send some sort of message," says Ceepak.

"A mob hit? From Skeletor and his biker buddies?"

"It's a possibility, Danny."

I look up and see Paulie Braciole hanging on the wall between a giant pink gorilla and a flock of floppy green ducks. His head is slumped forward, so, fortunately, I don't have to stare at his dead eyes. Whoever pinioned him to the wall had twisted the straps of his muscleman tee shirt into a knot that they then tied around a hook, leaving Paulie's neck limp, his head sagging. Dry blood streams down from a temple-high hole in his fade haircut, just in front of his left ear, and trickles across his shoulder and down both sides of his tight white tee.

I note a ring of brown circling his neck. Also—some of the blood smears upward, instead of dribbling down.

"What's going on around his neck?"

"Unclear," says Ceepak. "The circle, to some extent, resembles a ligature mark. But it is not a bruise. It is blood."

"What about those smears?"

"Perhaps the killer originally tried hanging Mr. Braciole with a noose. Discovering that he did not need the rope, he slipped it up and off his head."

"Streaking the blood upward."

Ceepak nods. "But all of this is pure conjecture on my part. I found no rope fibers. No noose. However, I did note dried blood on the floor."

Meaning Paulie was still dripping when the killer hung him out to dry.

Ceepak makes a hand chop toward the rear wall of the booth. "There is a trail of blood out back. I also noticed a set of footprints and a single tire tread."

"Like from a unicycle or something?"

Ceepak shakes his head. "Motorcycle, Danny. Two tires, one directly behind the other, leaving behind a single furrow."

Right. Duh.

"Botzong's team will want to plaster-cast both the footprint and the tire track." Ceepak pulls a miniature digital camera out of the calf pocket of his cargo pants. He always wears long pants when we're working a murder case. More pockets to stow stuff in. "Hopefully, they can also shed some light on the blood ringing the neck."

I look up at Paul Braciole, his limp arms dangling at his sides like one of those bright pink fuzzy orangutan things. Something silver and frayed is wrapped around both of his wrists.

"Is that duct tape?" I ask.

"Roger that," says Ceepak. "There is also evidence of it on both of his shoes. Mostly gummy residue with some filament webbing."

"So they tied him up with duct tape so they could execute him?"

"Uncertain at this juncture. Also, there is no sign of duct tape around either of his ankles, or his calves."

I nod. If you were tying up your victim, you wouldn't just bind up his hands and shoes, you'd secure his legs and feet too.

On the rear wall, in that farm-scene mural, I notice a seam cutting through horsey's snout and a doorknob poking up in the center of a flower.

"Was the back door locked?"

"Yes. But it was a simple hardware-store lock attached to a flimsy hasp. Judging from the splintering plywood where the screws ripped free, the killer was able to kick it open quite easily."

"Any security cameras?"

"Negative. The major investment in booth security was out here." He indicates the rolling steel gate, now stowed inside its overhead housing.

"What about the guy who discovered the body? Hugh Williams."

"Junior at the local high school. Became quite ill when he smelled all the bodily fluids that had seeped out of Mr. Braciole during the period of time he hung on the wall."

Okay. When Ceepak calmly downloads information like that, I know his big brain is off doing something else.

"Cameras," he mumbles.

"You said there weren't any."

He shakes his head. "At the house."

He doesn't mean police headquarters, even though we always call it "the house."

He means the Fun House.

They video everything, 24/7. That's how I know Soozy K and Mike Tomasino are now whoo-hooing with each other. I saw him crawl into her bed right under this creepy night-vision security cam at the end of the "stalker in the parking lot" episode.

"Dylan? Jeremy?" Ceepak calls to the Murray brothers. "Hold down the fort."

"You got it," says Dylan.

"Come on, Danny. We need to go visit our friends at Prickly Pear Productions."

Great. We're going to get a sneak preview of coming attractions. See if, last night, all those *Fun House* cameras had shot anything that might help us catch a killer.

12

WE RACE DOWN THE ISLAND TOWARD HALIBUT STREET.

I'm thinking Skeletor or one of his Creed biker brethren killed Paulie as payback for splashing them all over prime time TV Thursday night. That would explain the very public execution and the motorcycle tire tracks Ceepak had discovered out back behind the Knock 'Em Down booth.

"Let's not jump to conclusions," says Ceepak when I mention my suspicions. "Remember—a mind is like a parachute. It works best when it is open."

I would groan, but I'm trying to keep an open mind here.

We climb out of our cop car and clamber up those steps to the production trailer.

Inside, when our eyes adjust to the darkness (these guys could grow mushrooms in here), we see Marty Mandrake planted in his director's chair in a front of a TV monitor. He's munching grapes again. Organic, I'm guessing.

Grace, the woman with all the stopwatches draped around her neck, is the only other person in the room.

On the small screen they're both glued to, I can see Soozy K. She's wearing a black bikini under some kind of black knit wrap. She is also sniffling. Black mascara streaks down her cheeks, making her look like a wet newspaper.

"Paulie and I had something special," she says to that off-camera interviewer who's probably not even there. *"Sure, it hurt when he hooked up with Jenny, but that doesn't mean I didn't still have feelings for him. I didn't expect it to happen, but we made a connection, you know?"* Big sniff. *"I've never met anyone like Paulie. Never. I'd give anything for us to continue our journey, to have him flash me again."*

Marty Mandrake nearly chokes on a grape, spits it out like a little green cannonball.

"No, no, no!" he hollers into his walkie-talkie. I can hear his voice, a half-second delayed, echoing out of the TV screen. Soozy K pouts like an upset puppy.

"What the fuck?" she snaps, smearing the phony tears off her schnozzle. *"What's your fucking problem now, Marty?"*

"You're killing me here, babe," Marty screams into his walkie-talkie. "Jesus, kid—you're supposed to be in fucking mourning."

"So?" Soozy chomps her gum hard. Yep, she'd had a cud of Dentyne tucked up inside her cheek the whole time she was getting all choked up for the camera. *"Paulie screwed me over, Marty! We had an alliance! What's he doing bumping ugly with that skank Jenny Mortadella?"*

Ceepak steps forward. I can tell: he has heard enough.

"Sir?"

Mandrake glances over his left shoulder. Snorts. Then ignores us because, judging from his bright bulging eyes and fast finger snap, he just had a Big Idea. "I got it. This is brilliant, babe. Say 'I guess we weren't meant to be.'"

"At least not in this lifetime," adds Grace who, I'm guessing, reads a lot of those books about teenaged vampires.

"Beautiful!" Mandrake reaches over with both hands. Kisses Miss Stopwatches on her forehead. "I love it."

"Mr. Mandrake?" Ceepak again. Louder this time.

"What? I'm working here."

"So are we."

Mandrake sighs. Picks up his walkie-talkie. "Rutger? Take five. We have visitors."

They way he says "visitors," it sounds like we're the swine flu or something.

"How can I help you two today?" says Mandrake, sounding all sorts of snotty.

Ceepak gestures toward the monitor where Soozy K's blank-eyed face fills the frame. Her lips flap silently. She must be memorizing her new lines.

"Surely," says Ceepak, "you have canceled any future *Fun House* episodes."

"We thought about it," says Mandrake. "But then we realized that that would be the selfish reaction. The coward's way out."

"Come again?"

Mandrake gives us his I'm-so-earnest-it-hurts face again. "Officer Ceepak, this is a time of great sorrow for me and everyone connected to this show." Stopwatch Woman nods. Her timekeeping necklaces clack into each other. "Paul Braciole wasn't just a television star and cultural icon. He was a friend. He was family."

Why do I get the feeling Mr. Mandrake is trying out the official statement some network PR guy has just written up for him?

"However," he continues, "Paulie loved this show. *Fun House* was his home. To quit now, to disappoint millions and millions of Paulie's loyal fans, well, that wouldn't be the kind of legacy the Paul Braciole I knew would want to leave behind. No, sir. The show must go on."

"Mr. Braciole was murdered," says Ceepak. "His killer is still at large."

"Which is why, next Thursday night, we will be dedicating a full hour of prime time TV to honor Paul's memory and to help you guys track that killer down."

My turn to stammer. "What?"

"It's *Survivor* meets *Jersey Shore* meets *America's Most Wanted,*" says Layla Shapiro, who must've slipped into the room behind us. She's carrying a foam-core poster board. "The network art department just e-mailed me a JPG of the graphic they want to go with."

She flips it around to flash a scary Post Office wanted-poster portrait of Skeletor.

"We pulled his facial features off last week's episode," Layla bubbles on. "Had an artist enhance it. I love what she did with the cross-hatching and shadows. Not crazy about the typeface. You still want to call it 'To Catch a Killer'?"

"You bet," says Mandrake. "It pops. Got all those K sounds going on. Catch a Killer."

"Fine," says Layla. "We'll open with the 'Funeral for a Friend' graphic, slam it out with this."

Mandrake is up and out of his chair, admiring the gruesome graphic.

"And tell those idiots I want smoke when this image blows the other one away. We're all tinkle-tinkle piano music over the funeral logo and, then—boom. In comes 'To Catch a Killer!' The funeral logo needs to crumble like a wall of bricks. I want an avalanche!"

"Awesome," says Layla. "Oh—I'm talking to Elton's people. They might let us use his song for the open. He's a huge fan."

I'm guessing "Elton" is Sir Elton John. I think he wrote a song called "Funeral for a Friend." I know Springsteen sure didn't.

"I want Elton to perform it!" says Mandrake. "Live! I see candles everywhere. Blowing in the wind. Buffeted by the sea breeze. . . ."

"The cast joins him on the chorus!" adds Layla.

"Yes! They hold hands and sing!"

"It's Must-See TV!"

Once again, Ceepak has heard enough.

"You cannot be serious," he says.

"About what?" asks Mandrake.

"Putting all this on television."

"Grow up, Bubeleh. It's already on television. The newsboys are running with it big-time. And not just our network. Fox, CNN, MSNBC. They're all over it like mayonnaise on bologna."

Okay, judging by the jaw pops, my partner is now furious. "You should never have run that footage of Skeletor and the motorcycle gang. You may have provoked this attack on your 'family.'"

"Whoa. Ease up, cowboy."

"You gave us your word you would not utilize any of that footage until after the arrest of our suspect."

"When? I don't remember making any such promise."

I nod toward Layla. "Your associate did."

"You have it in writing?" says Mandrake.

"No."

"So you learned a valuable lesson. Always make people put their promises on paper. That's why God invented lawyers."

"We need the footage," says Ceepak.

Mandrake and Layla both cock their heads sideways.

"What footage?" she says it first.

"From your cameras inside the house and out on the deck."

"We need to piece together everything we can about the hours before Mr. Braciole's death," I add.

"It is quite possible," says Ceepak, "that your cameras caught him leaving the house with his killer."

Mandrake puts his hands together to make a prayerful pup tent under his nose.

"You're right. That would be amazing."

Layla's nodding. "Fucking incredible."

Mandrake runs his hand across the air imagining a movie marquee. "The last minutes of Paulie Braciole's life. Dead man walking. . . ."

"It would be fucking awesome," says Layla. "Unfortunately. . . ." She trails off.

"What?" demands Ceepak.

"Last night," says Mandrake, somewhat sheepishly, "we encountered technical difficulties."

"How so?"

"A genny glitch," says Layla.

"Pardon?"

"Our power generator," says Mandrake. "It died last night too."

13

Layla is wearing that tight white gym top with the low-slung shorts again—the ones that show off her flat abs and diving pelvis bone.

But I'm not falling for it.

Well, I might.

So I'm forcing myself to stare at Marty Mandrake. His belly button is completely covered by a trampoline-tight polo shirt. I believe said belly button is currently drooped somewhere over his belt buckle.

"You run all this on generator power?" says Ceepak, gesturing at the glowing TV screens and blinking buttons in the command center.

"Yeah," says Mandrake with an ironic chuckle. "Supposed to protect us against blackouts. Capturing real time, the last thing we need is to lose power when something amazing happens."

"But you did?" Ceepak's brow is knit with confusion.

"Go figure. Murphy's Law, huh?"

"Surely you have a crew member whose sole responsibility it is to keep the generator fully functional at all times."

"That we do," says Layla. "And the last guy who had the job got fired this morning at five A.M. when I rolled in and discovered we were completely dark."

"What happened?" I ask. "Somebody forget to swing by the gas station and fill 'er up?"

Layla shoots me a dirty look. "Yeah, Danny. That's exactly what happened."

"Officer Boyle," says Ceepak.

"What?"

"While engaged in official police business, kindly address my partner as Officer Boyle."

"Fine. Whatever. Jesus." And then she mutters, "Put down the corncob."

Yep. She is mocking me. This doesn't usually happen until sometime around the *fifth* date.

"The genny runs on diesel," says Mandrake. "The guy on the truck, what can I say? He's an idiot! The union will have to deal with him. I don't care if he is a fucking Teamster!"

"What about the handheld cameras?" I blurt out.

Layla ignores me; Mandrake grunts a "huh?"

"The cameras you take on location," I say. "They run on battery packs, right?"

"Yeah. So? They're not going to help you with when Paul left the house, kid. Those cameras in the bedrooms, they're all powered by the genny."

"We'd still like to see the footage from the portable units," says Ceepak, giving me the slightest head bob to let me know I done good.

"No problem," says Mandrake. "What's mine is yours. Last night, we sent the five remaining contestants to a dance club recommended by your mayor, Mr. Sinclair."

"Big Kahuna's?" I say, remembering how Sinclair and the owner of that dance barn, Keith Barent Johnson, III, are tight.

"Yeah. That's the place. We were shooting the opening scenes for our big dance competition, which was going to be the centerpiece of next week's show."

"So now it's *Jersey Shore* and *The Bachelor Pad* meets *Dancing with the Stars*?" I say before Layla can.

Mandrake shoots me a finger pistol. "You're good, kid. Of course, we're scrapping the dance-off. Giving everybody immunity this week. No one will get booted out of the house in Episode Eight."

"Was Mr. Braciole at the dance club?" asks Ceepak.

Mandrake shrugs. "I assume so."

"Yes, he was," says Layla.

Ceepak remains focused on Mandrake. "You weren't at the shoot last night?"

"No."

"Why not?"

Another shrug. "I took the night off."

Ceepak gives Marty Mandrake his trademark slow and quizzical head tilt—it's very similar to how a dog will cock its head when it doesn't understand what you mean by repeating "roll over" over and over.

"You ever take a night off, officer?" Mandrake says with a wink.

Ceepak doesn't wink back.

"I let Layla and Rutger run things."

Ceepak takes a step forward. "Where exactly were you, Mr. Mandrake?"

"What?"

Ceepak whips out his trusty notebook and stubby pencil. "We need to account for everybody's whereabouts."

"You saying I need an alibi?"

"No. I am asking: 'Where were you last night?'"

"I was down in Atlantic City. Trust me—I left a trail of credit card charges. A very *deep* trail. Satisfied?"

"For now. Yes."

Now Ceepak turns to Layla.

"Were you at the club, Ms. Shapiro? Big Kahuna's."

"For the pre-light and first roll. I, too, needed a night off."

"And where were you?"

She doesn't give Ceepak any guff, because she just saw how well that tactic worked for her boss.

"I had a date."

"With whom?"

"A guy."

"Does this 'guy' have a name?"

"They usually do."

Ceepak waits. Me, too. Curious to see who has replaced me in the whoo-hoo department.

"Phil. No, I'm sorry. Bill. Billy. I met him at the bar."

"Do you have proof to substantiate your claim?"

"You want to see the used condom?"

Ceepak's face reddens. "A local phone number will suffice."

She pulls out her iPhone. Diddles her fingers across the glass.

"I'll text you the text he texted me after I sent him home at three. Parental discretion is advised. Billy's totally into sexting. You *do not* want to open the attachments."

In my pocket, I can feel my cell vibrating. I let it roll into the message center.

Ceepak puts away his note pad.

"Where is the dance club footage?"

"Still in the cameras," says Mandrake. "The crew worked late. Didn't wrap until three, maybe four in the morning. We had to give them an eight-hour turnaround. It's a union rule. And then boom: Unit Two is down on the boardwalk, covering you guys doing your thing in the Knock 'Em Down booth; Rutger's here at the house rolling on reactions from Soozy; Unit Three's down on Ocean Avenue with Jenny."

"We'll talk to Mr. Reinhertz first," says Ceepak.

"Rutger?" Mandrake makes a big deal of looking at his watch. "Jesus, guys—you're killing me. We're on a tight schedule."

"Us too," says Ceepak. "We'll be with Mr. Reinhertz."

Ceepak and I head out the door and tromp down the metal steps. We start hoofing it around the corner, heading for the Fun House.

Suddenly, Ceepak stops in his tracks.

So I stop too.

Ceepak looks me square in the eyes. I have never seen so much parental concern; especially not from my parents.

"I'm sorry that didn't work out, Danny."

"Huh?"

He nods back toward the trailer. "Ms. Shapiro. Rita and I both imagined that you two might become romantically involved."

I shrug. "We only dated a few times."

Ceepak stuffs his hands into his pockets. Drops his head slightly. We shuffle up the block. All of a sudden, I feel like I'm on the cover of an L.L. Bean catalog, walking in the woods of Maine, having a man-to-man chat with my dad, who would never actually talk with me this much about "girl trouble." He'd just tell me to go see my mother or send me to the library to ask for a brochure.

"Given how you two met," Ceepak continues, "it is understandable that there would be an immediate and overwhelming physical attraction."

He means the fact that Layla Shapiro and I had met when, together, we defused a very tense hostage situation in the control room of the Rolling Thunder roller coaster. And, by defused, I mean we both could've been killed.

"Yeah," I say. "They say an adrenaline rush is a surefire aphrodisiac."

Ceepak nods. "But now young faces grow sad and old and hearts of fire grow cold."

I grin. The big lug has the heart of a poet. Or, at least, he knows how to borrow from one: Springsteen.

We say no more. We don't have to. The Boss and his music fill in all the gaps.

We keep walking.

Then Ceepak stops again.

There's a light bulb over his head. It's a street lamp, but I can tell he's having an idea too.

14

"We need to contact Gus Davis," says Ceepak.

"He was working the security detail last night?"

"Roger that. He would have been at the dance club with the cast. Might be able to fill us in on any details about what transpired there."

We move into a patch of shade under one of the few trees on the block so Ceepak can read his cell phone screen. He puts it on speakerphone mode so I can hear.

"I quit," are the first words out of Gus's mouth, before Ceepak says anything.

"Gus, this is John Ceepak."

"Yeah, I know. My grandkids figured out how to make this caller I.D. thing work. Freaking phone company."

"Danny and I need to ask you a few questions."

"You want to know how freaking sick I am of baby-sitting those drunken ding-dongs? You want to know how much I don't need their royal pain in

my butt? They're freaking animals. You don't need retired cops running security; you need zookeepers."

"Gus, have you heard the news this morning?"

"What? That crap about the school board?"

"No. Paul Braciole. From *Fun House*."

"Paulie. He the one with the drug problem? Always wants to flash you his high beams?"

"10-4."

"What about him?"

"He was murdered."

"Son of a sea cook. When?"

"Uncertain at this juncture. Most likely late last night or early this morning."

"Crap on a cracker."

"Were you there for the entire shoot at Big Kahuna's dance club?"

"Yeah. Didn't get home till three in the freaking morning."

"What can you tell us about Mr. Braciole's movements?"

"They're terrible. Dances like Travolta with three left feet."

"Did he go home with the rest of the cast when they finished filming?"

"No."

I glance up at Ceepak. He gives me the knowing nod.

"Gus? What happened?"

"He was at the bar, doing that T-shirt flasher bit with a hot toddy who looked totally tanked. Anyways, Paulie's over there, hiking up his shirt, wiggling her his nay-nays; she's impressed. They chug a few beers, knock back a few shots of Jägermeister, badda-bing, badda-boom, they're waltzing out the door looking to book the honeymoon suite at the Motel No Tell, if you catch my drift."

"Did you follow after them?"

"Nah. Couldn't. That other one, the one with the hair that looks like a dog bowl, he and the two loudmouth dames started in with some of the

locals. You know, John Broadwater and that bunch. I think Broadwater wanted to get his picture in the papers decking the smart mouth with the hair, Tomasino I think his name is. So I'm busy breaking that up, because Tomasino's going on and on about how he's going to win a quarter million bucks and hire Broadwater to wipe his butt with hundred-dollar bills, crap like that."

"So Mr. Braciole and this local girl—"

"She might've been a tourist. She was wearing high heels and one of those shiny sausage skirts that barely cover her ass, you know what I mean?"

Ceepak closes his eyes. Sighs. "Yes, Gus. I am familiar with the dress style you are describing."

"Yeah, I'm figuring she's a tourist. Local girls know better than to walk around town at midnight looking like two-bit tarts."

True. They usually have the decency to quit around eleven.

"Did Braciole and his date leave the dance club unescorted?"

"Yeah, I guess so. Like I said, I was busy breaking up that thing between Tomasino and Broadwater. I think Ponytail followed Paulie and his floozy out the door."

"Ponytail?"

"This mug lugging a camera. Has one of those hippy hairdos. He and two other yahoos went chasing after Paulie and Miss Hot Hiney. Some guy with a freaking bright light; another one holding out something fuzzy on a flagpole. Looked like a giant squirrel tail."

The squirrel tail on the pole would be a boom microphone. Layla taught me that. Back before she met whoever she'd hooked up with last night.

"Thank you, Gus," says Ceepak.

"You need anything else?"

"Not right now."

"Good. I've got fish to gut. Catch you later."

Ceepak thumbs the off button. Presses a speed dial.

"Who you calling next?" I ask.

"Prickly Pear Productions. Ms. Shapiro."

"She's probably still in the trailer." Which, I don't add, is only about fifty feet behind us.

"Danny, to be honest, I'd rather not go back in there again until we absolutely have to."

I nod. The feeling is mutual.

"Ms. Shapiro? John Ceepak. Quick question. Does one of your cameramen wear his hair in a ponytail?"

He nods so I can see that he has been answered in the affirmative.

"Where might Jimbo and Unit Three be now? Thank you. What? I understand. However, this is extremely urgent."

Now Ceepak does something I've never seen him do before: he makes a duckbill out of his left hand and flaps the thumb and fingers open and shut—giving me the universal "blah-blah-blah" sign.

"Right. Roger that. Okay. Thank you. We have to run."

Finally, he snaps shut the phone.

"Danny, do you know the Starfish Boutique?"

"It's on Ocean Avenue. Most expensive clothes on the island."

"Apparently the cameraman with the ponytail is named Jimbo Green. He is currently filming Jenny Mortadella at the dress shop because she 'doesn't have anything decent to wear.'"

Funny. I thought that was the whole point of the Fun House wardrobe: the more indecent, the better.

And then Ceepak adds the kicker: "She needs a black outfit for Mr. Braciole's funeral. They're filming it first thing Monday morning."

15

We head down to Ocean Avenue.

I'm behind the wheel, wondering what the "weekly competition" will be on *Fun House: The Funeral Edition.*

Casket-tossing?

Competitive pall-bearing?

Maybe they can do a "rose ceremony" with all the funeral flowers. They could form teams and run a gravesite floral-arrangement contest.

We park at the curb outside the Starfish Boutique. Their motto: "Why just be another fish in the sea when you can be the star?" It's painted on both display windows flanking the front door. The mannequins wear gowns worked over by someone with a BeDazzler.

The glow of a blindingly bright spotlight swings by the window on the left. Jenny Mortadella, led by a sales associate in what they call "glamorous resort wear," is being trailed by a full camera crew as she heads over to a rack of black garments. Judging by his pony-tail, the man operating the camera aimed at Jenny's badonkadonk is Jimbo Green.

Ceepak pauses at the front door. He's polite enough to let Jimbo finish his shot.

"What the fuck is this shit?" Jenny brays, slapping her way through the hanging black dresses.

"These represent the finest in funereal fashion," says the helpful assistant. "Remember, no matter how somber, funerals are, at their heart, social outings. And, just like weddings, there will be a lot of single, emotional people there. A long black dress with a steep neckline can be respectful *and* provocative."

"I'll fucking melt. You can't wear fucking black in the fucking sun!"

"Cut!" shouts Jimbo.

"We're cutting," echoes his stopwatch-clipboard guy. Off goes the floodlight. Down comes the squirrel-tail boom microphone. Ceepak pushes open the door.

"Mr. Green?"

Jimbo whirls around, camera mounted on his shoulder.

"Yeah?"

"I'm Officer John Ceepak with the Sea Haven Police Department. This is my partner, Danny Boyle."

"Yeah, sure! From the parking lot. 'Give me the fool gear.' Right on." He gives us a righteous-dude fist pump. "You two rock."

"Oh, um, *hey,* Danny!" says the sales associate.

I recognize her now, even though she's wearing grownup clothes. Her name is Lissa. We went to high school together. She always looked great in black, which is all she wore, because, back then, she was like our class's Goth chick poet. Wrote about sea gulls contemplating suicide a lot.

"We need to ask you a few questions," Ceepak says to Jimbo.

"Cool."

"Um, can I take my break now?" asks Lissa.

"Yes, ma'am," says Ceepak. "That might be a good idea."

"Five minutes, sweetheart!" says Jimbo. "And you did good with the script. Keep it up, you'll be a star."

"Ha," snarls Jenny. "Fat fucking chance."

Lissa ignores Jenny and breezes past Ceepak and me. I realize she still smells like patchouli oil and pot. I hear a locker bang open and shut in the storeroom. Probably where she stashes her bong or bowl. I guess she wants to stash her weed some place better so we don't find it.

"Hey—I'm fucking hungry, here, Jimbo," says Jenny, painting lip-gloss on her puckered puss.

"New Guy?" Jimbo says to one of the crew guys in khaki shorts and hipster ski cap.

"Yeah?"

"Fix Miss Mortadella a plate at the craft services table."

The new guy nods. Poor kid. He looks to be my age. Probably what they call a P.A., or production assistant. Lowest man on the TV-crew totem pole. Layla told me that was how she got started in the business.

"And grab me a half-apple," says Jimbo.

New Guy looks confused. "You don't want the whole thing?"

Jimbo rolls his eyes. "Where'd Marty find you, kid? The New Jersey Film School For Idiots?"

The other crew guys kind of drop their eyes. I get the sense that Jimbo, despite his peace-loving hippy hairdo, is a first-class buttwipe.

But nobody says anything.

New Guy stands there. Stoic. No emotion at all. But inside, I'll bet he's wondering about that fifty thousand dollars he still owes on his college loan so he could attend NYU film school and get a job stepping and fetching.

Ceepak steps forward.

"Apple boxes," he states with great confidence, because I'm sure that, as soon as *Fun House* landed on our beaches, he spent several nights researching production lingo, "are wooden boxes of varying sizes with holes on each end that are chiefly used in film production. The 'half-apple' is typically four inches tall, whereas the 'full apple' is eight inches."

"Well done, Officer," says Jimbo. "You want a job on my crew?"

"No, thank you."

New Guy nods thanks to Ceepak, tugs down on his knit cap, heads for the door.

"Half-apples are on the grip truck," says the man holding the microphone boom like a broomstick. "Round back."

"Craft services table is back there, too," adds the spotlight toter.

Guess these two both remember their first days on the job, working for a jerk like Jimbo.

"And, New Guy?" shouts the big man, Jimbo, so his crew will remember who's the boss.

The kid turns around.

"Hustle, baby. Hustle."

Out he goes.

Jimbo struts over to Ceepak. "We need to have Jenny stand on something. She's disappearing, ruining my shot."

"I heard that," snaps Jenny as she jabs out her hip, anchors her hand on it.

"I'm just trying to make you look good, babe."

"Why do I need to wear fucking black?"

"'Cause it's a fucking funeral," Jimbo answers. "We're back in five. Everybody chill. I need to chat with the police officers here."

"Back in five," yells the clipboard man.

Ceepak holds open the door. "Bring your camera," he says.

Jimbo does as he's told.

The three of us cluster around the front of our parked vehicle.

"What's up, bro?" Jimbo asks, giving his ponytail an artful flick.

"Last night," says Ceepak, "you followed Paul Braciole out of the Big Kahuna dance club?"

"That's right. Me, Chuck, and Rich. We peeled off from the pack. Rutger sent us after Paulie and his hot date. Very attractive local lady in an extremely tight skirt. Her butt shimmered, man. I wish we could've hosed down the streets, got that slick surface going, like we do in car commercials. But this is reality TV. No time to light right."

"Chuck and Rich?" says Ceepak.

Jimbo jabs his thumb toward the dress shop. "My sound and light guys."

"Where did Mr. Braciole and his date go?"

"A couple blocks north. 136 Red Snapper Street."

Ceepak makes a face to let Jimbo know he's impressed. "You're certain about the address?"

"Yeah. We were camped out in the front yard till like three in the morning."

Ceepak has his notepad and pencil out. "How so?"

Jimbo flicks his ponytail again. Maybe he's like a horse, uses it to swat flies. "Like I said, me and my boys, we tailed Paulie and his hot little honey out of the dance club, hoping to catch some hot and heavy action. Now, if they had headed back to the Fun House, we would have, you know, been able to follow them inside, tailed 'em all the way into the bedroom, might have even hung around to catch a little nookie action."

Ceepak's left eye twitches. "Go on," he says.

While he talks, Jimbo monkeys with buttons on his camera, peers into the viewfinder.

"This house on Red Snapper being the girl's abode," he says, while squinting into that little rubber-cupped box, "we can't go in without an invitation, which, you know, wasn't exactly forthcoming. In fact, yeah . . . here we go." He holds up the camera so Ceepak can peek at the playback. "Check it out."

Ceepak does.

"I see," he says after a few seconds. He pulls back from the camera.

"You see Paulie give me the finger?"

Ceepak just nods.

"I hope Marty cuts it into the show, seeing how I got the last fucking shot of Paulie before, you know, he got whacked by the stalker or whatever. But they probably won't use it. Paulie flipping me off doesn't fit in with this week's narrative. That 'Funeral for a Friend' jive Marty pitched the network. Ratings will be through the roof. Just like Princess Diana."

Ceepak reaches for the radio clipped to his utility belt.

"Excuse me," he says to Jimbo. "We need to send a unit over to the house on Red Snapper. Interview the woman."

"Cool. Can we roll with you dudes? We're pretty unobtrusive. We'd shoot you grilling the chick, catch it all guerilla gonzo style."

"Not gonna happen," I say as Ceepak radios in a request for the first available unit to respond to 136 Red Snapper Street, to hold a "blonde female, approximately five feet, two inches tall, one hundred pounds, with a mole on her left cheek" for questioning.

Ceepak. While watching a video of a drunken girl in a skimpy skirt bopping up a dark street, he keeps his eye on the distinguishing characteristics.

"Hey, if it helps," says Jimbo, "the chick's name is Mandy."

Ceepak, gripping his radio mic in one hand, cocks an eyebrow.

"She was wearing that T-shirt over her sausage dress," Jimbo explains. "You know—the one that says 'Remember my name. You'll be screaming it later.' So Paulie, he's such a joker, he says 'What am I gonna scream, baby?' and the chick with the hooters says 'Mandy.'"

Ceepak adds the name "Mandy" to his bulletin then clips the radio back on his belt.

"How long did you stay outside the house?" he asks.

"Till Mandy came back out, pretty close to three A.M."

"I take it Paulie was not with her?"

"That's right. She came out in this skimpy bathrobe, even shorter than that skirt she'd been wearing at the club. Told us we were wasting our time: Paulie was gone. 'I have a back door, numbnuts,' were her exact words." He holds up the camera. "You want me to find the clip?"

"No, thank you," says Ceepak. "We'll talk to her ourselves. I'm curious as to why Paulie left."

"Oh, I'm sure he wanted to stay. But the *Fun House* kids have this curfew. They can, you know, hound-dog around town all they want, but they have to be back in the sack at the shack on Halibut Street by 3 A.M.—gives Marty more R-rated action to shoot with all those locked-off night-vision cameras bolted to the ceilings."

Except last night, when the generator died.

"Thank you for your time, Mr. Green," says Ceepak.

"No problem. Hey, did Marty give you guys a bit for the funeral show?"

"No," says Ceepak.

"Hey, dig this: you two could go on camera and ask for America's help tracking down Paulie's killer."

"No, thank you. We'll leave any on-camera performing to the trained professionals."

That's Ceepak cracking wise.

Guess I've been a bad influence on the poor guy.

16

"YOUSE TWO MIGHT WANT TO HEAD BACK TO THE BOARDWALK, seeing how Officer McAlister says Mandy needs a few minutes to, you know, 'freshen up.'"

Yes, our dispatcher, Mrs. Dorian Rence, puts her motherly touch on all her official radio broadcasts.

Ceepak is working the radio in the front seat of our Crown Vic. I'm behind the wheel.

"10-4," he says to the mic gripped in his hand.

"Besides," Mrs. Rence continues, *"Detective Botzong, who's still in the Knock 'Em Down booth, he says his people found something very interesting."*

"Did he give you any indication as to what it is he discovered?"

"A video. From a security camera. You think it shows the killer?"

"It's a possibility, Mrs. Rence."

"Golly bum, I sure hope so. The phone here is ringing off the hook. I already talked to Billy Bush and Mark Steines!"

Ceepak glances over to me.

I fill in the blanks for him. "*Access Hollywood* and *Entertainment Tonight*."

He still looks confused.

"They're TV tabloid shows. Cover entertainment and celebrities."

Ceepak nods slowly like, oh, yeah, he's heard that such things exist. I figure that at 7 P.M. on weeknights he's usually watching *Cold Case Files* on A&E. He's just not as interested in Jennifer Aniston, the Jonas Brothers, or Brangelina as the rest of America.

"We had to dispatch six more auxiliary officers to the Fun House," Mrs. Rence continues on the radio. *"All the big shows are setting up camp to cover the story. I like that Billy Bush. He asks the questions I'd ask if, you know, I ever met Brad Pitt or that other one, Julia Roberts."*

Ceepak likes Mrs. Rence. Heck, we all do. But judging from the grimace on his face, he has heard enough.

"Dorian," he says, "please advise Officer McAlister that we are detouring back to the boardwalk and will join him and the witness—"

"Mandy Keenan."

"Come again?"

"That's her name, John. The girl who, you know, did whatever with Paulie Braciole last night."

"Thank you, Mrs. Rence. Tell Officer McAlister we'll join him as soon as we take a look at Detective Botzong's video."

"Roger that," says Mrs. Rence. *"10-4. Over and out."*

Mrs. Rence has only been on the job a few months. She's a fast learner, but, well, she kind of jumbles everything up into one big gumbo of police mumbo-jumbo.

"We caught a break," says Bill Botzong as he leads us up into the back of the State Police Major Crimes Unit's brand-new Mobile Crime Scene Investigation Unit. It's basically a one-hundred-thousand-dollar step-van with a ladder going up to the roof, where there's this little deck, a couple antennae, and more ladders.

I guess, in New Jersey, a lot of our forensic evidence is found in trees and other hard-to-reach places.

Inside the back of the new van, Botzong and his techies have all sorts of gear, including—my favorite—a Cyanoacrylate Fuming Kit for finding fingerprints with superglue fuming.

There is also digital video player.

And a box of Dunkin' Donuts.

"You guys hungry?" asks Botzong, gesturing at the open-lid tray. I see a toasted coconut with my name on it.

"No, thank you," says Ceepak.

"Danny?"

"I'm good."

Okay. It's a lie, but Ceepak doesn't notice. He's too eager to see what kind of lucky break Botzong has caught.

"What'd you find, Bill?" he asks.

"A quick clip of our killer bringing the body to the boardwalk. Seems there are security cameras in the parking lots of the three motels across Beach Lane from the boardwalk access point closest to the Knock 'Em Down booth," Botzong explains as he thumbs the remote for the video player to advance the digits to the point he wants us to see. "P.S.—there's a ramp at that entrance."

"For wheelchairs," I say.

"Or motorcycles," adds Ceepak.

"Exactly," says Botzong. "Anyway, one of those cameras, in the parking lot of the Flamingo Motel, is aimed in such a way that it picks up a little bit of street traffic, too."

"Beach Lane?" says Ceepak.

"Right."

"How fortuitous."

Yeah, I think. *And lucky, too.*

"At 3:17 A.M.," Botzong continues, "our killer putters through the frame."

"Motorcycle?"

"Yep. Which, of course, explains that tire track you found out back, behind the booth. Carolyn Miller pegs the ride as a 2010 Harley-Davidson Sportster 1200 Low."

Carolyn Miller, who helped us on the Rolling Thunder case, is probably the State MCU's top tire-tread analyst. I don't know how you become one of those. Probably hang out with the Pep Boys; ask Manny, Moe, and Jack a bunch of questions.

"Carolyn tells me she had to isolate the front tire pattern from the rear, even though they're almost on top of each other, as they are slightly different. A Dunlop 100/90 R19 57H up front, Dunlop 150/80 R16 71H in the back."

Ceepak nods like, somehow, it all makes perfect sense to him. Me? I'm still checking out the tread pattern on that toasted-coconut donut.

"If memory serves," says Ceepak, "the Harley-Davidson Low models have what I would call a long, cushioned seat plus footpegs over staggered shorty exhaust pipes to accommodate a second passenger."

"Exactly," says Botzong. "That's where the biker chicks usually ride. It also explains the duct tape you guys found on the victim's wrists and shoes, not to mention that ring of dried blood around his neck. Check it out."

He pushes the play button.

The image is grainy, but, in the background, we can make out a Harley hog with a helmeted driver and a helmeted passenger with his arms wrapped around the driver's waist.

The passenger is not a biker chick. It's Paulie Braciole. He's wearing an aerodynamic helmet with a tinted visor, just like the driver, but I recognize his white muscle-man T-shirt.

"Clever," says Ceepak. "To transport the dead body, the killer propped the helmeted Mr. Braciole in the passenger seat. . . ."

"And duct-taped his shoes to those rear footpegs," adds Botzong.

"Then the killer took their position in front of the dead body. . . ."

"Which had to be pretty hard to do," says Botzong. "Balancing the body to secure the feet. Then, I'm guessing, they had to brace Mr. Braciole by the helmet while they mounted the bike."

The motorcyclist in the video is wearing racing gear, a one-piece space suit deal that gives absolutely no hint as to who or what is inside; same with the aerodynamic helmet and padded gloves, which more or less blend right into the high-collared suit. Our killer could be a guy or a girl. He or she could be sixteen or sixty. Heck, he or she could be a very well-trained orangutan. The flight suit hides everything.

"Once the killer had taken their place up front," says Ceepak, "they reached around, grabbed hold of Mr. Braciole's limp arms, binding them together in front of their waist with more duct tape."

"Yep," says Botzong.

Wow. I'm impressed. First, by Ceepak and Botzong, who figured it all out. Second, by the killer. He (or she) had to be pretty nimble and quick to pull it off. Third, by duct tape. Is there nothing that stuff can't do?

"The neck roll of the helmet being forced over Mr. Braciole's head, of course, explains that ring of dried blood and the 'up-drips' around his neck," adds Botzong. "It acted like a temporary dam, causing the blood to pool in a circle until it was removed."

I nod because I figured it out maybe two seconds after Botzong said it.

"So," says the head of the State Police Major Crimes Unit, tapping the monitor screen, "do you guys recognize the motor scooter?"

I'm guessing Detective Bill Botzong, when not rehearsing amateur theatricals, spends his Thursday nights watching *Fun House,* so he saw me and Ceepak chasing the Creed motorcycle crew around the parking lot of Morgan's Surf and Turf.

"Several of the motorcycle gang members we encountered were, indeed, riding similar Harleys," says Ceepak. "However, I don't recall any distinguishing characteristics on any of the bikes that allow me to I.D. the motorcycle."

"What about Skeletor? Is that his bike?" asks Botzong.

"Sure looks like it," I say.

"It sure does, Danny," says Ceepak.

I'm waiting for the "But."

"But. . . ."

There it is.

"This low-slung Harley profile is quite common."

"Yeah," I say. Plus, the rider, disguised in a helmet and leather jumpsuit, is hunched over so much, gripping onto the handlebars like a motocross racer, there's no way to tell how tall and skinny he or she might be. It could be Skeletor on the bike. It could be anybody.

"Well, Skeletor and his Creed brethren are definitely on my most-wanted list," says Botzong.

Now Ceepak nods. "Ours too."

"Any word on his whereabouts?"

"Negative. We put out an APB immediately after our run-in at the restaurant."

"Which was almost a week ago," I add.

"We may need to cast a wider net," says Botzong.

Ceepak sighs. "Bill, as Chief Baines undoubtedly alerted you, the producers of *Fun House* want to go on air this week and devote a good deal of time to showing the drug dealer's face to their viewers."

Botzong screws up his face like it pains him to say what he's about to say. "Yeah. Buzz told me. I think it might help, John."

Ceepak reluctantly nods. "My wife, Rita, also agrees. This morning, she advised me that *America's Most Wanted with John Walsh,* a long-running program on the Fox network, has aided authorities in the capture of well over eleven hundred fugitives."

"So, tell me: You going to play the John Walsh role?"

"No, Bill. I was going to ask you to do it. After all, you have more stage experience."

"Sure. If the TV people want me, I'll dig out my black turtleneck and leather jacket."

Ceepak grins. "That'll work."

I'm smiling too.

I guess because I'm imagining Broadway Bill Botzong breaking into song and dance, halfway through the show. You know—it's *America's Most Wanted* meets *Glee.* I just hope Botzong isn't pitchy, a term I learned watching too much *American Idol.* It's all Randy Jackson ever says.

Botzong and his CSI crew continue combing the crime scene.

I'm pretty sure they won't find any fingerprints. The killer on the Harley, after all, was wearing very thick racing gloves.

Ceepak and I head back across the island (hey, it's only about a half mile wide) to chat with Mandy Keenan, who, as far as we know, was the last person to see Paul Braciole alive. We're hoping she can help us track The Thing's movements, because we need to find where he was killed before someone, maybe even Skeletor, strapped him onto the back of that motorcycle and hauled him over to the Knock 'Em Down booth.

Huh. I wonder.

"You think the killer picked the Knock 'Em Down on purpose?" I say as we crawl west on Red Snapper Street. "I mean, they could've picked any booth. The Frog Bog. Whack A Mole. Why the Knock 'Em Down?"

"An interesting question, Danny," says Ceepak.

"Maybe they were sending a message. You know, like that Springsteen song, 'Wrecking Ball.' It's a dare. Take your best shot, let me see what you've got. Go ahead, put me on national TV. And then, boom—the bad guy knocks Paulie down."

"A fascinating hypothesis. It would be in keeping with the very public execution of one whom Skeletor and The Creed obviously felt had betrayed them."

Yeah. You don't hang a dead guy up by his undershirt on a wall filled with stuffed animals unless you want somebody to find the body.

"So, it looks like Skeletor and The Creed are our top suspects?"

"Yes, Danny. At this juncture."

"That means we need to play along with Marty Mandrake, do the whole *America's Most Wanted* bit?"

Ceepak nods. "No matter how personally repellent, it appears to be the most prudent course of action currently available to us."

I pull into the driveway at 136 Red Snapper.

Up at the house, the front door swings open.

Officer Kenneth McAlister of the SHPD comes out, shaking his head.

Ceepak is up and out of our vehicle.

"What's the situation, Ken?"

"This Mandy?" He jabs a thumb over his shoulder. "Now she says the dead guy stole her car."

17

"He stole my fucking Mustang!"

This from Mandy Keenan, who, it turns out, is a real charmer—if, you know, you're charmed by women who wear T-shirts that say "Feel Safe At Night: Sleep With A Jersey Girl."

We're inside Mandy's living room. Or maybe it's her trash compactor. Empty rum jugs litter the floor, mingling with assorted thongs, beach wraps, flip-flops, boogie boards, skirts, shorts, and socks, not to mention all sorts of magazines promising "20 Top Sex Secrets," Cheetos bags, pizza boxes, Pringles cans, Tasty Cake wrappers, and maybe six dozen empty Starbucks Frappuccino cups with petrified foam bubbles caking their innards. When you walk across the green-gold-orange shag carpet, hidden crumbs crunch beneath your feet.

Mandy, whose parents must've really loved that old Barry Manilow song, sits in a cabana-striped chair. I think it's supposed to be a piece of outdoor patio furniture. She's blonde and built. If she's ever a murder victim, she'll be easy to I.D. Breast implants have serial numbers. I can tell she has slapped on her white lip-gloss and matching white eye shadow (with glitter) in anticipation of our arrival.

Ms. Keenan's car, we learn, had been parked around the block, up on Prawn Street, because "My fucking roommates and the ass-holes that rent upstairs took all the fucking parking spaces on the fucking lawn."

Yes, reality TV has infected real reality. Everybody thinks they need to sound like the hard-partying smut-mouths on prime time TV.

"I told Paulie he could borrow it, but he had to bring it back by noon on account of that's when I wake up. Plus, they're having this big sale at the Target on the mainland and I wanted to buy one of those George Foreman grills, because if Paulie and I are gonna have like paparazzi taking our pictures all over the place, I gotta keep off the poundage."

Ceepak turns to Officer Kenneth McAlister.

"Have you advised Ms. Keenan as to why we are here?"

McAlister shakes his head.

Great. Ceepak gets to do the honors.

"Ms. Keenan?"

She bats her eyes. Girls do that a lot when John Ceepak and his muscles are in the room.

"Please—call me Mandy."

Ceepak nods. He'll try. "Mandy, I take it you have not heard the news?"

"Not really. I mostly listen to W-A-V-Y. It's classic rock."

"Paul Braciole is dead."

"What?"

"He was murdered last night."

"Get! Out!"

"It's true," I pipe up.

"When?"

"After he left here."

"No fucking way! Some asshole killed him?"

"Yes, ma'am."

"Shit."

"Mandy?" says Ceepak, as best he can.

"Yeah?"

"We need you to tell us what happened last night."

"You mean with me and Paulie?"

"Yes, ma'am."

"We, you know, got busy. You want to see the video?"

"Not right now," says Ceepak. "Tell us how you met Mr. Braciole."

"Who?"

"Paulie," I say. "The Thing."

"Oh. Okay. I had heard the *Fun House* crew would be at Big Kahuna's, so I put on my hottest Fuck Me outfit, the one that always gets me laid." She cups her hands under her breasts to, I guess, illustrate the effect she had been striving to achieve. "Anyway, Paulie, The Thing, he comes over and starts showing me his pecs and shit, and I say I'm more interested in the muscle down below—"

Ceepak holds up a hand. "Let's jump ahead a little."

"Oh. Okay. To when? Like the second time we did it? Because that time, things got a little kinky—"

"How about when he left?" I say.

"Oh. Okay. Paulie had to be back at the Fun House by three, 'cause they have this bullshit curfew. And he couldn't walk all the way back to Halibut Street, and there are no cabs in this fucking town, not at two or three in the morning, so I told him he could borrow my Mustang. That asshole with the ponytail, the one lugging the camera, he was still out front after tailing us all the way from Big Kahuna's." Mandy shakes her kinky hair, lets it tickle the top of her fake gazongas. "Paulie had to slip out the back door and cut across the yards to get over to my car on Prawn Street."

"What time was this?"

"I dunno. Maybe two, two thirty, two forty-five."

"Can you be more specific?"

"Ha. I wish. My fucking watch broke. It was supposed to be waterproof, but I went into the ocean, just this one fucking time because of all the jellies, that was on Tuesday, I think, yeah, Tuesday, 'cause me and Kristen—she's one of my roommates—we went to the Pancake Palace on Tuesday before hitting the beach because you can get like two stacks of chocolate-chip pancakes for the price of one, so we like split it 'cause we figured we'd swim off the calories. You ever been to the Pancake Palace?"

"Yes, ma'am."

"Service sucks, am I right? Syrup bottles are always sticky and shit."

Ceepak jots a note in his pad. I see what he writes. It isn't about sticky syrup bottles: "2:00–2:45."

"Were any of your roommates here last night?" Ceepak asks.

"Kristen and Coco? No way. Only one of us at a time can hook up with a guy here, that's the rule. Since I left the club first, I got first dibs, which was cool with Kristen, because she was totally into this guy Brandon, who I think goes to college part-time and has his parents' place down here for like three weeks and Coco, well, she was so blitzed, she probably stayed at the club until it closed or they started serving breakfast or maybe she hooked up with the bartender because she just found out that this guy she'd been seeing, this very hot local stud named Eric Hunley, well, Eric's been hooking up with that skank Soozy K. And Coco used to be a belly dancer. Coco Ihle, you ever heard of her?"

"No," I say because I canceled my subscription to *Belly Dancing Monthly* years ago. "But the Soozy K who stole her boyfriend. You mean the girl from *Fun House,* right?"

"Yeah. That bitch has Eric wrapped around her pretty little finger."

She shows me her pinky to make her point. The nail has a sparkly butterfly painted on it.

"Anyway, Coco was looking for a revenge fuck. Told me she was going to take whatever she could get."

"Fascinating," says Ceepak—just to shut her up, I think. He's really not that interested in the modern mating rituals of today's twenty-somethings. "Do you have a photograph of your vehicle?"

"Butch?"

"Pardon?"

She does a quick giggle wiggle. It's supposed to be cute. "I give all my cars nicknames. I called the Mustang 'Butch' because it's a hunk." Now her eyes shift to sultry. "And, if you don't mind me saying it, so are you."

Ceepak just nods. Puking isn't really an option here.

"We'd like to show the photograph around," I hop in. "See if anybody's spotted it."

"Can I be in the picture?"

"Sure," I say.

"Awesome! I have one of me in a bikini just, you know, hanging out, leaning against Butch's hood. I look smokin' hot."

"That'll work," I say, because Ceepak, the hunk, still doesn't look like he's fully recovered from Mandy's giggle-jiggle.

"It's in my phone."

"Forward it to me," I say.

We work out the details. I forward the photo on to Dorian Rence at headquarters. She'll download the file and send it out to all our street units, post the picture on the bulletin board in the dayroom.

The hunt is on for Butch, Mandy's manly mustang.

"Should I call the insurance company?" Mandy asks. "Tell them Paulie stole my car?"

"Probably a smart idea," I say. "But we don't think Paulie stole it."

"Then why isn't it back where I told him to park it? I looked out the kitchen window and couldn't see it!"

I just smile. Why tax her brain past its limit?

"Ken?" Ceepak says to McAlister.

"Yeah?"

"Please stay with Ms. Keenan. Help her fill out the stolen vehicle report."

Yeah, we're leaving McAlister holding the crappy end of the stick. But he'll deal with it. He's a cop. It's what cops do.

"Come on, Danny," says Ceepak.

We crunch across the carpet.

"Officers?" Mandy calls after us. "Is that picture of me and Butch going to be on TV?"

"Hopefully," says Ceepak, "we will locate your vehicle before *Fun House* airs again."

"But if you don't?"

"Then we might indeed need to widen our search and broadcast the photograph."

"Awesome!" says Mandy like she just won the lottery.

I'm reminded of that Disney World commercial they always run at the end of the Super Bowl:

Mandy Keenan, your last lover was just murdered, what are you going to do next?

"I'm going to be on TV!"

18

We climb back into our Crown Vic cruiser.

"You want to swing by Big Kahuna's later?" I say as I crank the ignition so I can blast the AC before the heat radiating off the seats bakes us into a pair of crispy cop cookies. "My friend Bud, the bartender, might've seen something when the film crew was in there last night."

Ceepak nods slowly, the way he does when he's half-listening to what I'm saying because he's busy thinking about something much more important.

"You remember Bud?" I say. "He helped us back when your father was—"

"Danny?"

"Yeah?"

"Let's go grab a black-eyed pea cake and a plate of tofu scramble."

I glance at the dashboard digital. It's 3 P.M., 1500 hours in the Ceepak Time Zone. But he's not thinking about a late lunch or early dinner.

He wants to go talk to the person who first tipped us off to Skeletor's drug dealings.

Gladys at Veggin' On The Beach.

We met Gladys a couple summers ago when Ceepak and I were working our first case together. She was a homeless person living out of a shopping cart in the crumbling remains of The Palace, which had once been a grand old hotel, at the northern tip of the island.

Back then, Gladys was dating a druggie drifter everybody called Squeegie. Gladys refused to call him that, because she found the nickname demeaning, "likening a human soul to a tool capitalist pigs use to wipe away the grime of greed warping their windows."

She's probably what people whose job it is to shout at each other on cable TV all day would call a commie pinko or a Nazi, even though Ceepak has informed me that commies and Nazis are "polar opposites on the political spectrum."

This is why Ceepak and Rita spend more time at Veggin' On The Beach than I do. The restaurant is way too intellectual for me. Besides, I like meat in my sandwiches, not tempeh bacon, pan-seared seiten, or hiziki seaweed.

We head east, cutting across the island, aiming for Ocean Avenue and Hickory Street. The restaurant, which always smells like stewed beets, is set up in a brightly colored cottage right in front of the sand dunes.

We pull into the parking lot where Stan The Vegetable Man—a ten-foot-tall plywood portrait of this dude with a smiling pumpkin head, tomato torso, carrot legs, and corncob feet, greets us. There are about a dozen newspaper machines lined up in front of the porch, because Gladys thinks all newspapers print nothing but lies fed to them by "the man" so maybe if you read enough of them you can cobble together the truth for yourself.

I check out the headline peeking through the window on *The Sandpaper* box (our weekly newspaper). Apparently, "Fun Hou$e =

Be$t Touri$t eaon Ever!" Cash registers up and down the island are having sunny, funderful days. It's amazing what a hit TV show will do for T-shirt and trinket sales.

We climb the plank-and-beam steps, push open the screen door.

Ceepak enters first like he always does when we're heading into dangerous territory. Hey, it's a scientific fact: soybean products, such as tofu, make people fart. The last time Ceepak decided we should grab lunch at Gladys's, there were so many butt barks I thought we'd walked into a trombone recital.

Gladys is behind the counter, wrangling with a sagging sack of sweet potatoes she means to steam on an August day when it's already 95 and extremely steamy outside. Oh, Veggin' On The Beach doesn't believe in air-conditioning. It's bad for the ozone, not to mention the electric bill.

"Good afternoon, Gladys," says Ceepak as he strides up to the counter.

"Easy for you to say. You're not the one hoisting a damn fifty-pound sack of yams."

Ceepak goes over to the stove to lend a hand. Even he has trouble getting a grip on the bag as the gnarly tubers tumble around inside the burlap.

"Careful, jarhead. You bruise a sweet potato, it turns to mush fast."

"Roger that." Finally he is able to hoist the burlap sack up and over the steaming kettle and empty out a rumbling rockslide.

"Thanks, John," says Gladys, who is a small woman. In fact, she's so short, I wonder how she dumps anything into her stockpots without climbing on a stepstool or calling Ceepak for backup. Today, she's wearing a tie-dyed T-shirt with no sleeves and no bra underneath. She's also sixty-something with boobs bigger than the Casaba melons on the brunch menu, so I think, maybe for the first time in my life, a bra here would be a good thing.

"What are you making?" asks Ceepak.

"Spicy sweet potato and coconut soup. Marty Mandrake and a bunch of those other jerks working on *Dumb House* love organic vegan food. We've been mobbed since they rolled into town from La-La Land. I shouldn't complain—but, if I didn't, then I wouldn't be me."

Ceepak grins.

"So, how the fuck you boys been?"

Gladys may be sixty-something, but she's not what you might call grandmotherly about it.

"I've had better days," says Ceepak.

"Really? So now you know how a dairy cow feels, artificially inseminated year after year so she'll keep on pumping out milk even though her newborn calf is snatched away from her two seconds after it's born because the farmer man doesn't want her to waste any of her milk on her own children, leaving more for those assholes at Skipper Dipper so they can make fifty fucking flavors of ice cream out of the life-giving nectar leeched from her teats!"

Ceepak just nods. Guess he's used to Gladys's rants.

Vegans are much tougher than vegetarians. Don't like the exploitation and abuse of animals that fills half the refrigerator cases at the Acme Supermarket. There's a bumper sticker slapped to the back of Gladys's cash register: "Heart Attacks. God's Revenge For Eating His Animals."

"You want some apple crisp?" She gestures to a pan of gloppy brown goo on a cake plate under a dome.

"No, thank you," says Ceepak. "Is Jerry here?"

Jerry is Squeegee's real name.

"He and the dog took the truck and headed over to the mainland," says Gladys. "Jerry says he found a deal on some juicing equipment up near New Brunswick."

"I see."

"I think they're really in Bridgewater. There's a Fuddruckers."

Ceepak gives her a confused cock of his head.

"It's a burger chain, meathead! They sell hamburgers with two thirds of a pound of chopped beef squatting on the bun! They make milkshakes—in one of those machines where the steel blades scrape against the steel canister, which should fucking remind people of the pain inflicted when we steal milk from the udders of exploited mothers."

"The cows?" I say, just so I'm clear.

"That's right, Boyle. How would you like some asshole dairy farmer sticking a fucking vacuum cleaner to your man boobs every morning, sucking them clean?"

Okay, just for the record, I don't have moobs. Gladys is being extremely hypothetical here.

"Jerry is no longer vegan?" asks Ceepak.

Gladys flaps up both hands and I wish her T-shirt didn't have such giant armholes. The Casabas are flopping up and down and around.

"He's cheating on me, John. Every now and then, he gets an uncontrollable craving and comes home with cooked cow on his breath." Now she gives a dismissive flick of the wrist. "Guess he couldn't kick all his addictions at once."

"Speaking of Jerry's former addictions," Ceepak says, quite smoothly, I might add, "we'd like to ask you a few questions."

"What? About that skeeve Skeletor? I saw you and him on TV last week. You two cowboys hot on his trail?"

"Yes, ma'am."

"Jesus, don't start in with that ma'am shit again, John. It's not polite, it's patronizing."

"Sorry. I suppose using that term is my bad habit."

"Yeah, yeah. Eat some fucking apple crisp." She lifts the lid off the pie plate. Ceepak, brave soldier that he is, takes the oozing wedge she slides onto a paper plate, nibbles at the edges.

Gladys wipes her hands on her stained prairie skirt, finding the one spot she hasn't already used as a dishrag.

"Skeletor," Gladys huffs. "I can't stand that skinny son of a bitch. Bastard's got a mean streak. Used to rip Jerry off like crazy back in the day, back when he liked to dip and dab Mexican Mud."

That means Jerry used to mess around with heroin.

"And when Jerry couldn't pay what he owed?" Gladys waves at the blank TV screen. "Skeletor would unleash those douchebag bikers who chased you two around that fucking parking lot on TV. Those Creed assholes would roar into town on their Harleys, find Jerry, rough him up. This one time, I thought he was gonna die, they messed up his face so bad. Kicked in a couple ribs, too."

Ceepak nods grimly.

"I remember one February, Jerry was sleeping off a high up in one of those Tilt A Whirl cars at Sunnyside Playland, they marked him, man. Marked him bad. He still carries the scars."

"How so?"

"Next time you see Jerry, ask him to roll up his sleeve and show you the '88' they carved in his arm with a knife." She taps her shoulder.

"Why 88?" I ask. "Is that how much he owed them?"

Ceepak shakes his head. "The eighth letter of the alphabet is H. 88 becomes HH, which represents the phrase 'Heil Hitler.'"

"The Creed?" says Gladys. "Bunch of white supremacist assholes. You need to bust these dudes, John. If you don't, I will." She clutches a melon-chopping butcher knife to make her point.

"Gladys," says Ceepak, "do you know where Skeletor has been operating of late?"

"You mean ever since you two burned down his Hell Hole hideout?"

Actually, we weren't the ones who burned it down, but Ceepak lets it slide. Gladys is not lying, she's just operating with faulty intelligence, something, Ceepak says, the Army has to do all the time.

"We know he is still in operation," says Ceepak. "He has been supplying steroids to members of the *Fun House* cast."

"Figures. You don't get meat like that the natural way. Did you know that two thirds of America's beef comes from cows pumped up with steroids? All those hormones in hamburgers, that's why girls are going into puberty at age ten these days."

Somehow, Ceepak stays on point. "What about Skeletor?"

"From what I hear, ever since the fire, he's a floater. Moves around. But Jerry said he saw the skinny turdpole hanging out behind that fried candy stand on Pier Two. Right across from the Fun House. The All American Snack Shack, the guy calls it. Jerry says Skeletor was up to his old tricks, dealing dope out of the back of the stall."

"When was this?" asks Ceepak, probably wondering why we didn't know about it.

"Couple weeks ago. But like I said, Skeletor's a floater. Only his regular customers know when he'll come back to any particular spot."

Ceepak puts down the apple crisp. Wipes his hands on a brown napkin.

"The candy stand, you say."

"Yeah. Pier Two. That red, white, and blue booth where they fry Oreos and Snickers and all sorts of shit filled with poly-hydrogenated chemicals people can't even pronounce."

"Danny?"

We're off to Pier Two.

At least fried Oreos smell better than boiled beets.

19

Cruising north on Beach Lane toward the boardwalk we get a call from Dr. Rebecca Kurth, the county medical examiner.

She tells us what we already know, what Ceepak and MCU Detective Botzong figured out staring at the hole in Paul Braciole's head: He died instantaneously from a single bullet that pierced both hemispheres of his brain. He was then hauled from that crime scene to the boardwalk on the back of a motorcycle. The collar of dry blood ringing his neck and the droplets smearing up toward his cheeks were a result of a helmet being forced down over his head and then, later, pulled off.

Of course the killer didn't give Paulie his spare helmet for protection; it was to hide The Thing's famous face—even though it was bloody and lifeless—from anybody else driving around town at three in the morning.

That's when Dr. Kurth says Paulie died.

Not too long after leaving Mandy's place.

"We need to find that Mustang," says Ceepak when we're done checking in with the ME.

"You think that's where Skeletor killed him? In Mandy Keenan's car?"

"I think that when we find the car Mr. Braciole borrowed to drive home, we should also find clues pointing us to where he was murdered."

Right. One step at a time. That's the Ceepakian way. Me? I like landing on squares with a chute or ladder so you can skip a few of the boring back-and-forth moves in between.

We take a quick detour over to Big Kahuna's Dance Club. Bud is behind the bar, slicing limes, prepping for what he tells us "might be the busiest Saturday night in shore bar history." News of Paulie's death is all over the TV, radio, Facebook, and Twitter. The island is jammed with *Fun House* fans, all of whom want to say they hit the last club Paulie Braciole ever busted a move in.

Ceepak reminds him that, per state and local fire regulations, occupancy by more than 855 persons is considered dangerous and unlawful.

"We'll keep it to 854, tops," says Bud, trying to make a joke.

Ceepak nods. "Be sure you include yourself and the rest of the staff in the head count."

Bud nods very slowly. "Right."

"So what can you tell us about the big *Fun House* shoot last night?" I say.

"Not much. They had like three camera crews crawling all over the place. Ton of guys lugging lights and microphones around behind other guys lugging cameras." He shrugs. "Other than that, it was the usual crowd. Guys in muscle shirts and hair gel. Girls in whatever shows off their tan best."

"Did you notice anybody unusually tall?" asks Ceepak.

"You mean like a basketball player?"

"How about anyone super skinny?" I ask.

"Oh, sure."

"Yeah?"

"You remember Lindsey? From high school?"

"Yeah. Kind of."

"Dude, I think she's gone all anorexic on us. Total gristly chicken."

Bud's got nothing we can use.

We leave Big Kahuna's, head up to the boardwalk. When we pull into the municipal parking lot bumping up against the entrance to Pier Two, Bill Botzong calls Ceepak on his business cell.

"I'm putting you on speaker," he announces. "Danny's here with me."

"Well, great to have an audience," says Botzong, his smooth voice sounding tinny coming out of the tiny telephone. *"But I don't have much to report. We've been studying the duct tape."*

I guess I laugh.

And Botzong hears it.

Ceepak too.

"Danny," he says, "as you might recall, duct tape analysis helped lead to the arrest of two-year-old Caylee Anthony's killer."

"And the sticky side's great at picking up dead skin cells and fingerprint residue," adds Botzong. *"Of course, you have to dip the sample in liquid nitrogen, freeze it to three hundred and sixty degrees below zero so you can slop on the liquids."*

Ceepak's nodding.

Man. I really need to spend less time watching *TMZ,* more with *CSI.*

"Were you able to I.D. the type of duct tape utilized?" asks Ceepak.

"Yep. It's the same stuff they sell in every Ace Hardware up and down the East Coast. We've got nothing."

Ceepak sighs.

Because we're basically in the same boat with Botzong.

"Bill, it looks like we're going to need you to go on TV Thursday night," Ceepak says.

"Yeah. I just wish I was playing a different role for my network debut."

"Roger that. We'll arrange a meeting with Prickly Pear Productions."

"Who are they?"

"The folks responsible for *Fun House.*"

The way Ceepak says "responsible," it's like they were the rats that carried the bubonic plague to Paris or wherever.

The oily odor of French-frying pancake batter hits us at fifty paces.

Across the boardwalk from the clown-mouth Fun House, I see a red-white-and-blue booth, with red-white-and-blue striped banners, red-white-and-blue blinking light bulbs, and side panels cluttered with hand-lettered red-white-and-blue menu items: Deep Fried Oreo Cookies, Deep Fried Twinkies, Deep Fried Snickers, Milky Way, Reese's Peanut Butter Cups, and Ho-Ho's.

America's two favorites. Junk Food and Deep Fat Frying.

One menu item catches Ceepak's attention.

"Deep Fried Pepsi Balls?" he mumbles.

Being a junk-food junkie, I explain: "You make the batter with Pepsi syrup, flour, eggs, and butter. Roll the dough into balls and drop 'em into the French fryer. Then you top them with powdered sugar and more Pepsi syrup."

"Fascinating," he says.

We approach the booth.

I see an older guy with white bristle-brush hair and wraparound sunglasses bossing two acne-riddled kids rigging up a sheet of cardboard behind one of the gurgling oil vats so the grease won't splatter into the tub of powdered sugar.

They're attaching the cardboard to the back of the fryer with duct tape.

I glance at Ceepak.

He sees it too.

"Don't jump to conclusions, Danny," he whispers.

The boss turns around and looks like he has Pepsi Balls for lunch every day. He's wearing an American flag golf shirt that shows off his sagging laundry-sack abs. I'm pretty positive Skeletor wasn't feeding him free steroid samples.

Mr. America smirks when he sees us.

"Ha! Give me the fool gear!" he says with a belly laugh. The two young kids working the fry baskets turn around to see what's so funny.

"Dude!" says one, whose American flag polo shirt is splattered with what looks like baby poop shot out of a blender without a lid. "Put down the corn cob!" He jabs a basket full of sizzling Oreos at me. It splashes a few droplets of hot grease on his co-worker's canvas All-Stars.

"Shit!" says the co-worker, hopscotching in place. Scalding hot oil seeps through canvas every time.

"What do you need, boys?" asks the boss. "A pair of fresh Balls?"

He chuckles again.

Ceepak doesn't chuckle back. In fact, he is in glare mode.

"I meant Pepsi Balls," says the fry guy. He jerks a thumb to the sign offering "Two Giant Balls" for two bucks.

"Are you the proprietor of this establishment?" asks Ceepak.

"Yeah."

"I'm Officer Ceepak. This is my partner, Officer Boyle."

"I know who you two are." Mr. America isn't smiling any more. "I seen you on TV." He holds up two fingers. "Twice. The Skee-Ball thing, and the thing with the brothers on the bikes."

"Then, I take it, you remember the slender man we were pursuing as well?"

"Skeletor. Yeah. Sure. I remember him. Catchy name. Skel-e-tor!"

"Do you remember him working here?" asks Ceepak.

"Who?"

"Skel-e-tor," I say, because Ceepak wouldn't mock the guy as much as I do.

"What the fuck you talking about?"

"Perhaps we should step around to the rear of your booth," suggests Ceepak. "Away from public view."

"What? So you two can jackboot me into saying something I don't want to say?"

"Pardon?"

The guy in the booth knuckles both fists on the counter so he can lean forward and get in Ceepak's face.

"This is America," he says. "I have my rights."

"Indeed you do, sir. And it is our sworn duty to protect your rights. It is also our duty to apprehend those who would break the law."

"What? Selling dope to jigaboos and mud people? You ask me, maybe these so-called drug dealers are doing America a favor. Thinning out the herd of jackals and illegal immigrants infesting the ghettos. Reclaiming this country for the people who founded it."

"Seriously?" I say. "Allowing Skeletor to sell smack and steroids out of the back of your stall here is going to help fix America?"

"The tree of liberty must be refreshed from time to time with the blood of patriots and. . . ." He whips off his sunglasses dramatically so he can glower at us. "Tyrants! Thomas Jefferson said it first, not me. Now get outta here, boys. You're scaring away my customers."

"We will leave. As soon as you tell us about Skeletor."

"What about him?"

"When will he back?"

"Who said he was ever here?"

"We have our informants."

"Of course you do. Who? Some junkie from up in Newark you pay to tell you what you want to hear?"

"When will Skeletor be back?" Ceepak asks again.

"He was never here."

"Sir. . . ."

"I only know him from TV." He gets this manure-eating grin on his face and jams his hands into the front pockets of his jeans so he can rock back on his heels and gloat at us a little. "You two shouldn't mess with a hornets' nest, or we'll swarm out to sting you."

"We?" says Ceepak.

"Go away. I'm busy here. Got Ho-Ho's to fry."

"So you admit that you are a member of The Creed?"

"I don't admit shit."

"You don't have to."

"What?"

"Earlier, when you were leaning on your fists, I noticed the eights tattooed above your knuckles, two on each hand."

"That's when I graduated high school. '88. 1988."

"If true, your school spirit is commendable. However, I suspect you are lying to us about this, as well as your knowledge of Skeletor's whereabouts."

"Prove it."

"We will. And when we do, trust me, sir, you will answer our questions or you will be incarcerated. Danny? Let's go. We've learned what we needed to know. Be advised, sir, your booth will be under constant police surveillance."

"What? What for?"

"Drug trafficking. Kindly inform Skeletor that, when he returns, he will be arrested."

"Hah! He's not coming back here. He's not stupid."

No, but some of his friends sure are. The guy just basically told us that, yes, Skeletor has been selling drugs out of his candy stand.

Of course, he's also right.

We won't catch Skeletor hiding behind the Pepsi Balls. The guy has slipped out of our grip more times than an oily Snickers bar.

We really only have one shot.

Playing the *America's Most Wanted* card. Putting his bony face and Mandy's Mustang on TV.

20

Monday, we go to church.

For Paul Braciole's funeral.

We're working crowd control and traffic outside Our Lady of the Seas Catholic Church, which more or less resembles a brick school building with a steeple and stained-glass windows. Don't worry. Judging from the television satellite trucks lined up around the block, you'll be able to watch highlights on all the major entertainment news shows, not to mention this week's "Funeral for a Friend/To Catch a Killer" edition of *Fun House*.

We're on a bit of a break. The TV anchor types are all in their satellite vans, waiting for the funeral to end so they can mob folks streaming out of the church, including several celebrities who dropped by to remember Paulie, a "young man of enormous talent who was taken from us too, too soon," according to the church-lawn eulogy delivered by Marty Mandrake for the gaggle of reporters jabbing microphones in his face before the services started.

Prickly Pear Productions has hired about a dozen beefy guys in EVENT STAFF windbreakers to keep the crowd of mourning fans behind a hastily erected barricade of interlocking fences running up the sides of the church steps. Since it's a somber occasion, all the looky-loos are behaving. Holding candles and sobbing. Making memorials out of stuffed animals, flowers, and, yes, tubs of bodybuilding protein powder.

We're in our police cruiser, parked right at the curb in front of the entrance steps. Even our radio is quiet. Perhaps Dorian Rence is observing a moment of silence in Paulie's honor.

Ceepak's cell rings. The personal phone. He always wears two so he doesn't "blur the line between my private life and my professional responsibilities."

"Hello?" he says. If it was the business line, he'd say "This is Ceepak. Go."

I do that slight head-tilt thing that I always think will make it easier for me to eavesdrop.

"I'll have to call you back," he says.

Whoever's on the other side says something that sounds like a mosquito singing: "Bizz bizz-bizz bizz."

So much for my head-leaning eavesdropping technique.

"Oh," says Ceepak. "You saw it?"

The mosquito, I think, says "yes" or some other one-syllable buzz.

"Have my television appearances made you reconsider your job offer?"

Okay. It's the sheriff from Ohio. The one who wants to steal Ceepak away from me, make him head of a detective bureau when he needs to stay here, chasing down skinny drug dealers and babysitting reality TV stars.

"Really? I see. Well, let me say that I am seriously considering your proposal."

Geeze-o, man. What will I do without Ceepak? I mean, besides make a fool of myself on a regular basis? The guy's been my partner since day one on the job.

"Thank you, and in a spirit of full disclosure, you should know that Mrs. Ceepak is not overly enthusiastic about making the move."

Yay, Rita!

"Correct. She is somewhat reluctant to leave the town that has been her home for close to twenty years."

A smile creeps across my lips. Rita is a total Jersey girl, the kind Springsteen sings about. And, as Ceepak has obviously learned, nothing else matters in this whole wide world when you're in love with a Jersey girl. I don't think there's a song about Ohio Gals, unless you count "Hang On Sloopy," the state's Official Rock Song, which was written by The McCoys about a singer named Dorothy Sloop of Steubenville, Ohio, who sometimes used the stage name Sloopy.

It's amazing what you can learn at bar trivia contests.

Rita Lapscynski-Ceepak (yes, her married name sounds like it could be a breed of small, fluffy dog) came to the beaches of Sea Haven when she was in high school and in trouble. People here were good to her. She made a life. She raised a son. She found Ceepak. No wonder she never wants to leave.

The Ohio mosquito buzzes in Ceepak's ear a little longer. He glances at his watch.

"Roger that," he finally says when the buzzing bloodsucker runs out of gas. "I will. Yes. Before Labor Day. You too."

He closes the clamshell.

Clips it to his belt.

And squints out the side window at the church.

"Well?" I say.

"That was the sheriff of Lorain County, Ohio."

"But Rita wants to stay here, right?"

He grins. "Officer Boyle, your evidence-gathering skills continue to impress me."

"Hey, you taught me everything I know. So they want an answer by Labor Day?"

"That is correct."

"That mean's you've got, what? Two weeks to change Rita's mind?"

"Something like that."

"Not gonna happen."

"It might."

"No way. Rita's a Jersey girl."

"They're offering us a very substantial pay raise."

"Really? What, a twenty-, thirty-percent bump?"

Ceepak shakes his head. "Double what I make here."

Geeze-o, man. Double?

"Well," I stammer, "you'll never get to eat decent seafood again."

"Perhaps. However, Danny, as you may have heard, they now fly fresh seafood into the heartland of America on a daily basis."

"What? You mean Red Lobster? Bubba Gump Shrimp?"

"Lake Erie is very close to where we might live."

"There's no shrimp or scallops in Lake Erie—"

"Did you know, Danny, that every Friday during Lent, several restaurants and churches in the Cleveland area host a fish fry. It's a northeastern Ohio tradition."

"Yeah, but—"

We'll have to save the second half of our New Jersey–Ohio seafood debate for later. The front doors of the church swing open. So do the back doors on two dozen news trucks.

"Let's split up," says Ceepak. "You take the front. Lend a hand to the security detail, should they require official intervention."

I nod. Check my official intervention device, also known as my sidearm.

Ceepak makes a hand chop to the side of the building. "I'll swing around back and make certain that the funeral home personnel are allowed to perform their somber tasks with a modicum of dignity."

"Sounds like a plan," I say as I yank open my door and head up the steps, letting my hand brush the stock of my Glock. I always like to make sure it's still where I put it.

As I make my way up the steps, I notice that some of the fans behind the barriers are decked out in those "Put Down The Corn Cob" T-shirts. Nice. Everybody's getting rich off of my catchphrase except me, the guy who created it.

As the celebrities start streaming out the door, I can hear organ music. Yep. It's Elton John's "Funeral for a Friend"—the sad riff at the top, not the "love lies bleeding in my hand" bit near the end.

Fans start shrieking. Here comes this year's Bachelorette from that other reality show, the original cast members from *Jersey Shore* plus the lady who sprained her ankle on *Dancing with the Stars* and that fashion critic who makes snarky on-camera comments about what everybody else is wearing but never looks in the mirror long enough to check out how weird he looks.

Yes, I feel like I'm working the red carpet at the Oscars or the Emmys or The Reallys, an award I just made up for reality TV shows. I see Soozy K and Jenny Mortadella in their outfits from the Starfish Boutique. Good thing Our Lady of the Seas Catholic Church doesn't have any nuns left on its staff. They'd be blushing. Jenny and Soozy look like they're on their way to Satan's own cleavage convention.

In front of them is Ponytail, walking backward so he can keep his camera trained on the two girls as they sob and shimmy down the church's marble steps.

Off to the side, out of the camera lens's field of vision, I see Layla Shapiro. She's wearing tight black slacks, a black silk blouse, and a wireless headset.

"Smooth out the move," she whispers at Ponytail, her voice cutting through the squeals and screams from the mob lining the steps, who have apparently forgotten this is a funeral, not a Justin Bieber concert, even though I think he was here to sing "Amazing Grace," the Elvis version.

"Come on, Soozy," Layla coaches. "You just lost the man of your dreams. Let America see how that makes you feel."

Soozy starts sobbing louder. She even blubbers a high-pitched "Boo-hoo" like a caption in a cartoon.

I catch Layla's eye.

She smiles. Shoots me a wink. I'm guessing Paulie's funeral is one of the happiest days of young Ms. Shapiro's life.

Me?

I just want Layla to leave me and my hometown alone.

If she doesn't, maybe I can move to Ohio too.

Maybe Chief of Detectives Ceepak will need somebody to fetch his coffee and seafood.

I see Layla again around 6 P.M.

We'd set up a six o'clock meeting with Marty Mandrake at the Prickly Pear production trailer to discuss the details for Bill Botzong's pre-taped appearance on the show Thursday night.

Of course Mandrake can't see us when he said he would, because some big honchos from network headquarters up in New York have dropped by "unexpectedly" for a "major confab."

Layla tells me all this when I am sent forth as the emissary from the cop car to the trailer steps, where she sits thumbing her BlackBerry. Detective Botzong and Ceepak hang back.

"Why aren't you in the meeting?" I ask.

Layla shrugs. "Marty asked me to leave when they started firing up the cigars."

"I thought you were his right-hand man."

Okay, the "man" thing is my little dig. Layla lets it fly on by.

"He doesn't want me stealing his thunder."

"I see."

"Besides, he has Grace Twittering all the details already." She shows me her smartphone screen, but I don't want to lean in to read it.

"What's it say?"

"Basically, that he hit the numbers for his trigger clause."

"Huh?"

"The network promised Prickly Pear a bonus if he delivered a certain ratings target. He's off the charts, thanks to you and me and Ceepak."

"Really? What'd me and Ceepak do?" I ask, even though I think I know the answer: we made for must-see TV.

"Ever since that Skee-Ball scene," says Layla, "working the police into the plotlines—hauling Paulie off to jail, that bit with the biker boys in the restaurant parking lot—*Fun House* has become the surprise smash hit of the summer."

"And that was your idea? Having the kids do stuff that would get them arrested?"

"I put a bug in Marty's ear. No one had ever done a reality romance-slash-cop show. It's a can't-miss hybrid."

"What about the steroids? Did you plant those?"

"No comment."

"Did you tell Skeletor to bump off Paulie? Was that another plot twist?"

"Jesus, Danny! That was just a lucky fucking break. Who knew Skeletor would get that pissed off about his fifteen minutes of fame?"

A lucky break?

Geeze-o, man. Ms. Shapiro is twisted. She's spent too much time inside TV, what my father calls the idiot box. It's turned her into an idiot too.

She jabs a thumb over her shoulder at the trailer. "You know what's going on in there?"

"What?"

"Marty The Old Farty's career is about to rise from the ashes."

"Well, have fun rising with him."

"Me? No way. Prickly Pear was just a foot in the door. I have feelers out. When people hear how I turned this turkey around, they'll be begging me to work for them."

I've heard enough. Hollywood, especially the New Jersey branch office, makes me sick.

"Let us know when Mr. Mandrake's ready to talk about Detective Botzong's bit," I say. "I'm sure it'll help boost your ratings even higher."

"Will do," says Layla, not even looking up at me, diddling with her BlackBerry keys some more.

Shoulders slumped, I head back to the Crown Vic, my mind swimming in its deep end of dark thoughts.

Marty Mandrake gets a big bonus plus a couple new TV shows.

The TV network gets to charge advertisers more for airtime on Marty Mandrake's hit show.

Layla probably gets her pick of production jobs.

Even Ceepak's salary gets doubled when he flies to Ohio following his guest appearances on the reality TV show.

Yep, everybody's cashing in on this thing except me.

And, of course, Paulie Braciole.

21

THURSDAY NIGHT, THERE'S A BIG *FUN HOUSE* WATCHING party at the Sand Bar, this nightclub with about fifteen giant plasma screen TVs downstairs and a dozen more up on the canopied deck, all of which are usually tuned to whatever sport is currently in season.

This is where me and my friends used to hang. Jess, Olivia, Mook, Katie, Becca. We'd sit around a bucket or two of beers and toss back crabcake sliders and fried zucchini strips so we could tell our mothers we were eating our vegetables. Now Jess and Olivia are married and have moved up to New Brunswick, where she's finishing med school. Becca is still in town, helping her folks run the Mussel Beach Motel. Mook and Katie are both dead. Murdered.

I've been to too many real funerals for a guy my age.

So, tonight, off duty, downstairs at the Sand Bar, it's just me and my old friend Bud. Not the bartender from Big Kahuna's; the long-neck bottle of beer.

It's been a lousy week. We still have no clues. Skeletor has not returned to the red, white, and blue grease pit. We're not closer to catching Paul Braciole's killer.

Yeah. I'm in what they call a maudlin mood. That'll happen when you're surrounded by mammoth speakers pouring out sappy music and everybody around you is sniffling back tears. Death. It's a real buzz-killer.

"Tonight," croons Chip Dale, the *Fun House* host, in his best "let's-do-this-for-the-children" telethon voice, *"we mourn the passing of a friend. Peter Paul Braciole. A young man so full of life, no one ever thought it could be snatched away from him so quickly."*

The screen fills with a slow-motion video montage of Paulie when he was alive. Tugging up his T-shirt. Flashing his pecs. Repeatedly. The wiggling chest muscles look even weirder at half speed, like some kind of underwater balloon ballet.

"I am The Thing you want," we hear him say over a syrupy orchestra of strings. *"The Thing you wish you could be!"*

Here's Paulie smooching Soozy K in the hot tub. Paulie and Soozy laughing as they pluck live crabs out of a tank at Mama Shucker's Seafood Shop and, then, Paulie aiming the crab's snipping pincers at Soozy's boobs. Paulie flexing his biceps, Soozy pretending to do chin-ups off his bulging arm. The back of Ceepak's head is in the next shot, one of Paulie stuffing Skee-Balls down the fifty hole.

I look around. People are simultaneously smiling and sniffing. One guy is dabbing at his eyes with a paper napkin. Then he blows his nose into it.

Nobody is nibbling their free popcorn.

Fried clams are going cold. Sliders are going unslid. The Sand Bar resembles a funeral home with bad lighting.

"But the end of one man's life," croons Chip Dale, shifting into ominous announcer mode, like the guy who does all the movie trailers, *"marks the beginning of the hunt for another man: Paulie's killer!"*

Cue the dramatic music.

And the explosion sound effects.

Boom. Here come those animated graphics. And a very scary shot of Bill Botzong, arms crossed in front of his chest, glaring at the camera from under the brim of his New Jersey State Police hat, a hat I've never seen him wear before. Guess the Prickly Pear Productions people didn't like his black-turtleneck-and-leather-jacket look.

"This is Fun House*!"* says Chip, strolling down Halibut Street until he's right in front of the Italian-flag garage door. *"Tonight? A special double feature edition: Funeral For A Friend."*

Another boom as that type crumbles to dust.

"To Catch A Criminal!"

He really hits the "K" sounds in both words, just like Marty Mandrake wanted.

Geeze-o, man. I wish Ceepak were here. But he and Rita are watching the program at home. Probably so they can talk about what furniture they should take with them when they move to Ohio. If Rita's feeling the way I am right now, she might be ready to split, because she doesn't recognize Sea Haven anymore. The TV has taken everything we love and flattened it out or glossed it up.

And still I can't stop watching this drek.

We see Paulie and the gang having fun at Big Kahuna's. *"What should have been the most amazing dance competition ever,"* says Chip, *"waltzed off the floor and out the door when Paulie left the club with an adoring fan."*

We see Mandy Keenan flirting with Paulie, who, in the edit, looks like he only tugged up his T-shirt to flash her his pecs because Mandy kept begging for him to do it.

In one angle they cut to, in the background I can see Ponytail and his whole three-man crew. Now we go tight on Mandy's face. I'm thinking Ponytail's team got that shot.

"Meet Mandy Keenan," the announcer continues. *"A young woman who had a little too much to drink last Friday night. An eager admirer Paulie had hoped to let down gently, gracefully."*

"WTF?" I think so I don't have to bleep my brain. Paulie had hoped to bang her, pardon my French, not "let her down gently."

"Paulie Braciole was the sweetest man I ever met," says Mandy, all dolled up for the cameras, a squiggle of black mascara trickling down her cheek. Somebody must have brought in a bulldozer and cleaned all the crap out of her living room. Instead of crusty Frappuccino cups and crinkled Cheetos bags, I see fresh-cut flowers and one of those Kinkade cottage paintings.

As I'm shaking my head in disbelief, I see Mr. America, the white-haired white supremacist from the French-fried version of *Candyland.* He's at the bar, signaling for the bartender. She gestures back. Wants the guy to cool his jets, probably till the next commercial break. She's glued to the TV screen.

Me, too, mostly because I can't believe how unreal this week's version of reality has turned out.

"He, like, walked me home," says Mandy.

Yes, in the background, they are playing a slow, piano-only instrumental version of the Barry Manilow number. "Mandy." Pure dentist-office music.

We see grainy, handheld camera footage of Paulie and Mandy stumbling up the walkway to her front door. They cut out before Paulie flips Ponytail the finger.

"I made us both some coffee," says Mandy with a slight giggle. *"Believe me, we needed it. Well, I did. I drank more than I usually do, because I was so excited about meeting a celebrity. Anyways, Paulie, was a total gentleman. He looked at me with those big brown Bambi eyes and told me his heart was already spoken for. He said he didn't come to the Fun House to find love but, at the Fun House, love found him."*

Soft dissolve to Soozy K and Paulie all tangled up together when they played Twister on the beach during Episode Four. Cross-dissolve to gauzy footage of the two them splashing each other in the hot tub. Another dissolve, and they're playing Frisbee with a puppy—but that footage is shot so you can't see "Paulie's" face, because I think they shot it after Paulie died with a body double and a rented dog.

"Soozy K and he were hoping to take their relationship to the next level," says Mandy. *"I respected that. Sure, I wanted him all to myself; what woman wouldn't? But his heart could never be mine. I could see that. I felt it. Here."* She taps her own chest, I guess to give the camera a reason to go in tighter on her bazoombas. *"So, seeing how Paulie was sober and I was still kind of blitzed, I lent him the keys to my car so he could run home and be with Soozy. His soulmate."*

Geeze-o, man.

At least the next thing the hidden manipulators of reality cut to is a snapshot of the car we're really looking for: Mandy's silver Mustang coupe, the car she calls Butch. We're treated to several cheesecake shots. Seems Mandy liked to pose next to her car in several different bikinis in several different seasons, so this segment about the missing Mustang resembles a video version of one of those pinup calendars hanging in the oil-change bay at a skuzzy gas station.

"I hope someone finds my car," says Mandy when they cut back to her. *"I hope it helps the police catch Skeletor."*

Up comes a black-and-white title: WHO IS SKELETOR?

Back comes Mandy with the answer: *"He's the man who murdered Paulie Braciole."*

Boom! She's wiped off the screen by the "To Catch a Killer" graphics.

"More from the funeral," says the breathlessly excited announcer, *"and how you can help the police catch Paulie's killer—after the break!"*

Then, believe it or not, they roll a Ford car commercial.

For their new Mustang model.

I've seen enough. I'm ready to head for home.

But when I turn to leave, Mr. Deep Fried Pepsi Balls is standing there, two beers in one hand. He head-bobs toward the other chair at my table.

"Anybody sitting there?"

"Nope. You can have both seats. I'm out of here."

He holds out one of the beers.

"I bought you a beer."

I check out the bottle gripped between his fingers, mostly so I can check out those knuckles Ceepak noticed. Yep. They're both there. 8 and 8.

"Thanks," I say, "but I'm not really thirsty."

"I talked to Thomas."

"Who?"

"Skeletor."

22

OKAY.

The guy knows how to get my attention. I sit back down.

The man from the All American Snack Shack looks exhausted and sort of sick. Maybe he has a queasy stomach from inhaling coconut-oil fumes all day. He's wearing a navy blue polo shirt, his bottle-brush white hair looks like it's wilting and needs watering, and, when he takes off his black-rimmed glasses, I can see bright red marks the nose pads have left behind. He takes the seat across from me.

On the TV screen over his head, I can see Elton John playing the pipe organ inside Our Lady of the Seas Catholic Church. Wow. He was really there.

Now my unexpected visitor takes a long pull on his beer. It's beechwood-aged Budweiser, of course. No fancy European import brewskis for this patriotic American. I guess as the day drags on, I'm losing my edge. I don't bust his chops about Bud being a Belgian beer, seeing how the folks in St. Louis sold out to InBev, a company based in some place called Leuven, which I'm told is near Brussels, home of the sprouts. And their CEO is a Brazilian.

"Thomas did not kill Mr. Braciole," the guy says when the beer has given him enough courage to talk.

"So why doesn't he turn himself in?"

"He's scared."

"How come?"

"They ostracized him."

"The Creed?"

He nods.

"So," I say, "what exactly does that mean? Ostracization or whatever."

"They cut him loose. No one is covering his back. Thomas is completely on his own."

"How come?" I ask, even though I think I know the answer.

Mr. America tips his white fuzzy head toward the closest plasma-screen TV glowing with more somber footage of Paulie's casket being carried up the center aisle of the church.

"This much publicity is bad for business," he says. "We like to keep a low profile. That thing in the parking lot at Morgan's? Well, that was fun. Nobody got busted. But this? This is bad. Thomas is attracting way too much heat."

I peer at the guy. Something about this isn't right.

"You know I'm a cop, right?"

"Yeah." His lip can't help but curl a little, like he just smelled sour milk.

"So, you talking to me. The Creed finds out, won't they ostracize you, too?"

"Maybe. But it's the chance I have to take for my brother."

"You'd go against all your Creed brothers for the sake of one?"

"Yeah."

"Why?"

"Cause he's my brother."

I must look confused, because I am.

Bushy-head helps out: "My *real* brother."

Now my face telegraphs that I'm not buying it. I see absolutely no physical resemblance between this tubby guy and the towering Skeletor.

"Same mother. Different fathers. His was tall. *Very* tall."

Oh. Okay.

"Why'd you think I let him sell that shit out of the back of my booth after some asshole torched his Hell Hole hideout?"

Ah, brotherly love. It knows no limits. No wonder they named a city after it.

"So, what does Thomas want?" I ask.

"The same thing you want: to turn himself in. Before something horrible happens. Before some hardass state trooper guns him down in cold blood."

Man. This guy actually believes all the conspiracy crap on cable TV.

"How soon can Thomas surrender?" I ask.

"You and your partner free Saturday?"

"Why Saturday? Why not tomorrow? Why not tonight?"

"He's got some shit to take care of."

"What kind of 'shit'?"

"There's this lady friend. Maybe a baby. I'm not sure."

Geeze-o, man.

"Look," I say, "the sooner Thomas turns himself in, the sooner we can start protecting him."

"I know, but my baby brother has an extremely thick skull."

I take a sip of the beer the guy brought me and think about the Unabomber, Ted Kaczynski, and his brother, David, the guy who, basically, turned the nutjob in. It can't be an easy thing to do.

"Is Thomas in immediate danger?" I ask.

"No. If the Creed wanted him dead, he'd already be dead. They're just cutting him loose. Letting you guys do their dirty work for them."

I glance up at the TV screen.

Bill Botzong, head of the New Jersey State Police Major Crimes Unit, is on. He looks very professional in his starched dress uniform, golden shoulderboards, and admiral-style hat. He asks the public for any and all assistance they can offer as to the whereabouts of the drug dealer known to state and federal law enforcement authorities only as Skeletor, a prime suspect in the murder of Peter Paul Braciole.

And, it turns out, to make things even more interesting, the producers of *Fun House* are offering a fifty-thousand-dollar reward for information leading to the arrest and conviction of *"this man."*

When Botzong says that, the screen fills with a very scary sketch of our gaunt-faced friend in his floppy-billed Boonie hat.

"Did Thomas serve in Vietnam?" I ask his half-brother, who's swigging from his beer bottle, not even glancing at any of the dozen TV screens surrounding us. "Is that why he likes the hat?"

"No. The Army wouldn't take him." He taps the side of his head. "He has issues, you know what I mean?"

"Yeah." I push my beer bottle away. "Look, I need to talk to my partner. Organize things."

"Sure." Mr. America stands up. Extends his hand. "I'll bring Thomas to the police station first thing Saturday morning. How's eight? Too early?"

"No. Eight is cool."

I guess we're making a deal here, so I go ahead and take his hand. Shake it. "You want us to arrange for a lawyer?" I ask.

"You know a good one?"

"Couple. Yeah."

"He can't afford to pay much."

"I know somebody good in the public defender's office."

"Thanks. Appreciate it. I'm Gabe."

"Danny." Then I remember my official position and how this isn't just some dude I'm meeting over a cold one. "Officer Boyle."

"Okay. Officer Boyle."

We break out of the handshake.

"You know where to find me if your partner has a problem," he says.

"Yeah. We'll probably swing by your stand tomorrow. Iron out any logistics."

Gabe nods. "Thanks. Enjoy the rest of the show."

He slips out of the bar as Chip Dale strides onto the sundeck of the house on Halibut Street.

"And so we say farewell to Paulie. The Thing. The young man who lived his life with such joy, such gusto, such . . . liveliness. Sad to think that, only a few short weeks ago, Paulie was right here, on this sundeck, doing what he liked best: playing beer pong with his buddies, making them smile." Chip gives a sincere shuck of his head. *"Let's hope they have a pong table for him up in heaven. Next week?"* Man, this guy can shift gears faster than a drag racer stoked on methamphetamines. *"It's double elimination time! The four remaining contestants all had immunity tonight. But next week? Two contestants will be seven days closer to a quarter-million dollars while two of their housemates will be packing their bags and heading home. We hope you'll be watching. We know Paulie will. Until then, this is Chip Dale for* Fun House. *Be safe, be who you are, and be sure to have some fun at your house! Good night, America."*

As they roll the credits, they put up Skeletor's image again and superimpose a title done up in Wild West type: "WANTED. REWARD: $50,000."

I don't call Ceepak right away to tell him about Skeletor's brother. Hey, they gave the show two full hours tonight, pushed back the local news. It's eleven o'clock. The Ceepaks have lights-out at twenty-two hundred hours. I don't think he actually blows Taps on a bugle, but they're pretty rigid about it.

On the drive home, I start wondering about the $50,000 reward. Maybe Gabe will get it for turning in his brother. He could do a lot of good with the money. Donate it to a Clogged Artery Charity.

I stop thinking about the reward money when my phone rings at 6 A.M. Friday morning.

It's Ceepak.

The TV show worked.

Somebody found Skeletor.

There's only one problem: he's dead.

23

Ceepak tells me to meet him at Oak Beach.

In Sea Haven, we name our beaches after the streets they dead-end into. I have a lot of history on this particular plot of sand: it's where my friends and I used to hang out when we were teenagers, born to run, like Springsteen says, from everything we knew in New Jersey.

Of course, I never did run. I'm still here.

But Oak Beach was where we plotted our escape and talked big about what we'd do and who we'd become. I think I was going to become a rock star. More specifically, I was going to play trombone with the E Street Band, even though, as my late girlfriend Katie pointed out, "they only have a saxophone player."

"That's why they need me!" I told her.

But I quit blowing the bone before the end of my freshman year in high school. There was an unfortunate marching band incident. My slide took out the tuba player. Spit valve to the neck.

We laughed about that all summer long.

Every day in June, July, and August, after working our various crummy jobs catering to tourists, we'd all march down to Oak Beach and hang out together. We'd plant our umbrella in whatever patch of bare sand we could find, hide the cooler of beer we were too young to legally drink under a beach towel, and spend the end of the day shooting the breeze, smelling the salt air, dashing up to the dunes every time the guy with the ice cream truck tinkled his bell, honestly thinking we would live that Dylan song Springsteen sings sometimes and stay "forever young." Our glory days would be like the waves crashing against the shore. Endless.

Oak Beach is also where I fell in love. Several times each summer.

If I want to re-connect with my first girlfriend from seventh grade, I don't have to do it on Facebook. She's just up Shore Drive, at the Mussel Beach Motel, fluffing pillows and wrapping crinkly sanitary paper on top of bathroom glasses. Becca Adkinson is kind of like me: we swore we'd get out when we were young and, instead, ended up hanging around town forever.

I guess I'm clinging to my memories because I'm about to march into another crime scene that, I'm pretty sure, will make me hate Oak Beach for the rest of my life.

Thomas, a.k.a. Skeletor.

Dead. In a lifeguard chair.

It's still early. Too early for much beach traffic. In time, the scrubby sand alongside the boardwalk path cutting through the dunes will be cluttered with kicked-off sandals and flip-flops. People just leave them here when they first hit the beach, pick them up on their way back to their rental houses for lunch—probably a sandwich made with cold cuts from the supermarket deli on a nice soggy roll.

Surprisingly, nobody ever steals the footgear. It's the shore's unwritten code. This is a place to escape all that, all the pushing and shoving and stealing and lying.

Well, in my memory it is.

I can see Ceepak standing on the other side of a corral of fluttering yellow police tape stretched out between flagpoles, the ones the lifeguards stake in the sand to mark how much beach they're keeping an eye on. My partner is staring up at the lifeguard chair, a bright yellow perch about six feet off the ground. A lanky body is flopped sideways in the wooden seat, its legs and arms dangling down like a rag doll a kid has tossed on the edge of a couch. The head droops sideways.

Whoever put Skeletor in his high chair must've cinched up the chinstrap on his Boonie hat: it's buffeted by the sea breeze, but it's not blowing off his dead head.

I duck under the police tape, check out the pattern of footprints in the sand, and find the path most likely left by Ceepak's shoes so I can use his trail like stepping stones. I'm sure Bill Botzong and his MCU crew will be plaster-casting all these dimples and divots, hoping the killer left us some kind of footwear impression we can use to track him down.

"MCU is on the way," says Ceepak.

I nod. "Who found the body?"

"Early-morning joggers." He points to a waffle-wedge impression in the sand. "They like the Nike LunarGlide running shoes."

"How'd he die?" I ask.

Ceepak taps his left temple. "Single bullet, shot from a distance of two to three feet. Exit wound slightly lower on the right side, suggesting a downward firing angle."

"Just like Paulie Braciole."

"Roger that." Ceepak has shifted into his more robotic mode. He usually does this when confronted with the horrors of death. I think it's how he made it through Iraq without totally losing his mind.

"Was this where he was killed?" I ask.

"Doubtful. The beach, although officially closed at midnight, still attracts quite a few night visitors."

True. I'd say fifty percent of my Oak Beach memories took place after dark.

"Also, Danny, as you can see, there are no bloodstains on the lifeguard stand itself." Right. If they shot Skeletor while he was sitting up in the elevated chair, there'd be blood splatter stains and dribble marks all over the bright yellow paint.

"Most likely," Ceepak continues, "Skeletor's body was dumped here sometime shortly before dawn. The joggers called 9-1-1 at 5:30 A.M. When the first responders realized who the victim was, they immediately notified Chief Baines at home. The chief called me."

And Ceepak called me.

Before I could call him. Geeze-o, man. I almost forgot.

"His name is Thomas," I say.

"Come again?"

"Skeletor. His first name is Thomas. He's Gabe's brother."

"And who is Gabe?"

This happens sometimes. My mouth races ahead of my brain.

"The guy with the Heil Hitler knuckles from the candy stand."

Okay. The brain still hasn't quite caught up.

"You mean the gentleman we spoke with yesterday at the All American Snack Shack booth?"

"Yeah. I bumped into him at the Sand Bar last night. I went there to watch *Fun House.* He came over with a peace offering of a couple beers. Said he wanted to arrange his brother's surrender."

"May I ask why you didn't notify me immediately?" Ceepak asks, more puzzlement in his voice than criticism.

"I would have, but Gabe said Thomas couldn't turn himself in until tomorrow morning, Saturday. Lady-friend problems."

"I see."

"This all happened around eleven o'clock," I say, without adding, "after your bedtime."

"Did Gabe suggest that his brother, Thomas, a.k.a. Skeletor, had reason to fear for his life?"

"No. Not really. He said the Creed had ostracized Skeletor. But if they had wanted him dead, he'd be dead already."

"Indeed," Ceepak says thoughtfully. "Do you know his last name?"

Damn.

"No," I say. "Sorry. Should've got that. Sorry."

"Don't 'should' on yourself, Danny."

Ceepak slips a digital camera out of the thigh pocket on his cargo shorts, puts the viewfinder to his eye, and activates the zoom.

"Fascinating," he says.

"What?"

"There is a square of folded paper pinned to the Boonie hat with a beach badge."

Beach badges are what people pin to their swimming suits or beach bags to prove they've paid their way onto the sand. They cost like five bucks a day or thirty-five for the whole season. The money collected pays for stuff like lifeguards, cleanup crews, and the salaries of the beach patrol kids who come around to see if you have your beach badges.

"You want me to climb up and see what it says?" I offer.

"Negative. We shouldn't disturb the body until MCU's had a chance to examine it."

And so we wait.

For Botzong and his crime-scene investigators to literally comb the sand for clues. Yes, they find some footprints—but, in truth, there are far too many to be of any use to us.

They dust the lifeguard chair and Skeletor's clothes for fingerprints. They find none. Just like with Paulie's body in the Knock 'Em Down booth.

They drag all sorts of high-tech gizmos out of the back of their van. Hanging on to the high chair, they vacuum the dead man's clothes, hoping to pick up a stray hair or fiber. They take their own photographs. They check under his fingernails.

But mostly, Bill Botzong, dressed in a Windbreaker and baseball cap instead of the dress blues he wore on TV last night, shakes his head.

"Whoever did this is good," he says grudgingly.

"Do you suspect, as I do, that we are looking for the same person who killed Paul Braciole?" asks Ceepak.

"Yeah. The gunshot wounds are almost identical."

Ceepak nods. "And both bodies were 'dumped' in very visible, extremely public places."

"What about the piece of paper pinned to his hat?" I ask because I'm hoping it's some kind of super clue, like the killer's business card or something.

"Yeah," says Botzong. "We should definitely look at that." He calls over to two of his team. "Weitzel? St. Claire? We need to, very carefully, take the body down from the chair, get him on a gurney."

"We can help," say two guys in lab coats who, I think, work for the county medical examiner.

All four guys work their way up the side beams of the lifeguard chair like they're climbing a jungle gym and try to figure out how to best extract Skeletor's body from its elevated perch. Watching them work with Skeletor's floppy but stiffening body, I'm reminded, first, of Ceepak wrestling with that sack of sweet potatoes at Gladys's restaurant, and then that old movie *Weekend At Bernie's,* the one about two young dudes who prop up their dead boss and cart him around a swanky beach resort. Hilarity ensues.

This morning? Not so much. Nobody's laughing.

The whole scene is extremely grim. Like the stations of the cross, the second to the last one, the thirteenth, I think. The one where Jesus' body is taken down from the cross. I'm reminded of a prayer the nuns taught us for Good Friday: "May the souls of the faithful departed, through the mercy of God, rest in peace."

Hey, somebody has to pray for the Skeletors of this world.

The dead body is laid on a black vinyl body bag supplied by the team from the morgue.

Botzong puts on sterile gloves; works open the beach-badge safety pin.

"There appears to be something bulky stuffed inside his shirt pocket," says Ceepak.

"Yeah," says Botzong. "We'll extract that next."

"What's on the paper?" I ask.

"Writing. A note." Botzong fumbles in his shirt pocket for a pair of reading glasses. He studies the tiny slip of paper like it's the fortune cracked out his cookie at a Chinese restaurant.

"'I killed Paulie,'" Botzong reads without emotion. "'I killed Skeletor.'" He hesitates.

"And?" says Ceepak.

Botzong finishes: "'Next, I will kill Soozy K.'"

24

I HAVE NO IDEA WHAT WE'RE DEALING WITH HERE.

A crazy fan? Some kind of copycat killer? Are the two murders really linked, or is it just some sicko's warped way of glomming on to Paulie's murder?

I glance to my right. Ceepak is holding a pair of stainless steel forceps. They're usually stored in the left shin pocket of his cargo pants so they don't snap when he sits down. Yes, one day—a very slow one, as I recall—I asked Ceepak if he had a system for loading his work pants. He did. And it only took him about an hour to explain it.

"Shall I do the honors?" he asks Botzong.

"Yeah. I left my forceps in my other pants."

Ceepak crouches down, works the silver tongs into Skeletor's right front pocket.

"Fascinating," says Ceepak as he extracts what, at first, looks like a tennis ball made out of green felt. Then I see the googly eyes and, finally, the yellow-and-red striped legs, the floppy webbed feet. It's a plush, if crumpled, duck—one of the smaller prizes hanging on the wall of the Knock 'Em Down booth next to Paulie Braciole's body.

"Clearly," says Ceepak, "the killer is attempting to confirm their claim by linking this death to that of Mr. Braciole."

One of the CSI guys holds out a paper bag. Ceepak deposits his prize.

"We'll do a fiber scan," says Botzong. "Make sure it's a match with what we found in the booth near Braciole."

Great, I think. *All that fancy new gear in the back of the State MCU van will be utilized to positively I.D. a stuffed duck.*

"We should notify his next of kin," I mumble, hoping nobody thinks I mean the duck.

"Skeletor has kin?" says Botzong.

"Roger that," says Ceepak. "A local business owner who introduced himself to Danny last night."

"You want us to handle it?" asks Botzong.

"No, thank you," says Ceepak, looking down at Skeletor's body, which, I swear, has stiffened in the last fifteen minutes. Lying on the ground on top of the black vinyl body bag, he looks like a cardboard Halloween skeleton somebody dressed with a camouflage Army hat. "You have enough to deal with processing this crime scene. Danny?"

Yeah. We need to dump my Jeep at the house and then head north to the boardwalk to let Gabe know that, unfortunately, Saturday morning will be too late for his brother to turn himself in.

Gabe has lost most of his bluster and all of his swagger.

He's sitting in the back of the All American Snack Shack on top of a stack of Snickers cartons. Slumped forward, he takes off his thick-rimmed glasses and rubs at his eyes.

His booth isn't open yet. The young fry jockeys haven't clocked in yet. There is no sound of batter-dipped candy bars sputtering in oil. All I can hear is Gabe steadying his breath.

"Who did it?" he asks.

"We don't know, Mr. Hess," says Ceepak because he was sharp enough to quickly glance at the guy's vendor license when we stepped up to his stall to deliver the bad news. "However, rest assured, we will find out."

"Bullshit."

Ceepak does that confused dog head-tilt of his again.

"You two don't give a fuck about Tommy. To you and every other fucking cop, he was just some kind of derelict drug dealer. You're probably glad somebody else took him off the streets for you."

"Mr. Hess, I assure you, the Sea Haven Police Department and the New Jersey State Police will do everything in our power to track down and apprehend your brother's killer."

"Yeah, yeah. Tell your lies to somebody who hasn't heard 'em before."

"My partner never lies," I say.

Gabe stares at me. "What?"

"My partner never lies."

"Oh. I see. He's George Fucking Washington?"

"No. He's John Fucking Ceepak."

Ceepak shoots me a look. Slowly shakes his head, like I shouldn't have given him that particular middle name. I shrug. He's right. My bad.

But Mr. Hess ticks me off. I would have said he "pisses me off," but Ceepak wouldn't like that either.

"Here." I say, handing Hess one of our business cards. "If you want to help, call a few of your friends, then call us."

"What do you mean, 'my friends'?"

"Officer Boyle is suggesting that you make contact with your other brothers—the members of The Creed motorcycle gang."

"Why?"

"We have reason to suspect," says Ceepak, "that your brother's death is directly linked to that of Paul Braciole."

"That jerk from the TV show?"

"The young man found murdered in the Knock 'Em Down booth."

"The Creed didn't do that."

"Well, somebody riding a Harley sure did," I chime in.

"Says who?"

"A video from a nearby security camera," says Ceepak.

"I don't care what the fuck you think you saw. The Creed would not waste their time on that steroid-popping punk, and they sure as hell wouldn't kill Thomas."

"Are you one hundred percent certain of that, Mr. Hess?"

Hess doesn't answer right away. Instead, he actually thinks before engaging his mouth. He tucks the business card I handed him into his star-spangled shirt pocket.

"I'll make a few calls."

"We'd appreciate that," says Ceepak. "In the meantime, it would be helpful if you could come with us to Oak Beach."

"What? You want me to identify the body?"

"Yes. If you'd rather wait until your brother's body has been moved to the county morgue. . . ."

Gabe stands up. "No. Let's do it now. Get it over with."

We walk out of the booth.

I can't help checking out the deep fat fryers.

The cold grease pits have congealed icebergs of black-flecked lard floating on the surface. Guess that's what dead fried Oreos look like after rigor sets in.

We shuttle Gabe Hess to the beach and, then, back to the boardwalk.

Now the chief is back on our radio.

"John? Swing by the Fun House. ASAP."

"Do we have a situation?"

"No. We just need to discuss production details moving forward."

I'm behind the wheel but turn to look at Ceepak, who's turning to look at me because we're both thinking the same thing: *moving forward?*

"Surely," he says into the radio mic, "with the newly discovered death threat against Ms. Kemppainen, Mr. Mandrake is shutting down his show."

The chief hesitates before responding. *"Swing by the house, John. The mayor's waiting."*

So I flip on the roofbar and we jet down to Halibut Street.

In the driveway, I see Marty Mandrake, Layla Shapiro, Mayor Hugh Sinclair, and Chief Buzz Baines huddled around a foldout picnic table, jabbing at some kind of rolled-out plans. Mandrake is strutting around, making grand arm gestures. Layla is dutifully nodding her head and taking notes.

Ceepak and I climb out of our cruiser and stroll down to join the brain trust.

"John, good," says Chief Baines. "I want Prickly Pear to run you through their production schedule for the next seven days."

"No problem," says Layla, thumbing the BlackBerry, which, I think, has been surgically attached to her hand. "This week will be a busy one. Starting today, we shoot footage for the quarterfinals show, slated for next Thursday's regular airdate. We also simultaneously gear up for a special Friday night finale."

"We're doing it live!" says Mandrake, shooting up both hands like exploding starfish to give the word "live" a little more pizzazz.

"Excuse me?" says Ceepak.

"The finale," says Mandrake. "It'll be a live broadcast. A week from tonight."

"Surely you jest," says Ceepak, because he can say stuff like "surely you jest" without people sniggering at him.

"Huh?" says Mandrake, stuffing a sugar-coated cruller into his mouth. As usual, there are all sorts of snack food items spread out on the makeshift meeting table.

"Surely, Mr. Mandrake," says Ceepak, "you can't seriously consider exposing Ms. Kemppainen to that kind of risk."

"We're giving Soozy automatic immunity in the quarterfinals shows," says Layla. "We'll keep her under wraps and out of public places. She'll just talk about the threat and how it makes her feel, maybe she does a one-on-one sit-down with Chip."

"Beautiful," says Mandrake. "But I need her in the fucking live finale on Friday."

"Obviously," says Layla. "Since she's guaranteed to be one of the two finalists."

"That's what the fuck I'm saying, Layla!" Mandrake looks around for a servant who isn't there. "Where's my goddamn mochachino?"

Layla turns to Ceepak. "We'll be out of your hair in seven days, officer. Next Friday night, we do our season closer live from the Fun House on the Sea Haven boardwalk."

"*Fun House*—live from the Fun House!" says Mandrake, seeing another movie marquee blazing across the sky. "It's so fucking poetic." He pivots to Baines. "Chief, I'm sure you and your men can keep Soozy safe for one more week. She thinks so, too. Soozy K is totally on board with our production plans."

"What a trouper," says Mayor Sinclair, who's bouncing up and down on his heels. "That young girl is an inspiration to us all."

"Again," says Ceepak, "I must protest."

"Save it, John," says Chief Baines, sounding kind of snippy, the way people do when their bosses order them to do crap they don't really want to do. "The mayor, the town council . . . it's been decided."

Marty Mandrake struts over to Ceepak. "Officer, I understand your trepidation. But hell—*Fun House* is the number one show in America. The whole country is pulling for the four kids upstairs. We can't let America down."

Ceepak turns to Chief Baines, his eyes pleading for sanity.

The chief's mustache wiggles like a queasy dust bunny. "I need you to head this thing up, John. Unfortunately, I promised some folks down in Florida I'd swing by before the end of summer. Can't be here for the final shows. Wish I could. But, well, I gave my word. You know how that goes."

Before coming to Sea Haven, Chief Buzz Baines ran a police department in the Sunshine State. Guess he needs to go home periodically to guzzle some O.J. or wrestle a gator.

"But—" is all I can stammer before the mayor gives me The Hand.

"Save it, Officer Boyle. You're either with us or against us; and if you're against us, well, you're not who we want with us, are you?"

Mayor Hugh Sinclair does not like me or my partner very much, not since back in June when, thanks to our crack investigatory skills, the mayor's wife found out what he'd been doing with a few of his curvier constituents in a hot tub.

"If we call off the show," Sinclair continues, "the local economy will suffer an incredible blow, and, worst of all, the terrorists will win."

Okay. He has completely lost me now.

Ceepak, too. "Terrorists?" he says, arching up both eyebrows.

"This death threat. Whoever delivered it is a terrorist, trying to terrorize us. Well, this is Sea Haven. We don't cave in to terrorist threats."

"Soozy wants to remain in the competition," says Layla. "Her family could sure use the money. Her little brother needs an operation. . . ."

Geeze-o, man. What next?

"And the finale," says Mandrake, "will raise tons of money for charity. Each contestant gets to pick their favorite. Whoever wins, their charity wins too! Big-time."

"Papa John's is donating pizzas!" says Mayor Sinclair. "Budweiser's giving us beer!"

Fortunately, the radios on our belts start squawking.

"Unit A-12, this is base. Base for A-12."

Ceepak is a faster draw than me, at least when it comes to angrily whipping a walkie-talkie up to his mouth.

"This is Ceepak. Go for A-12."

"A-12, see the woman Becca Adkinson. Mussel Beach Motel. She says she has located the missing Mustang."

25

The Mussel Beach is a two-story, horseshoe-shaped motel owned and operated by the family of my friend-since-forever Becca Adkinson.

Becca's dad, Andrew "Andy" Adkinson, was and is his own general contractor for all renovations, which is why it took him five years to fix the crack in the swimming pool. He also handled the interior decorating, so most of the motel's rooms come with a shellacked swordfish on the wall between two mass-produced-in-a-Chinese-factory seashore oil paintings. It's also why the faux-marble counter in the lobby is a swirled blue you usually only see in bowling balls. I think they were having a sale at Countertops "R" Us.

As for the five-foot-tall stuffed Batman doll with its chubby legs splayed out in the lobby window, its limp body propped against the glass so the caped crusader's pointy ears bump into the neon NO VACANCY sign, that's Becca's decorating touch. Her most recent boyfriend won it for her by squirting a water pistol into a clown's mouth. That was during the first fifteen minutes of their date. Then Becca made the guy lug it around the boardwalk all night.

Mr. Adkinson is behind the counter when Ceepak and I enter the lobby.

"Hey, John," he says to Ceepak, "is it true what I'm hearing on the radio? Somebody killed the killer you guys were looking for?"

Mr. Adkinson is pretty buff for an old guy (he has to be at least fifty). Works out every day. Keeps his silver hair cut short. Always wears one of those "Life Is Good" T-shirts with the stick-figure man playing golf with his dog or whatever. At the gym, he and Ceepak sometimes spot each other on the bench press. Or so I've heard. I don't actually go to the gym enough to see these sorts of things.

"Andy, to be quite honest, we were never convinced that Thomas Hess, a.k.a. Skeletor, was responsible for the death of Paul Braciole."

"Really? Wow. It just goes to show you, huh?"

Ceepak nods. I guess he knows what the heck Mr. Adkinson means, even if I don't.

"They cancelling the show?" he asks.

"Sad to say, they are not."

"Shut the front door," says Mr. Adkinson, which is what he always says when he really wants to say something else. "Who's the lamebrain behind that decision? Wait, don't tell me—Mayor Hubert H. Sinclair."

"Indeed. The mayor is eager to have *Fun House* continue filming, no matter what. Apparently, the program has been very good for businesses on the island."

"Son of a biscuit. That arrogant idiot is gonna ruin this town."

Ceepak actually nods. "It's a possibility."

Now Mr. Adkinson rummages around in a junk drawer under the check-in counter. He pulls out a clipboard with a sheet of paper clamped to it. Clicks a ballpoint pen.

"What's on the clipboard?" asks Ceepak.

"My petition. I need two hundred signatures to get my name on the ballot for mayor this November. Somebody's gonna have to clean up Sinclair's mess. He's had eight years to screw things up and, brother, that's the one job he actually knows how to do. You two want to give me your autographs?"

Ceepak purses his lips. "Actually, Andy, as much as I would like to support your candidacy, I do not think it is wise for public servants, such as Danny and myself, to become engaged in partisan politics."

"Yeah," I say. "Sorry."

"Sure, sure. I understand. No problem." Adkinson tucks the clipboard back under the counter. "You have to serve to the best of your ability, no matter who's running the show."

"However," says Ceepak, "should you or your campaign team find yourselves canvassing the area around the Bagel Lagoon, be sure to stop by our apartment and ask Rita to sign. I'm certain she would support your candidacy. Now then, the car?"

"Come on. Becca's around back, guarding it."

We head out of the office, scoot around the lip of the pool, and head through an arched breezeway with waves painted on the walls that takes us under the second-floor sundeck and out to the rear parking lot.

"Hey, Danny. Hey, Ceepak."

Becca is dressed in a short shirtdress over her bathing suit, the better to show off her tan.

"Hey," I say.

"Ms. Adkinson," says Ceepak.

Usually, when the two of us drop by, Becca starts flirting like crazy with my partner because she has long been an admirer of the chiseled male physique. Today, despite her billowy shirtdress and funky ant-eyes sunglasses, she seems a little more subdued.

"There's like a bullet hole or something in the door over there," she says.

Mr. Adkinson drapes his arm over his daughter's shoulder. "Come on, sweetheart. Let's head back inside. Let Danny and Ceepak do their jobs."

Becca tries to smile. "Thanks, you guys."

After the Adkinsons leave, Ceepak crouches down, peers through the open window.

"We better call Botzong," he says. "Ask him to send over his best ballistics tech."

"Right."

As I'm reaching for my radio, a state police car comes crawling around the corner, crunching the tiny shells scattered across the asphalt.

"Guess they read our minds," I say, re-clipping the walkie-talkie to my utility belt.

"Or they were monitoring SHPD transmissions, as they typically do."

Okay. Or that.

One of Botzong's CSI techs climbs out of the back seat lugging an attache case, the kind copier-repair people carry.

"Officers Ceepak and Boyle?" she says. "I'm Detective Jeanne Wilson, MCU. Bill sent me over."

Ceepak gestures at the Mustang. "It's all yours. We're going inside to interview the witness who called it in."

We're in the small office off the front counter, the room where the night clerk does up everybody's bills on the computer.

Becca looks a little odd, sitting behind the big gunmetal-gray desk her dad picked up at the thrift shop over in Avondale. She's taken off the sunglasses but, with her blonde hair done up in a topknot like Pebbles Flintstone and that shirtdress draping off one shoulder, she still looks like a beach bunny pretending to be a grownup. Mr. Adkinson is behind her, leaning up against the credenza, monitoring the sputtering coffeemaker that's brewing us all a fresh pot of caffeinated mud.

"When did you first notice the vehicle's presence in your parking lot?" asks Ceepak.

"This morning, when I was taking a load of towels out to the laundry room. I mean, it's probably been parked out back for a while, but cars always are. I don't really pay much attention to them. Sorry."

"I take it the Mustang did not belong to a registered guest?"

"Nope," says Mr. Adkinson. "I ran the plates through our records. Unlike a lot of motels, we have more spaces than rooms. Sometimes families take two units, but arrive in one car. A minivan or whatever."

"So there are typically empty spaces in your lot?"

"Yeah. Except Saturdays, when the day-trippers show up. If they behave and we have space, I let 'em park."

"For free," Becca adds, sounding astonished.

Her dad smiles. "It's good for business. Maybe not mine, but, well, Skipper Dipper across the street sells a couple extra ice cream cones and maybe, one day, they recommend my motel. It all comes out in the wash."

"Can I ask a question?" I say.

"Certainly," says Ceepak.

"You guys ever see any motorcycles parked back there?"

"Sure," says Mr. Adkinson. "Sometimes."

I keep going. "You ever hear one pull in at like two or three in the morning?"

Becca gasps. Her cheeks flush red. "Shut the front door!"

Like father, like daughter.

"How did you know that, Danny?"

"I—"

"Daddy, do you have a security camera aimed at the pool?"

"Yeah. For—"

Becca whips back at me. "Danny—did you see me naked?"

26

"What?" I sort of sputter.

"Did you see me naked?"

"Not in the pool—"

"I can *not* believe this. . . ."

"Sweetheart?" says her dad, reassuringly, "I turn the pool camera off when we lock it up at eleven P.M."

"Oh. Then how did you know, Danny?"

I toss up my hands. "Know what?"

"A week ago. Last Thursday night. I'd been out on a very bad date. Jim and I broke up. For good this time."

"Thank goodness," her father editorializes.

"Daddy?"

"Sorry."

"Afterwards, I couldn't get to sleep. So, at like three in the morning, I came down, opened up the pool and, you know, took a dip."

Me and Mr. Adkinson sort of nod slowly.

Ceepak, however, has his note pad out and needs the facts. "Naked?" he says.

"Yes." Becca is blushing like she's swallowed a stoplight. "When I need to unwind, sometimes I skinny-dip."

"Did you adjust the chemicals afterwards?" asks her father.

Becca sighs. "Yes, Daddy. I showered off before jumping in and I adjusted the chemicals after I got out, okay?"

Mr. Adkinson holds up both hands to make the classic "hey-I-was-just-asking" gesture.

"Did you see or hear anything?" asks Ceepak.

She nods. "I heard a motorcycle pull into the parking lot, just like Danny said."

"At 3 A.M.?" says her dad.

"Or a little after."

Guess she wasn't even wearing a watch.

"Did you go out back to see who was pulling in at that hour?" asks Ceepak.

"No. I was naked. I swam over to side of the pool and tried to hide."

Ceepak leans forward in his chair. "What did you hear, Becca? This is very important. Try to remember everything."

"Okay." She closes her eyes. "The motorcycle cut out its engine. I remember thinking, 'Oh, great. Whoever it is, they're gonna come through the breezeway and see me.' So I dunked my head under the water. When I came back up for air, I heard a car door open and slam shut. And then . . ." She squeezes her eyes tighter. "Another car door thunked open."

"You're sure?" says Ceepak.

"Yeah, because then I heard it thunk shut again."

I glance over at Ceepak. This doesn't make sense. Why did Paul Braciole drive the Mustang over to the Mussel Beach Motel when he left Mandy's place? Why did he get out of the car, and then go back and open and shut the door again? Did he have something in the car the killer on the motorcycle wanted?

"Did you hear a gunshot?" I ask.

"No," says Becca.

Okay. Maybe the killer used some kind of noise suppressor on the muzzle of his weapon.

"Perhaps a soft popping sound?" asks Ceepak.

"Nope," says Becca. "There were no more sounds for a while, except, of course, the water gurgling down the drain."

"What did you do then?"

"I waited. Like five or ten minutes. Then, since everything was still quiet, I figured whoever it was had gone down to the beach or whatever. So, I climbed out, found my towel, grabbed my clothes, and ran up the steps to the second floor."

She pauses.

"What is it, Becca?" I say.

"When I got to the top of the staircase, I had to cut across the sundeck to get to my room. I wrapped myself up in the towel and tiptoed as quietly as I could. That's when the motorcycle started up again." She puts her hand to her heart. "It startled me. So I looked down. Saw the two people on the motorcycle."

"Two?" says Ceepak.

"Yeah. The driver and a passenger behind him, hanging on tight to his waist."

"You're certain the motorcyclist was a man?" says Ceepak.

"No. Not really. He had on one of those tinted racing helmets and like a leather jumpsuit, so I guess he could've been a girl."

"And the passenger?"

"Oh. He had on a helmet, but I could tell: he was definitely a guy. He was wearing a muscle shirt to show off his biceps and junk—just like Paulie always did on *Fun House*."

Becca's eyes go wide.

"Omigod. That was him, wasn't it? On the back of the motorbike. Right before he died."

"Perhaps," says Ceepak.

Because it could have been Paul Braciole right *after* he died.

Right after somebody shot him in the rear parking lot of the Mussel Beach Motel.

27

WHEN WE LEAVE THE MUSSEL BEACH MOTEL OFFICE TO CHECK in with Detective Wilson, the CSI tech working over the Mustang in the rear parking lot, Ceepak has that look on his face.

The one he always gets when something about a case is bugging him. It's like indigestion mixed with intense concentration. Makes him look like a grumpy old man sizing up his sock drawer, wondering why he has so many argyles that don't match.

"What doesn't fit?" I ask, since he usually gets these queasy squints when one piece of the puzzle won't lock into place with all the others, no matter how hard he tries to force it in around the edges.

"The sounds. The motorcycle cuts out its engine. A car door opens and closes. A second car door opens and closes."

"Maybe Paulie knew the guy on the motorbike. Maybe Mr. Motorcycle wanted something Paulie had in the car, so Paulie went back to get it."

Ceepak's head is nodding, even though his brain has raced off to wrestle with the illogic of it all.

"Maybe Paulie wanted to give the guy an autographed bobblehead doll."

This brings Ceepak back to earth. "A bobblehead?"

"Yeah. They make them of the whole *Fun House* cast. I bet Braciole had a bunch of his that he signed and gave away to people."

"I see. But why would Ms. Keenan keep a supply of these Paulie dolls in her car?"

Oh. Right. It wasn't Paulie's ride. It's Mandy's Mustang. So, unless he had bobblehead dolls stuffed in his trousers, my idea is basically idiotic.

So I shut up and let Ceepak woolgather while we walk around the pool and head through that arched breezeway for the back parking lot.

Detective Jeanne Wilson is standing near the Mustang's driver-side door, peeling off her latex gloves. She hears us approaching, turns around.

"This is where he was killed," she says.

"The parking lot?" says Ceepak.

"No. Sorry. I should've been more specific. From my examination of the evidence, I can state with a high degree of confidence that Paul Braciole was murdered inside this vehicle. Where it was parked at the time of his death, however, I cannot say with any certainty."

"Can you even be certain it was *parked* when he was murdered?" asks Ceepak.

"I believe so," says Detective Wilson. "Otherwise, well—we would have found this car wrapped around a telephone pole or totaled in somebody's front lawn."

Ceepak nods. He agrees. You shoot someone while they're driving, there's usually collateral damage.

"I still want to match the blood," says the CSI tech, gesturing through the open window toward the passenger-side door and the bullet hole in the upholstery. "I was able to scrape a tiny sample from the interior of the bullet hole."

"Did you also extract a bullet?"

"Nope. I think the killer took it. Then he tried to swab out the hole with a cloth wrapped around his gloved index finger, but he missed a few drops. I found them. They were baked in pretty good."

"Suggesting," says Ceepak, "that the vehicle has been parked here for some time."

"I'd say at least a week. With the windows open."

"Interesting," says Ceepak, crouching down into a squat to peer across the front seat and gaze at the crater in the quilted padding above the passenger-side armrest.

"Why would they roll down the windows?" asks Ceepak.

"I don't think the killer did that. I suspect Mr. Braciole had his window down before the bad guy shot him; otherwise the glass would be shattered."

Ceepak peeks down into the thin window channel. Pulls out his Maglite so he can check out whatever lurks down in the darkness of the door.

"I see no signs of the glass being punctured. No radiating fissure lines."

"Exactly," says Wilson.

Ceepak stands up. Pockets his miniature flashlight.

"Have you dusted the interior for fingerprints?"

Wilson shakes her head. "Not yet. But I'm pretty sure we won't find any."

"Bleaching?" says Ceepak.

"I think so. There's no smell of it. Another reason to leave the windows open—let the car air out till somebody found it ditched in a parking lot behind a motel. We'll do a luminol test. See if we can find any residual traces of blood. But the killer wiped things down pretty good. I only found the blood droplets because they were hidden deep inside that hole."

"Wait a second," I say.

Both Ceepak and Detective Wilson turn to look at me.

"If Paulie was shot in the car, how could he be opening and closing the door to give away bobblehead dolls?"

"Exactly," says Ceepak.

"Huh?" says Wilson.

"Sorry," says Ceepak. "My partner and I have been hypothesizing possible scenarios based on information obtained from a witness who may have seen the killer drive away with the victim's body."

"The motorcycle?"

"Right. It is possible," Ceepak continues, spitballing an idea to see if it makes enough sense to stick, "that the doors opening and closing our witness heard were connected to the killer removing Mr. Braciole's body from the car."

"So you think he *was* murdered here?" says Wilson.

"We can't be certain at this juncture." Ceepak glances around the parking lot. "And, after a week, it's doubtful that we'll find any evidence suggesting this parking lot was, indeed, the murder scene. No shell casing, for instance."

"The killer probably picked it up," adds Wilson. "Just like they dug the bullet out of the door."

"Okay," I say, "the first opening and shutting was to drag Paulie's body out the driver-side door. The second set was so they could gouge out the slug from the passenger-side door."

"It's a possibility," says Ceepak, like he always does when my answer may not be the only one—or even close to the real one.

"You guys remember Mr. Braciole's bullet wound?" asks Detective Wilson.

Ceepak taps his left temple. "In front and slightly above his left ear."

"Correct. Then it exits somewhat lower on the right side of his skull." She taps her right cheek, just above the jawbone. "If you imagine Paul Braciole sitting in the driver seat, line up that hole in his temple with the hole in the door panel."

She stands about a foot away from the door. Holds up her right hand and turns it into a finger pistol aimed so it's pointing down at a slight angle to the hole in the passenger-side panel.

"This was a very clean kill," she continues. "One bullet to the brain. The shooter was good; knew precisely where to place their single bullet. An amateur would've probably blown through a whole magazine of shells."

Ceepak nods.

"Here's how I figure this thing plays out, wherever it took place," says Detective Wilson. "Paulie parks somewhere or stops at a red light. Our killer is tailing him, probably on that motorcycle. When they see their chance, maybe at a stoplight, they stop, dismount, and stroll up beside the car. Very cool, very casual. Or, maybe they stumble a little—to pretend they're drunk and weaving their way home, which would explain why they're walking in the middle of the road, coming up on the driver side of the car.

"Paulie's behind the wheel. Maybe fiddling with the radio. Adjusting mirrors, trying to figure out where everything is on this girl's car. When our doer gets to the window, he or she whips up their pistol in two seconds flat. They aim and fire—one shot that goes clean through Paulie Braciole's skull and embeds in the far door."

"Your hypothetical killer is quite skilled," says Ceepak.

Detective Wilson nods. "The best."

"You've seen this sort of killing before?"

"Once or twice. It's a quick and clean execution technique perfected by a rebel group in the Philippines called the National People's Army. They used to target U.S. troops and diplomats.

The assassin walks up to your car window while you're waiting at a stoplight, whips out their rod, and bam. You're dead before red changes to green."

This makes no sense.

"So," I say, "we're looking for somebody from the Philippines?"

"Doubtful," says Ceepak.

"Yeah," adds the techie. "The NPA may have invented the move but, these days, the technique's very popular with all sorts of professional hit men."

A pro.

The kind of killer who would know precisely where to place a single shot to ensure a quick death. The kind of professional hit man a motorcycle gang like The Creed probably has on its roster.

"So," I say, "if that's what happened, then this has to be where Paulie was murdered, or else the car wouldn't be parked here, right?"

Ceepak doesn't answer right away. He just keeps staring through that open window. Detective Wilson does the same thing.

Finally, Ceepak speaks. "Such is our conundrum, Danny. The riddle we must answer."

"Well," I say, "what if the murder took place back here but *before* Becca went swimming, and all she heard was the motorcycle and the killer opening and closing car doors while he cleaned up any evidence and hauled Paulie's body out of the car?"

"That is definitely one answer," says Ceepak.

The way he says it? I know he doesn't think it's the right answer.

28

CEEPAK'S STILL RACKING HIS BRAINS WHEN, ONCE AGAIN, WE are called to the set of *Fun House*.

"Ceepak?" It's Gus Davis on the radio, sounding grumpier than the dwarf in the Disney movie after Sneezy blows boogers in his beard. Guess he's back on the unarmed-security detail. *"Get your butt over here. There's this jerk harassing the girl what got the death threat. Soozy K."*

"Where are Reed and Malloy?"

I'm guessing those were the two full-time cops on security duty today.

"Mayor Sinclair yanked them away for some kind of press conference down at Borough Hall. Mandrake went too."

I'm betting Gus can hear Ceepak crushing the radio microphone in his hand. He's that ticked off.

The mayor thinks he and Mandrake need the armed security guards more than Soozy? I don't care what Ceepak says, the next time Mr. Adkinson pulls out that petition, I'm signing it.

"Settle down, son," we hear Gus say to somebody, probably the jerk. "Ceepak?"

"10-4," says Ceepak. "We're on our way."

"He might be the nincompoop you're looking for."

"Come again?"

"The idiot drove here on his freaking motor scooter."

Sirens wailing, we fly up Shore Drive, even though there are these cute signs that say stuff like "IF YOU'RE IN A HURRY, YOU'RE ON THE WRONG ROAD" and "DRIVE SLOW, SEE OUR SIGHTS—DRIVE FAST, SEE OUR JUDGE."

The signs were Chief Baines's idea. Good Public Relations, which seems to be why we do all sorts of stupid stuff in Sea Haven these days, like let a bunch of drunks puke all over us on national TV and haul security details to Borough Hall when the primary threat is on Halibut Street.

We whip around the corner to the TV house. I see Gus and his partner, another retired cop named Andrew Stout. They're double-teaming this big dude in a fringed leather vest that shows off his arm muscles. Behind the guy is, of course, his motorcycle: a Harley-Davidson with high handlebars and a banana seat.

Gus and Stout are unarmed. However, Gus Davis is scrappy and, like he always says, he won't take "no guff from nobody." He stands his ground with both fists up and his feet firmly set, aping the Fighting Irish boxer pose from Notre Dame. Stout, who looks like he still runs three miles every morning, has both hands up, the way blocking linemen do in football. The two of them may be retired, but they still know how to keep a bad guy at bay.

I slam on the brakes. Tires squeal. Our rear end fishtails a little to the left.

This gets the lumbering lunatic's attention.

He turns his thick neck around, looks in our direction.

Ceepak's up and out of his door before the car stops sliding sideways.

"Come on kid," I hear Gus shout. "Give me a reason to knock your block off!"

"I just want to talk to Soozy!" the guy pleads.

"So buy a baby doll and name it Susan!" counters Gus, moving his fists around in a circle under his chin.

Ceepak pulls his Glock up from his hip. Locks it into a two-handed grip. "We've got this, Gus," he shouts, aiming his weapon at the big bruiser's left thigh. "On the ground!" he shouts.

Motorcycle man hesitates. You can see the "Huh?" etched on his face.

So Ceepak repeats himself: "On the ground! Now!"

I think the guy is slow—as in stupid. He puts his hands over his head.

This is not what Simon said.

"On! The! Ground!" I'm shouting it too, as I come around the nose of the car, my hands going for the plastic FlexiCuffs hooked to my belt.

"Kiss the dirt, douchebag!" shouts Gus. The guy finally comprehends. He drops to his knees.

"Down!" shouts Ceepak.

The lunkhead lies on his stomach. It takes him a while. Finally, he puts his face in the pea-pebble lawn.

"Hands behind your back!" barks Ceepak.

The horizontal dude obeys.

"Danny?"

Ceepak keeps his weapon trained on the ox while I work my way behind him, slip the plastic loops over his hands, and tug up on the zip straps like I'm bundling monster cables behind my high-def TV.

"I just need to talk to Soozy," the guy grunts into the gravel, so it comes out kind of mumbled.

"You ever hear of a telephone?" says Gus. "Next time, drop a dime!"

The guy isn't struggling as I fasten his hands behind his back, so I glance up. Ceepak is actually chuckling. Gus will do that to you.

Up on the sundeck, over Ceepak's shoulder, I can see Layla with Soozy K. The other three contestants are behind them: Mike Tomasino, Vinnie Martin, and Jenny Mortadella.

I hear feet crunching across gravel. Someone coming up behind Ceepak.

He hears it too.

Quick as a cat hunting Coke caps, he spins to his right, bringing his weapon around with him.

It's the freaking camera crew.

Geeze-o, man. Looks like we're going to be on TV again.

About ten, fifteen minutes later, Eric Hunley is so accommodating and apologetic that Ceepak tells me to cut him out of the plastic restraints.

Yep, the guy who tooled over to the Fun House on his Harley is the "very hot local stud" that Mandy Keenan told us about, the one who dumped her roommate Coco so he could hook up with a reality TV star, Soozy K.

"She broke my heart, man," Hunley says to Ceepak as he rubs his wrists. Guess I tugged a little too hard on those plastic zip strips. "I thought we could take our relationship to the next level."

I roll my eyes. Ceepak closes his.

Does everybody in town have to talk like they're being interviewed for this week's episode of *Fun House*?

"She got what she wanted," Hunley goes on. "She used me."

"How so?" says Ceepak.

"It's all a game to her," he head gestures up toward the house. Soozy K and the cameras have gone inside. I believe Gus Davis saying "get that freaking camera lens out of my freaking face or I'll jam it where the freaking sun don't shine" prompted Layla and Rutger Reinhertz, the director, to "wrap" filming in the front yard, move the shoot to a new location. Indoors.

Gus and Andrew Stout went inside with the cast and crew. "I need to hit the head anyways," Gus said as he galumphed away.

"Me too," said Stout.

From what I hear on TV, if you're a guy, when you get old, you spend a lot of time in the bathroom.

"Mr. Hunley," says Ceepak, "what exactly did Ms. Kemppainen want from you?"

"Who?"

"Soozy K," I translate for Eric.

"Oh. Sex, mostly. She's half nympho." He says it like it's an ethnic group on the census form. "And she wanted me to help her get rid of her competition."

Ceepak arches an eyebrow. "Paul Braciole?"

"Nah. She was using her new TV boyfriend, Tomasino, to take care of Braciole. They had an alliance or a strategy or something. She needed me to deal with the last girl standing in her way, the Mortadella chick. Wanted me to Tonya Harding her."

"Come again?"

"You know—the ice-skating chick whose ex kneecapped that other ice-skating chick with a nightstick."

"Nancy Kerrigan," I say, since obscure sports trivia is another one of my pop culture specialties.

"Yeah," says Hunley. "So, anyways, Soozy says I should do something like that on the only other hot chick left in the house, because she figures the producers have got this show rigged so it ends up being one hot guy and one hot girl in the big finale; they make it two hot guys, it comes off a little too homo, you know what I'm saying?"

Now Ceepak and I both close our eyes, just to give ourselves a half-second to cringe in privacy.

"She suggested I use my aluminum softball bat."

"On Ms. Morgan?" says Ceepak.

"Who?" says Hunley.

Time to translate again. "Jenny Mortadella. Her real name is Morgan."

"Really? Like the pirate captain? The one with the rum?"

"Yeah," I say, just so we can move on. It's 95 degrees out today. No shade. No trees. Just a lawn full of hot pea pebbles.

"But despite Ms. Kemppainen's suggestion, you two did nothing?" says Ceepak.

Eric tugs up on his belt. "I wouldn't say we didn't do nothing. But once Paulie got whacked, she didn't seem so interested in me busting up Jenny."

"Did she say why?"

"No. But then again, she didn't seem too interested in me anymore neither, so we didn't actually, you know, discuss matters much."

"And why did you come over here today?" asks Ceepak.

"Because for like a week, Soozy wouldn't answer my calls, my texts, nothing. Then, today, she sends me this text. Two letters. 'GL.'"

"What does that mean?" asks Ceepak.

"Either 'good luck' or 'get lost,'" I say.

"Exactly," says Eric. "Or maybe God I Love You, Eric."

Yes, the man is a dreamer who doesn't really understand how abbreviations work.

"The correct answer was 'Get Lost?'" says Ceepak.

"Yeah. So I take a ride up here, we have a face-to-face, then Soozy calls for the two rent-a-cops and they call for you."

"What did Ms. Kemppainen say during your talk?"

"That she don't need or want me no more. That if I show up again, it'll piss off Tomasino and she needs him to think they have something going on. That's her strategy or whatever, at least up to the finals. Then she'll screw the guy over because, trust me, that girl will do whatever it takes to win the big bucks. Quarter million dollars can make a person do some crazy shit, you know what I'm saying?"

"Did she tell you anything else?"

"Yeah. That I should 'climb back on my fucking tricycle and get the fuck out of her life.' That kind of made me mad." He drops his eyes and fiddles with a fringe flap on his vest. "Sorry if I gave those two security guards a heart attack or whatever."

"They will be fine," says Ceepak. "They are both retired police officers and, even unarmed, know how to handle themselves in crisis situations."

Ceepak doesn't say it, but what he means is: "Gus Davis and Andrew Stout would have whipped your leather-fringed ass, biker boy."

Instead, Ceepak turns to stare at Hunley's bike.

He walks over to it.

Touches the seat. Runs his hand along the long leather cushion.

"Danny?"

"Yes, sir?"

"Let's head back to the Mussel Beach Motel. I want to run an experiment."

"Am I free to go?" asks Hunley.

Ceepak snaps out of his temporary trance. "Do we have your word that you will stop harassing Ms. Kemppainen?"

"Who?"

Geeze-o, man, this guy is thick. "Soozy K," I say.

"Oh. Yeah. I'm pulling for Jenny Mortadella now. She's way hotter. I dig tattoos on chicks."

"Do not come within one hundred yards of any of the show's contestants," says Ceepak.

Hunley puts up his hands. "Don't worry, dudes. I'm out of it. Fucking reality chicks are too phony for me."

Ceepak nods. "Mr. Hunley, are you free for the next hour?"

"Huh?"

"You could be of great service to us and Sea Haven."

Hunley shrugs. "Sure. I'm free. Besides, I figure I owe you guys one."

"Then kindly follow us on your motorcycle down to the Mussel Beach Motel."

"Cool."

"Danny?" Ceepak gives me a head-bob toward our police cruiser.

Guess we're escorting Eric Hunley back to Becca's motel to run some kind of experiment.

I just hope it's not that one about the pool water changing color when you pee in it.

29

WE'RE CRUISING SOUTH ON BEACH LANE.

I glance up into the rearview mirror.

Eric Hunley is right behind us, tooling along on his Harley, leather fringe flapping in the breeze. He looks like one of the old hippies in that movie *Easy Rider.*

Over in the passenger seat, Ceepak is cogitating, a form of heavy thinking that, in his case, involves a knuckle pressed to his lips and a partial shuttering of his eyelids.

"So," I say, "you think, maybe, Soozy killed Paulie?"

The knuckle stays up, but the half-open eyes peer over at me. "Pardon?"

"Eric says Soozy will do anything to win the quarter-million dollars. You think she bumped off Paulie?"

"Firing one perfectly aimed bullet to the head, then hauling his body on the back of a motorcycle to the Knock 'Em Down booth, where she hung him up on the wall in the middle of the stuffed animal prizes?"

Okay. When you say it like that. . . .

"Well," I say, refusing to quit while I'm behind, "maybe she borrowed Eric's motorcycle. Maybe Eric did the shooting. Maybe they did it together."

"Interesting. Apparently, Danny, you and I are hypothesizing along parallel paths."

We are? I thought I was just saying stupid stuff to get him to tell me why the heck he's over there chewing his knuckles.

But he just turns back to his window, stares at the buildings blurring by.

I pull into the parking space out front you're supposed to use when registering at the Mussel Beach Motel. We're right outside the floor-to-ceiling plate-glass window of the office. I can see Becca inside, aiming a remote at the television set mounted in the corner, right above the window air-conditioner Mr. Adkinson decided to hang through the wall because the only window that slides open was too far away from an electrical outlet.

Ceepak's already out of the car and looking through the window at the TV set.

"I wonder if that's the press conference," he mutters.

On cue, Marty Mandrake and Mayor Sinclair appear on the screen. They're outdoors, standing behind a Plexiglas-topped podium in front of an ugly white wall where blocky letters spell out "Borough Hall, Sea Haven, N.J."

Eric Hunley putters into the space next to our cop car, takes off his helmet, shakes out his shaggy hair. In his bare chest and vest, he looks a little like a bloated version of one of those beefcake cover boys on the romance novels my mother likes to read and then store in her bathroom on top of the toilet tank near the dish of pink soaps shaped like seahorses.

"Mr. Hunley?" says Ceepak. "If you don't mind, I'd like to catch a little of the news conference before we get started with our experiment."

"No problem. I'll hang here. Need to give my tan a booster shot." He closes his eyes, flaps open the vest, leans back to soak in the rays.

"Danny?" says Ceepak.

"I'm with you," I say and we head into the motel office.

"That's not him," says Becca when we whoosh open the glass door.

Ceepak and I must look confused, because she clarifies:

"That guy on the motorcycle. That's not the guy I saw out back that night. He's too big. The guy I saw was more, you know, average. Five-seven, five-nine. Slender waist."

"Thank you, Becca," says Ceepak. "That's very helpful." Now he gestures up to the TV. "Have they started?"

"Yuh-huh. Mayor Sinclair said he hopes everybody is having a sunny, funderful day, and that, to let the terrorists know they can't scare us, the show must go on."

On screen, Marty Mandrake steps to the podium. He has to adjust the two gooseneck microphones on the podium because he's taller than Mayor Sinclair. Then again, so are many Chihuahuas.

"Thank you, Mayor Sinclair. Ladies and gentlemen, as my esteemed colleague just said, Soozy K has received a death threat. . . ."

"I can't believe they're announcing it like this," grumbles Ceepak.

Me? I believe anything. TV people have no shame. You ever watch that show where people who weigh five hundred pounds dance? Or that one where parents send in video clips of their kids slipping on ice?

"But," Mandrake continues, *"the show must go on. With the help of the Sea Haven Police Department, who have beefed up security around*

our Fun House, we will complete our exciting summer season, despite the heinous death threat leveled against Soozy with a special, two-night season finale spectacular next Thursday and Friday."

Somebody applauds. My guess? Mandrake brought along his script girl Grace, the lady with all the stopwatches around her neck.

"You know," Mandrake continues, giving the cameras an aw-shucks shuck of his head, *"it was Soozy K, herself, who, just this morning, came to me and said 'Marty, we can't quit now. If we do, the bad guys win. And then what was all our sacrifice for?'"*

Ceepak is shaking his head slowly. I think he's heard this argument one too many times. He has also seen its consequences. My partner spends a lot of his vacation days and holidays visiting Army buddies in VA hospitals or, worse, cemeteries.

"And it isn't just about winning the quarter-million dollars for Soozy," says Mandrake, *"because, in the finale, our two remaining contestants will also be playing for their favorite charities. Whoever wins, their charity wins too! Ten thousand dollars!"*

The assembled crowd of reporters and assorted Borough Hall hangers-on applauds, even though it sounds like the charities are kind of getting stiffed.

"Soozy has already picked her charity: SPF!"

"Yes!" says Becca, pumping her fist in the air. "Whoo-hoo!"

Okay. I have no idea what an SPF is or why it makes Becca so happy.

Then Marty Mandrake explains:

"The American Skin Cancer Prevention Fund wants to make sure everybody tans safely."

"I'm president of the local chapter," says Becca.

Of course she is. Tanning is her life.

"Mike, Vinnie, or Jenny will also be playing for a favorite charity," says Marty Mandrake. *"That is, if your votes put them through to the final round."*

I wonder what charity Jenny Mortadella picked. The Italian Deli Meat Anti-Defamation League?

"Now, to play it safe," Mandrake says, *"the network and I have reached a unanimous decision: Soozy K will receive immunity in next Thursday night's show. She's going straight to the Friday finals, which will be broadcast live from the Sea Haven boardwalk behind a ring of steel; the tightest security ever thrown up around a network TV show! We'll make it fun, but we'll keep it safe!"*

More applause.

I shake my head.

Mandrake sounds like a condom commercial.

30

"THEY'RE PUTTING HER THROUGH?" SAYS THIS GUY WHO JUST walked into the motel lobby, toting a cardboard carton.

"Yeah," says Becca.

"That means only the other three compete next Thursday?" The guy puts his box on the counter.

"And two of 'em get cut," says Becca who, apparently, watches *Fun House* religiously. "Because they already did that immunity deal for the funeral show, so two heads have to be on the chopping block."

The guy nods, pulls out his cell phone.

"Don't worry, Mr. Tomasino," says Becca with a big, bright smile. "Mike's going to make it to the finals, too. He's got my vote!"

"Thanks, Becca." Now he looks up from his phone, realizing that there are two police officers in the room with him. "You two with the SHPD?"

"Yes, sir," says Ceepak.

"Thanks for all you're doing to keep our kids safe and the show on the air."

"Actually," says Ceepak, "I had recommended that the show be cancelled."

Mr. Tomasino shakes his head. "You heard the mayor. We do that, the terrorists win. Thanks again for your service."

He heads out to the parking lot where the cell reception is better. As I watch him walk into a sunny spot of asphalt, I glance over to Eric Hunley, who's still sitting on his bike, eyes closed, holding open the sides of his vest so his chest can soak up the sun.

"You guys seen enough?" asks Becca, remote aimed at the tiny TV.

"Roger that," says Ceepak.

Becca presses the "OFF" button. Marty Mandrake and his smiling goatee shrink down into a tiny white dot.

"That was Mike Tomasino's dad," says Becca. "They live in Philly, so Mr. T rented a room with us for the show's final week."

So, I guess even The Mussel Beach Motel is making money off *Fun House.*

"Are you guys gonna like bring me more suspects to check out?" Becca asks, flicking her blonde head toward the window and the biker outside. "Is this what they call a line-up?"

"Actually, Mr. Hunley is here to help us conduct an experiment of sorts." Ceepak gestures at the five-foot-tall stuffed Batman propped up against the front window. "Becca, if you don't mind, we'd like to borrow your Batman doll."

"Um, okay. Oh, can you ask Mr. Tomasino what he wants me to do with his inflatable Ab Balls?"

"Come again?"

"Mr. Tomasino and his son, Mike, they're marketing these inflatable Ab Balls. I guess if Mike wins, they'll be huge." She pulls a limp orange, white, and yellow striped beach ball out of the box. On the white panels there's a screen-printed logo: "Mike Tee's Hard Body Ab Ball."

"Is that a beach ball?" asks Ceepak.

"I guess. Mr. Tomasino calls it a 'prototype.' He's been sending them out to investors. Very important people in New York and Hong Kong and Las Vegas." Becca puts the floppy vinyl wad back into the box. "The cool thing about this kind of exercise equipment? Extremely portable. You can like put it in your purse and exercise anywhere you go."

I just nod.

Ceepak, on the other hand, wraps his arms around Batman and hoists the caped crusader up off the floor.

"What's up?" I ask as he lugs the doll out the front doors and heads past the NO VACANCY sign for Hunley and the motorcycle.

"One minute," he says when we reach Mr. Tomasino.

"Don't worry," we hear him say to whoever is on the other end of his phone call. "Call China. Up the order. Mike's going to make the finals. It'll be him and Soozy. They have like a pact."

Finally realizing that we're standing right there, Mr. Tomasino cups a hand over his cell. He also sort of sizes up Ceepak, who is standing there hugging a giant Batman snuggle toy.

"Can I help you, officers?"

"Yes, sir. Ms. Adkinson asked us to remind you that you left your box in the office."

"Oh, right. Thanks." He glances at Ceepak's gut, even though it is partially obscured by Batman. "You guys work out?"

"Some," says Ceepak.

"A little," I add.

"You want a free Ab Ball? I can hook you up."

"No, thank you," says Ceepak.

"They retail for $29.99 on TV."

Really? I think, because, at Wal-Mart, cheap inflatable beach balls cost like three bucks.

"It's against our code of conduct to accept gratuities of any kind, no matter how generous the offer," says Ceepak, giving Mr. Tomasino the best two-finger salute he can without dropping Batman on his padded butt.

Mr. Tomasino nods like he gets it, returns to his phone call, and strolls back into the office.

"So, what exactly are we doing with Becca's Batman?" I ask.

"Something has been bothering me, Danny, ever since I watched the CSI team lower Thomas Hess's body out of that lifeguard chair."

Ceepak adjusts his grip on the dummy. Hikes it up a couple inches.

"Mr. Hunley?"

The sun-worshipping biker snaps to.

"Yes, sir?"

"Would you mind dismounting?"

"Sure. No problem." He swings his leg up and over, hops off the scooped seat.

Ceepak lowers the Batman doll onto the back of the bike.

"Danny?"

"Yeah?"

"How tall would you say this doll is?"

"About five feet."

Ceepak nods. Hefts the dummy up and down a few times. "And I'd say it only weighs twenty, maybe thirty pounds."

Yeah, I think, unless your girlfriend makes you lug it up and down the boardwalk all night, then it weighs more like a ton.

"Shoot," says Ceepak.

"What?"

"Could you run back inside, Danny, and ask Becca if she has a roll of duct tape we might borrow?"

"Um, okay. Can I ask why?"

"Of course. In the death of Paulie Braciole, we have, thus far, assumed that the killer positioned his lifeless and, therefore, limp, body—a body much taller and heavier than this one—onto the back of a Harley-Davidson motorcycle seat, strapped his shoes to the footposts below, then, somehow, kept the dead weight of Mr. Braciole's body from flopping sideways while climbing aboard, and, finally, wrapping the dead man's arms around their waist while, simultaneously, unrolling more duct tape to secure Mr. Braciole's wrists in front of their belt buckle."

"Right," I say.

"Well, Danny, I would like to see if I can do all that without any assistance from an accomplice."

31

He can't.

And if Ceepak can't do it, neither can anybody else.

Batman keeps sliding off and flopping down to the parking-lot asphalt.

Eric Hunley is enjoying the show. Laughing. Saying "Dude!" a lot.

First, Ceepak has to figure out how to steady the torso of Batman's body while he bends down to wrap the duct tape around his booties to secure them to the footposts. He finally figures out he has to pre-tear the tape strips, line them up on his sleeve, and then hoist the "dead body" up into its sitting position.

I start chuckling the third or fourth time Ceepak tries to steady Batman's head with his left hand while making a very graceful, almost balletic, backwards move that sends his right leg swinging up and over the motorcycle seat so he can hop on.

When he lets go of the head to quickly reach down and grab for both of Batman's wrists for the waist embrace, the stuffed superhero slumps into a spine-bending tumble off the back of the bike. Ceepak would have to be the Flash to strap Batman in.

And not even the Flash could do it with a real dead body.

A couple cars cruising past the Mussel Beach Motel toot their horns. They're enjoying the show, too.

"So," I say, when Ceepak finally gives up, "you think Paulie was killed by two people?"

"At least," he says.

"But you don't think it was Soozy and . . ." I do a subtle head jab toward Eric Hunley, who's hunkered down near the rear wheel of his Harley because he volunteered to clean up the gummy duct tape residue Ceepak's experiment left all over his rear footposts.

"Highly doubtful," says Ceepak. "Neither of them, to the best of my knowledge, is a skilled enough marksman to pull off the single-shot execution technique described by the CSI ballistics expert."

Yeah. Hunley would probably point to his pistol and say "Yo, dude, check it out" before firing his first round.

"What about Skeletor?" I ask. "Thomas Hess. Was that a team killing, too?"

"Most likely. The assassination technique was the same. Also, transporting Hess's body from wherever he was slain to the lifeguard chair would, once again, take at least two people to pull off."

I glance back at the motel.

"So, one guy killed Paulie, most likely right after he climbed into Mandy's Mustang on the back street behind her place, when Paulie out of camera range. . . ."

Ceepak nods.

"The killer then, what, got in the car and drove it over here and waited for his partner on the motorcycle to show up?"

"Such is my supposition," says Ceepak. "Undoubtedly, they were in radio or cell phone contact, coordinating their movements, keeping to a predetermined timeline."

"Okay. So that first door opening that Becca heard, that's the shooter-driver getting out of the Mustang . . ."

"Roger that."

". . . and the second door is them hauling Paulie's body out the passenger-side door."

"So it would seem," says Ceepak. "The driver-shooter then helps the motorcyclist secure Mr. Braciole's body to the back of his bike."

"And walks away."

"Or walks to a second car he has parked somewhere down the street."

"And Becca is up on the sundeck after that guy is already gone, when the second guy is getting ready to take off on his Harley."

"Such would be my conjecture."

Ceepak's conjecture gets an unanticipated assist when our radios start buzzing with a call from Bill Botzong.

"You boys been around back lately?" he asks.

"Negative," says Ceepak. "We've been conducting an experiment in the front parking lot."

"Well, you might want to go visit Detective Wilson. Her luminol test paid off, big-time."

Luminol is a chemical used by forensic investigators—on TV and in real life—to detect trace amounts of blood left at crime scenes, even ones that have been wiped down. It reacts with the iron found in hemoglobin, which, I guess, is the globby hemo stuff in blood. When the luminol spray hits what they call "an activating oxidant," it emits a faint blue glow that lasts about thirty seconds, which is why the CSI folks always roll video or snap photographs when they spray it on.

"Did the trace evidence show a smear pattern across the seats and/or headrests, as if Mr. Braciole's body had been shoved from the driver side over to the passenger side of the car?"

We have radio silence for a couple seconds.

"Yeah," Botzong finally comes back. *"How'd you know?"*

"Danny and I have hypothesized that Mr. Braciole was murdered by, at the minimum, a pair of very skilled, perhaps professional, killers, one of whom shot Braciole as he sat behind the steering wheel and then pushed his body out of the way in order to drive the Mustang here to the Mussel Beach Motel, where he was joined by his accomplice on the motorcycle."

Yeah. That's what I was hypothesizing. Except I had Soozy K cast as the "very skilled" trigger person, Eric Hunley on the motor scooter, and hadn't actually worked out all that shoving stuff.

"Well," says Botzong, *"it fits. So now what?"*

"I think we need to re-focus on The Creed," says Ceepak. "They would have the means and manpower. We can assume finding two skilled hit men in their ranks would be quite easy."

They also had the motive. Both Paulie and Skeletor were screwing with The Creed's very lucrative drug-distribution empire. Attracting too much attention. Making their pharmaceutical operations as well known as those drugs they sell on the evening news that might help you quit smoking if you don't kill yourself first.

Exasperation leaks out of the tinny radio speaker. *"My friends up in the Narcotics and Organized Crime Bureau have been trying to crack The Creed for years. They don't like to talk to strangers. And the last guy we almost got undercover almost got dead first."*

"Danny and I will work the one angle open to us," says Ceepak.

"Hess's brother?"

"Roger that," says Ceepak. "He has a vested interest in seeing that justice is done, no matter the consequences for his Creed brethren."

Looks like we're heading back to the All American Snack Shack to talk to Gabe Hess.

This is a good thing.

It's been a long day. We haven't even taken a lunch break.

Some deep-fried Pepsi Balls would definitely hit the spot.

32

CEEPAK ISN'T CERTAIN GABE WILL BE AT HIS FRIED-FOOD STAND.

"After all," he says as we bound up the boardwalk, "he may be at the funeral home, making arrangements for his brother's burial."

I nod, just as someone behind us shouts out "Good afternoon, officers. Where you guys going in such a rush?"

We turn around.

It's Layla Shapiro and a couple of her production-crew flunkies.

"Hey, Danny," she says. "I thought I recognized your butt."

"Officer Boyle," says Ceepak, sternly.

"Oh. Right." She taps her heart like she's a Dominican baseball player. "Respect. Let me try again: I thought I recognized your butt, Officer Boyle."

I'm about to say something about how I recognized her smart-ass mouth when my inner Ceepak kicks in. "What brings you out to the boardwalk, this afternoon, Ms. Shapiro?" I ask calmly.

She head-nods toward the horizon. "The Fun House. We're scouting it for the live finale. It'll be awesome."

"Totally," chimes in one of the flunkies, a dark-haired vixen with shiny red lips who's maybe a year or three younger than Layla and probably already scheming about how she can shove Layla aside and take over her job as Mandrake's right-hand gal, the way Layla, obviously, bumped out whoever stood in *her* way. Working in TV is a lot like Roller Derby—only without helmets or shin guards.

"Whoever makes it through to the final round, will have to make it through the Fun House with their charity partner to claim the grand prize," Layla continues excitedly. "We'll stagger the contestants. Time them—"

Ceepak, apparently, has heard enough. "Good luck with that," he says. "Danny?"

"Have fun," I say.

Layla and her posse head off to the Fun House and its big clown mouth entrance. Ceepak and I, following the scent of sputtering oil, head over to the All American Snack Shack.

There's a line. I guess mid-afternoon is when everybody hits the candy-bar machine when they're at work. When they're on vacation, they just hit the deep-fried candy-bar booth, instead.

I see Gabe, sitting on a thirty-gallon tin canister of cooking oil, back near the double deep-fat fryers. Misty grease fogs his glasses. His wrinkled flag shirt looks like it is flying at half-mast.

"Mr. Hess?" says Ceepak.

The sad-eyed man looks up.

"We need your help."

Hess nods. Motions for us to come around to the rear of the booth.

We do.

"I've made a few calls," says Hess.

Ceepak nods.

"The Creed did not do it."

"Are you sure?"

"Yeah. We don't lie to a brother, cheat a brother, or steal from a brother. That's the only way you can trust that your brother is your brother, you know what I'm saying?"

"Yes, sir," says Ceepak, choosing not to use this moment to discuss his own code of honor and ethics, which, of course, is way stricter than "screw the world but don't lie to, cheat, or steal from your biker buddies."

"So now this has become an honor issue for The Creed as well," says Gabe. "We will find out who did this thing."

"How?"

"Don't worry. We, like you, have our ways."

Geeze-o, man.

Why do I think The Creed's ways don't involve reading suspects their Miranda Warning or, for that matter, letting them live?

Of course, Gabe Hess and The Creed talk tough, but that doesn't mean they can deliver.

At least, not for seven long, frustrating days.

33

It's Thursday.

Nine P.M.

Time, once again, for *Fun House.* Tonight: The Semi-Finals.

And Ceepak, the New Jersey State Police, the FBI, and I are still no closer to catching Paul Braciole's or Skeletor's killers.

All evidence points to a professional hit involving, at the very least, two assassins: a triggerman and a getaway guy on a motorcycle. So everybody is looking at The Creed, the Garden State's most nefarious motorcycle gang. To hear Christopher Miller talk, the FBI guy who's heading up the Fed part of the investigation, The Creed are connected to what the Fibbies used to call La Costra Nostra, the Italian mafia, including the Pelagatti's and a Squarcialupi Family underboss named Bobby "Baby Fat" Marino.

The Creed is, in a way, like a mobile Rite Aid. They only *sell* the drugs, while other people, the kind who like to whack anybody who gets in their way, import the actual product from overseas manufacturers in places like Afghanistan, Peru, Mexico, Bolivia, and anywhere else the War On Drugs should be waving the white flag.

Ceepak thinks that the mob may have been the instigators of the dual hits. "They were, undoubtedly, furious when The Creed pulled that publicity stunt in the parking lot of Morgan's Surf And Turf."

Miller, the FBI guy, agreed. "Somebody had to pay for that. Big-time."

That's the theory of the day: Paulie Braciole and Thomas Hess were sacrificial lambs.

"Maybe," speculated Miller, "to keep doing business with the families, The Creed had to perform an act of penance by killing the TV kid and one of their own."

Geeze-o, man. When I went to confession during my days at Holy Innocents Elementary School, the priests just made us say an Act of Contrition and maybe five Hail Mary's if, you know, we were having impure thoughts or whatever. They never asked us to bump off one of our buddies on the playground.

Anyway, tonight is a night off from all that.

After six days of dead-ends, FBI and MCU meetings, not to mention repeated runs to the All American Snack Shack (I am officially sick of deep-fried anything, especially Tasty Kake Butterscotch Krimpets), Ceepak and I are, in his words, "recharging our batteries."

"Sometimes, Danny, the best way to solve a problem is to walk away from it and let your subconscious chew on it for a while," he says.

So, being romantically unattached, I headed over to Casa Ceepak to hang. John and Rita, plus their cat Gizmo (full name Hideous Gizmideus) and ancient dog Barkley (known to fart more than all the soy lovers at Veggin' On The Beach combined), live in a one-bedroom walk-up apartment over a shop called the Bagel Lagoon. Their place always smells like onions and garlic.

And, of course, dog farts.

Earlier, we charred some burgers on the grill on the tiny patio behind the Bagel store. Rita served her world-famous potato salad. I brought over a couple pints of Cherry Garcia ice cream from the Ben & Jerry's on Ocean Avenue. We pigged out. Then, after dinner, we headed upstairs to watch the second-to-last episode of *Fun House.*

Hey, if the show is going to ruin our lives, we might as well watch it.

Nursing my second beer of the night (Ceepak always asks that I allow an hour between brewskis so I never drive buzzed), I notice a stack of glossy *Discover Ohio* magazines with articles about "Everything Walleye," "Lake Erie Wine Country," and "Autumn Adventures: 8 Million Acres of Woods Would Like to Say 'Hello.'"

We don't have much of an autumn down the shore. Scattered evergreens shed needles. Flowers die of frost or thirst, whichever comes first. Lawns turn browner.

"So, you guys really gonna move?" I say.

Ceepak sips on his non-alcoholic Coors, a beverage he learned to love while serving in Iraq.

Rita sighs. "I don't know, Danny. Ohio looks nice."

"Sure does." I gesture at the magazine on the top of the pile. "They've got all those walleye."

"Indeed," says Ceepak. "In fact, in Port Clinton, Ohio, the Walleye Capital of the World, they drop a twenty-foot-long, six-hundred-pound fish on New Year's Eve. It's much more exciting than that ball in Times Square."

It's interesting to hang with Ceepak when he's off duty, boots off, stocking feet stretched out in front of him. He's actually pretty funny.

Of course, I say we're off duty because we're off the clock, but John Ceepak, being the American cousin to Dudley Do-Right, keeps his police scanner humming softly in the background.

From the TV, we hear the *Fun House* theme song. All eyes swing to the screen.

"Welcome to Fun House," says Chip Dale, the host, *"the number one show in America!"*

Soozy K, with her death-threat immunity and guaranteed entrance into the final round, is watching the show live with us. Well, not at the Ceepaks' place. They have her on a live remote from her heavily guarded bedroom at the house on Halibut Street.

"I wish I could've taken part in this week's competition, Chip," she says. *"It sounds like it was awesome!"*

"Indeed it was, our best challenge yet," teases Chip, because they like to do that a lot on these shows: hint that something good is coming. In fact, they do more hinting and teasing than actual entertaining.

Officers Dylan and Jeremy Murray are in the background of Soozy's secluded bedroom, looking tough, their arms akimbo, which is one of those words that doesn't sound like what it is. "Akimbo" should be a type of Latin dance, not a way of standing "with hand on hip and elbow bent outward," unless that is, of course, a Latin dance.

Chip Dale is back, promising us the fun will get started *"right after the break."*

When they cut to commercial, we tune out the sales pitches and pick up our conversation—the way it's done in living rooms all across the country.

"I'm not all that eager to move," says Rita.

"I thought everybody born in New Jersey was eager to escape from it," teases Ceepak.

"You listen to too much Springsteen," I say.

"Or not enough," adds Rita.

She's right. You listen to enough Bruce songs, you eventually hear a heartfelt love of his home state. Guess that's why he still lives over in Rumson when he's rich enough to live on Mars.

"I, too, like New Jersey," says Ceepak. "In fact, there are certain aspects of the Garden State I absolutely adore."

Over on the couch, he reaches out his hand to Rita. Here in my cushy chair, I gulp beer because a frothy adult beverage always helps when you think you might gag.

"So why do you want to take a job in Ohio?" I ask.

"Most of my adult life, Danny," says Ceepak, suddenly sounding serious, the way he does on the job, "I have lived and worked wherever my duty took me. Korea. Germany. Iraq. I only came here, as you recall, as an interim step, a waystation between my military life, which was ending, and my civilian life, which had not yet begun."

And then Ceepak stayed in Sea Haven because duty, once again, called and people needed him. Not too long after that, he met Rita. I think *he* needed *her.*

"This opportunity," he says, "presents a chance to work in the state, which, for better or worse, is my true home."

I nod. I know the "worse": his father, John "Sixpack" Ceepak, the drunk who had driven a young Ceepak to find a home in the Army.

I guess the "better" must be all those walleye.

"They'd also double John's salary," says Rita. "That would be nice." When she says it, she kind of looks around their dinky apartment. Okay, living in a one-bedroom box over a bagel shop may not be the American dream, but, hey, breakfast is always hot and fresh.

"And I'd be closer to my mother," says Ceepak, who doesn't trust his alcoholic old man to keep his promise to quit harassing his ex-wife.

"She could move here," I say.

"That's what I suggested," says Rita.

Ceepak is about to comment when his cell phone chirrups.

The work phone.

"This is Ceepak. Go."

Rita and I stare at him, both of us with a "What happened at the Fun House now?" look in our eyes.

He covers the phone. Mouths "Chief Baines."

Rita and I relax a little. Watch a cell-phone commercial.

Geeze-o, man. *Fun House* runs a ton of commercials. Like five minutes of ads for every three minutes of show.

"I see," Ceepak says. "Understood. Will do. Roger that. Safe travels."

And then he hangs up.

"Well?" I say.

"Chief Baines will be detained in Florida over the weekend."

"So he's missing all this?" I gesture at the TV.

"Apparently so."

I'm reminded of that old saying: when the going gets tough, the tough go to Disney World.

"He's asked me to fill in in his absence."

"You're Acting Chief?"

"Roger that."

"So, can we have a casual Friday tomorrow?"

"Come again?"

"If you're Acting Chief, you can suspend the dress code for a day. It's supposed to be in the hundreds."

"Be that as it may. . . ."

"Hey, if we're going to do the jobs of homicide detectives, we need to dress like 'em."

Ceepak smiles. "You make a good point. Very well. Tomorrow is plain clothes Friday."

"Uh-oh, John," says Rita. "You didn't tell me you guys were going to be on the show again this week."

On TV, the show is back. Chip Dale has just introduced a film clip. Me and Ceepak. In the front lawn of the Fun House, Ceepak aiming his Glock at Eric Hunley's thigh, the big guy dropping to his knees and, finally, going facedown on the ground.

Ceepak sighs. And then, believe it or not, he lets out a mournful, "Geeze-o, man."

"To ensure the safety of our house guests," says the always-cheery Chip Dale, *"local authorities have thrown up a wall of steel. So, as Soozy bravely defies her death threat. . . ."*

They cut to Soozy up in her room. She waves at the camera. Behind her, Dylan and Jeremy Murray still have their arms akimbo.

I yawn. Maybe it's the beer. Maybe it's because "second-to-last" shows are never that exciting. Think about the first three *Star Wars*. The one in the middle was just a setup for the big finish.

To make matters worse, tonight's competition is the hokeyest yet. It's *Jersey Shore* meets *American Idol* meets *I Want To Vomit.*

The three contestants have to sing "Under The Boardwalk" with three very special guest stars. America—at least those Americans who love to repeatedly thumb text messages to TV shows—will vote on who they think did the best job.

Of course, all this junk is pre-recorded.

Unfortunately, the contestants aren't lip-syncing. They might sound better if they did.

Mike Tomasino goes first and, believe it or not, the kid can actually sing. Plus, he gets to do the number with the Broadway cast of *Jersey Boys*. He nails it.

Vinnie Martin goes next and has the dubious pleasure of doing a duet with Barry Manilow. Mandy Keenan is there, too—sitting on the piano bench, mooning at Barry, flipping sheet music pages for him.

Vinnie doesn't stand a chance.

Before Jenny Mortadella sings, they cut to more commercials, what Chip Dale always calls *"the break."* The interruptions grow longer and longer.

"How come there are so many commercials?" I grouse out loud.

"The higher the rating for a show," says Rita, "the more money the network can charge for commercials."

When *Fun House* returns, it's obvious that the producers have stacked the deck against Jenny Mortadella. She gets to sing with a lounge act from Atlantic City, the kind nobody listens to because they're too busy bopping slot-machine buttons or whooping it up at the bar.

When Jenny and her wrecking-ball partner are done destroying the song, Chip Dale promises that we'll hear who Soozy thinks totally nailed the song—right after the break.

More commercials.

"Geeze-o, man," I say, popping open my third beer because it's almost ten, "they're raking in the dough tonight."

"You guys should ask for a cut of the profits," jokes Rita. "After all, John arresting Paulie, the two of you chasing those motorcycle hoods around Morgan's parking lot, not to mention the two murders and, now, Soozy K's death threat—that's what made *Fun House* the biggest hit of the summer."

Ceepak bolts upright on the sofa. His eyes go wide. I'm thinking he is having a stroke or something when he finally speaks:

"Of course!" He kisses Rita full on the lips. "Thank you!"

I'm about to say "What?" when, on the TV, live, Soozy K is screaming *"Omigod, omigod!"*

Ceepak, Rita, and I turn to the screen, where Soozy is blubbering and staring at her cell phone.

"What is it?" someone—maybe Layla—asks from behind the camera.

"A text message," says Soozy. *"From the killer!"*

She shoves her phone toward the camera. The lens zooms in. We read what is written on the phone screen in pixellated type:

"TOMORROW NIGHT. THE SHOW WILL BE LIVE.
YOU WILL BE DEAD."

34

WE'RE IN CEEPAK'S TOYOTA.

He's behind the wheel because he, unlike me, has not been imbibing beer.

He's also remarkably calm.

"It's all part of his play," he says.

"Who?"

"Mr. Martin Mandrake." He reaches down to his belt, unclips his cell phone, and hands it to me. "Danny, could you please press speed-dial fourteen?"

"Sure," I say. Since New Jersey has a handheld-cell-phone law, no way is Ceepak dialing while driving. "Who is it?"

"Christopher Miller."

The FBI guy.

"You want me to put it on speakerphone?" I ask after pressing the speed-dial digits.

"Roger that."

And that, my friends, is how you make a hands-free cell-phone call without tearing apart the interior of your car and doing a bunch of fancy wiring.

"Hello?" A little girl answers the phone.

"Angela, this is your father's friend, John Ceepak."

"Hello."

"Is your daddy home?"

"Yes."

"May I speak with him?"

"Okay."

And we wait. We hear the Miller family phone clomping to the floor or a very hard kitchen counter, and Angela, who's probably ten, screaming *"Daddy? It's Mr. Pea Pack."*

Kids. I guess they're cute when you're not in a hurry to find out why your partner said "Of course!" and kissed his wife after she said we should have a profit-sharing deal with Prickly Pear Productions.

"You have your badge?" Ceepak asks while we wait.

"Yeah." It's in the back pocket of my jeans.

"Put it on."

We hit a stoplight. Ceepak slips his shield into this nifty badge-holder he pulls out of the storage bin near the gearshift. He hangs the necklace around his neck. I pin my badge to a belt loop on my shorts. Ceepak and I are now, officially, plainclothes cops!

"John?" Christopher Miller comes on the phone. He's a big, hulking African American guy, a little over fifty, who still works out every day. He and Ceepak could be cousins if, you know, one of Ceepak's uncles had been black. *"What's up?"*

"My partner and I are on our way over to see Martin Mandrake."

"The producer on your TV show?"

"Roger that. We need anything and everything you might have on him."

"John, as I'm sure you're aware, we don't normally keep files on innocent citizens. . . ."

"We suspect that Mr. Mandrake may be implicated in the murders of Peter Paul Braciole as well as Thomas Hess, a.k.a. Skeletor, the drug dealer."

Miller hesitates. *"Care to elaborate?"*

"Certainly. But not right now. We are currently en route to the Prickly Pear production office."

"Okay. I'll see if we have anything on him. Maybe, if we're lucky, he cheated on his taxes."

"Appreciate it."

"You on your cell?"

"Roger that."

"Let me make a few calls. Get back to you."

"10-4. Thanks."

"Yeah."

And the phone call ends because, I can tell by the tone of his voice, Miller is already thinking about who he should call first.

I thumb the OFF button on Ceepak's phone.

"So," I say, "we think Marty did it?"

"The possibility looms large."

Okay. Usually he just says "It's a possibility" when considering a suspect for whom we haven't nailed down the means, opportunity, and motive.

"I think I get the motive," I say. "He used the killings to bump up the ratings for his show."

"Correct. And, as you recall, his career was in serious jeopardy prior to the success of *Fun House*."

True. Layla called him a "washed-up old hack" and "Marty The Old Farty" on numerous occasions.

"What about the means and opportunity?" I ask.

Ceepak sighs slightly as he makes the turn that will take us to the production trailer. "Admittedly, Danny, I am playing a hunch here.

However, remember that Mr. Mandrake is a producer. He knows how to put together the people he needs to get a job done."

"So, what, he hired a team of professional hit men to take out one of his stars to guarantee that *Fun House* would be a ratings hit and save his career?"

As we pull to the curb, Ceepak purses his lips and nods grimly. "Such is my supposition, Danny."

Wow. I think about this as Ceepak yanks on the emergency brake and I undo my seat belt.

Would Marty Mandrake really murder people to make sure his show was a hit? Maybe. The network bigwigs are already signing him up for more shows next year. He's gone from being a washed-up has-been to the next big thing, making millions because, all of a sudden, he has refound his Midas touch, the ability to turn crap into gold.

And all it took was a pair of dead bodies.

As soon as we're up and out of the car, Ceepak's cell phone chirps.

"This is Ceepak. Go." He listens. "That was fast. I see." Now he gets an earful. "Thanks, Chris. I owe you one."

He folds up the phone.

"Well?"

"Chris Miller knew exactly who to call."

35

"AND?"

I hate when he keeps me hanging like that.

"As I suspected," says Ceepak, "the FBI has quite an extensive file on Mr. Mandrake. It was first opened in 1971, the year he made his award-winning antiwar documentary about the Vietnam conflict. Apparently, the president at the time was not a fan of Mr. Mandrake's *Nixon Lies, Who Dies*?"

"So what can the Fibbies tell us?"

"That Mr. Mandrake likes to gamble."

"Right. We knew that. He was down in Atlantic City the Friday Paulie was murdered. Said he goes down there a lot."

"Indeed. However, Danny, even with all that practice, he is not very good at it. In fact, the FBI suspects he is deep in debt to certain members of the Lombardo crime syndicate."

Okay. That's a non-Creed crime family. I think. Those were the Pelagatti and Squarcialupi.

"The Lombardo people could help Mandrake hire two contract killers," I say. "Easy."

Ceepak nods. "Especially if he offered to pay back all that he owed on his gambling debts plus a substantial interest payment."

"Which he can do," I say. "Because the network paid him that bonus and hired him to produce a bunch of new shows."

"Exactly."

Okay. I would've kissed Rita, too, if I had figured all that out and, you know, been married to her.

Ceepak and I head up the steel staircase attached to the production trailer. Somebody's inside: I can hear laughter, the kind you hear outside a bar on a Friday night. Late.

When we enter, I'm gonna let Ceepak ask most of the questions because, when we turned into plainclothes cops, we were at his house, so he was able to strap on his Glock before we took off. My sidearm is secured inside the lockbox in my clothes closet, where it sleeps whenever I go out to grab a beer.

Ceepak shoves open the rattly door.

I see Marty Mandrake, Layla Shapiro, Rutger Reinhertz (the director), Grace the stopwatch lady, and about six assorted flunkies sitting around the conference table. The air is thick with cigar smoke. Someone pops open a bottle of champagne.

"Officers!" says Layla, raising her plastic champagne flute in our general direction. "Glad you could join us!" She has a big stogie stuck in her mouth, too. Puffs on it.

Marty Mandrake hikes his pants up over his belly as best he can and, cigar jiggling in his teeth, strides across the room to Ceepak. The tobacco tube comes out of his mouth with a wet smack. "Officer Ceepak! I just heard from Mayor Sinclair. I understand that Chief Baines has slipped out of town for a long weekend you're my new Acting Chief?"

Ceepak just nods.

"Great. You saw tonight's show? The kicker at the end?"

"Yes."

Mandrake winks and grins. Jams the cigar back in his pie hole. "Guess we better beef up security on the boardwalk tomorrow, huh?"

The room erupts in a chorus of phlegmy laughter.

"Oh, yes," says Layla, blowing smoke rings like a frat boy. "Soozy's life is in 'danger.'" She does what they call "air quotes" with her fingers when she says the word "danger."

I hate air quotes. I figure if you get to do air quotes, I get to do air exclamation points. With my middle finger.

The script lady, the only one in the crowded trailer not puffing on a stink bomb, has a finger to her ear, pressing an iPhone earbud down her ear canal.

"Mike Tomasino's lighting up the call center," she reports. "AT&T's about to melt down. He's doing double what Vinnie and Jenny are polling. Tomasino will be our second finalist, no doubt about it."

Mandrake rubs his hands together. "Excellent. America got it right."

"You mean they stuck to the script," jibes Layla.

"That's what I said, kid—they got it right!"

More laughter. Cigar smoke chugs out of mouths like these people are all related to Thomas The Train.

Mandrake grinds out the tip of his cigar in a cut-crystal bowl and turns to face Ceepak again—oblivious to how darkly my partner is glaring at him. "Champagne, boys? Cigar?"

"No, thank you," says Ceepak. "Mr. Mandrake, we'd like to talk to you—"

"About tomorrow? Sure, sure. Whose genius idea was it to go live with a one-day turnaround?"

"Yours!" says Layla with a hearty suck-up artist laugh.

Mandrake beams. "You bet, baby. Gonna be the biggest hit of the year. Ratings will be through the roof. Here's what you do, guys," he says to Ceepak and me. "Put your whole department on double overtime. Make it look good. Prickly Pear Productions will pick up the tab. Have your team seal off the boardwalk area around the Fun House, maybe put up a couple of those metal detector things, limit access to spectators with golden tickets courtesy of America's Golden Tan Spray-On Salons. . . ."

"It's a promotional consideration," Layla says to Ceepak and me, like we care.

"We're buying out the vendors and merchants up and down Pier Two," says Mandrake, using both hands to frame up every point he makes. "Shutting them down for the night."

"Except that fried-candy-bar asshole," says Layla. "He won't cooperate."

"Here's how we play this thing," Mandrake says to Ceepak and me. "We all act as if we're terrified that the crazed killer could make good on his threat to ice Soozy at any minute, even though, between you, me, and the bedpost, that kicker at the end? We texted it to her ourselves."

"It was my idea," says Layla. "Of course, Soozy thought the text was legit."

"Only way to get that honest of a reaction out of her," adds Reinhertz, the director. "Poor kid couldn't act her way out of a paper bag if you drew a map on the inside flap."

"It was our final booster shot," says Mandrake. "I guarantee we're gonna see Super Bowl-size ratings tomorrow night. So, we set up all the security, make sure all the news crews see it, build the buzz. But like I said, there's no real need for alarm; no new threat except the one Layla whipped up. Soozy's safe."

Now Ceepak gets an uncharacteristically devilish glint in his eye. "How can you be so certain of that, Mr. Mandrake?"

Mandrake looks a little flummoxed. "Because, like I just told you: we texted the threat ourselves. There's no real danger."

"That's one theory," says Ceepak. "Here's another."

Oh, man, Ceepak is pissed. I have never seen him jump this ugly in a suspect's face. Of course, this is the first killer we've confronted while he was popping champagne to celebrate his diabolical plot to cash in on a double homicide.

"What if," says Ceepak, "you, through your known Atlantic City connections in the Lombardo crime family, hired a team of professional hit men to murder Peter Paul Braciole?"

All of a sudden, the room goes silent.

"What if," Ceepak continues, "upon seeing the ratings success of that first murder, you requested another act of violence from your known crime associates to ensure your ongoing income stream?"

Now Marty Mandrake's nose twitches. "So, Acting Chief Ceepak, what the hell have *you* been drinking tonight?"

"Iced tea and non-alcoholic Coors beer, a taste I acquired while on combat duty in Iraq, dealing with individuals nearly as duplicitous as you."

Okay, as much as I've enjoyed seeing Ceepak get steamed, I'm realizing—it may not have been our smartest move. Mandrake is puffing up his chest. Tugging up on his belt.

"Grace?" he snaps.

"Yes, sir?" says the script lady.

"Call Rambowski. Tell him I want to sue this pissant cop for libel, slander, and whatever the hell they call it when a jarhead asshole says unsubstantiated crap he's gonna regret when I drag the sorry son of a bitch into court."

"You should also ask your lawyer to accompany you to police headquarters this evening," says Ceepak.

"What?"

"We need to ask you a few questions about your dealings in Atlantic City."

"You're fucking kidding me, right?"

"No, sir. I am in no way kidding."

Mandrake squinches up his eyes. “You know, Ceepak, this isn’t the first time jackbooted Gestapo thugs like you have kicked in my door and tried to frame me. I dealt with Tricky Dicky and his CIA goons back in seventy-one. I can sure as shit handle you.”

“Be that as it may,” says Ceepak, “I suggest you—”

Mandrake cuts him off. “Officer, am I free to go?”

“Excuse me?”

“Am I free to go?”

“We’d like you to come to police headquarters.”

“Officer,” says Mandrake, using the terse but polite tone some ACLU lawyer probably coached him to use back in the seventies when his anti-Vietnam movie came out, “you did not answer my question: Am I free to go?”

Ceepak’s jaw joint starts popping in and out.

Mine too.

Do we have “reasonable suspicion,” which would give us the right to detain Mr. Mandrake for investigatory purposes?

We have no hard evidence of Mr. Mandrake making contact with members of the Lombardo crime family.

We have no sales receipts from Murder, Inc. for the rental of two contract killers.

We have no confession from even one of the hired hit men, identifying Mr. Martin Mandrake as the person who paid for his or her services.

Basically, we have a hunch.

One Ceepak probably shouldn’t have played so publicly so soon.

“Officer,” says Mandrake, “I will repeat my question one last time: Am I free to go?”

Ceepak swallows hard. “Yes.”

And, without saying another word, Marty Mandrake walks out the production trailer door.

36

We sit outside the production trailer in Ceepak's banged-up Toyota for a few very long, extremely quiet minutes.

I can hear the ocean, and it's a block and a half away.

"Danny?" Ceepak finally says.

"Yeah?"

"I must apologize. I fear I let my personal feelings interfere with my judgment."

"Well, there's a first time for everything, I guess."

Ceepak shakes his head. "There shouldn't be. Not for that sort of unprofessional behavior."

The thing about Ceepak and his rigid honor code is this: he mostly imposes it on himself. My partner holds himself accountable to a higher standard than he'd ever hold, say, me. I think this comes from being in the military, where all your decisions could be life-and-death ones—for other people, not just for yourself. So when Officer John Ceepak occasionally blows it, it totally bums him out.

"Well," I say, digging through the treasure trove of sage Springsteen snippets, "tomorrow there'll be sunshine and all this darkness past." I go with "Land Of Hope and Dreams" because I know it's Ceepak's favorite.

Ceepak looks over at me. "I take it you have seen tomorrow's weather forecast?"

And then he finally cracks half a smile.

At least Marty Mandrake didn't skip town after he heard that we suspect him of masterminding two murders.

First thing Friday morning, when Acting Chief Ceepak and I show up on Pier Two to supervise the security detail (which is mostly for show, since we now suspect the death threat is a phony one), we see Mandrake working with his crew, organizing things up at the Fun House. I'm dressed in khaki shorts and a navy blue Engine 23 FDNY T-shirt that this guy who helped us out at the Hell Hole last summer, Captain Dave Morkal, sent me for Christmas. Even though I have my badge clipped to a belt loop, I look sloppy enough to work on Mandrake's crew.

Ceepak, in his golf shorts and white polo shirt, looks more like a Boy Scout working on his country club merit badge.

The big-shot producer is, of course, avoiding and ignoring us. And we can't force him to talk to us until we have some kind of incriminating evidence proving Ceepak's theory.

So Mandrake and his crew are running cables, rigging up cameras, acting important. I see another swarm of guys in baggy shorts, hiking sneakers, and T-shirts—with radios, tool belts, and duct tape hanging off their hips—pushing lights on rolling tripods, practicing camera moves, or noshing at the craft services table. All thirty or forty members of the *Fun House* camera crew have deer-hunter orange CREW I.D.s draped around their necks, showing that they have already been cleared through security.

I see that rookie, the guy in the knit hat, the one who didn't know what a "half-apple" was. He's hanging out under a pop-up tent munching on what appears to be a breakfast burrito, yukking it up with the ponytailed cameraman Jimbo, a guy leaning on his microphone pole, and another dude who's stuffing fistfuls of free popcorn into his face. Looks like the knit-hat kid caught on to how this production gig works pretty quickly: you work a little, then you stand around and snack.

Now Ms. Shapiro comes over to the tent, waves and points. I think they call it gesticulating. Anyway, Jimbo and his crew grab one last handful of Oreos and bright orange cheese balls, pick up their camera and gear, and head into the Fun House like Layla told them to. Knit Cap is in charge of lugging a cardboard flat of water bottles and soda pop for everybody.

I can see why Layla wanted to use the Sea Haven Fun House as the backdrop for the big finale. The brightly colored building looks like a three-story-tall clown castle with striped turrets topped off with colored pompoms: jolly birthday party hats jutting up against the sky. There are clown-face gargoyles all over the second and third floors, not to mention carousel elephants and circus animals, and, of course, red chaser lights spelling out FUN HOUSE in a wildly animated sequence of blinks, flashes, and strobes.

The main entrance to the castle is that wide-open clown mouth (picture Mick Jagger working for Ringling Brothers). The entryway is maybe fifteen feet tall, with a red-tongue carpet leading the way into the first mirror maze. To the right of the entrance is a "Shoot The Clown In His Mouth, Pop The Balloon" water gun shooting gallery. After the laughing clown dummies inside the Fun House torment you with their mirror mazes, spinning floor, DayGlo tumble tunnel, and slide-in-the-dark exit ramp, folks like to give the jokers a little payback.

At least that's how it was the summer I worked the Fun House. There was nothing better after finally escaping the madness than aiming your water pistol at a frozen fiberglass Bozo and bursting his balloon.

Ceepak, who used to run security outside the Green Zone in Baghdad, knows how to lock down the boardwalk surrounding the TV shoot. He has Joey Thalken, this friend of ours from the Sea Haven Sanitation Department, commandeer all sorts of salt-dumping trucks from maintenance yards off the Turnpike where the big, burly vehicles spend their summers dreaming about blizzards.

"Load them up with sand," Ceepak tells Joey T. "Park them there and there." He hand-gestures to the point where the boardwalk steps connect with the public parking lot. "Block all vehicular access."

"Okay," says Joey, "but how would, you know, a car with like a suicide bomber in it be able to climb up all those steps?"

"You make a good point, Joe," says Ceepak. "Give me a third truck at the bottom of the handicap access ramp in case, once again, the attack is mounted on motorcycles."

"Cool," says Joey T as he and his SHSD buddies set up a barricade of heavyweight dump trucks at all possible access points to Pier Two.

Meanwhile, half a dozen SHPD cops are linking sections of aluminum fencing together, stringing them across the boardwalk, leaving only a six-foot-wide access point, soon plugged with a pair of airport-style metal detectors rented from whoever rents them to the Secret Service when the president visits New Jersey.

While Ceepak supervises Joey T and the trucks, I amble over to the Fun House because I see Layla near the Squirt Gun Arcade. She's carrying a clipboard and talking to somebody through a headset wired to a walkie-talkie.

I'm hoping that, since we sort of had a connection once upon a time—oh, a few weeks ago—she might spill what she knows about her boss and his connections with a certain Atlantic City crime family.

"Hey," I say.

She holds up a hand to let me know she is busy but almost done barking orders at whoever's on the other end of her radio transmission. "I don't give a shit. Marty wants smoke in the mirror maze. The second one. Upstairs. Right. I don't care. Just do it." She's snarling. "Tell the fire marshal to take a flying fuck at a rolling doughnut."

Okay. Don't think Dunkin' Donuts is ever gonna use *that* as their slogan.

Layla jabs a button on the radio slung low on her hip, much like her cargo shorts. The girl likes displaying her ripped midriff. She tosses back her hair and smiles.

"Officer Boyle. Whazzup? You and your partner hatch any more harebrained theories about who killed Paulie and Skeletor?"

"Nah. We're sticking with the one we've got."

"That Marty did it?"

"No. That he hired other people to do it for him."

"So he could pump up our ratings?"

"Hey, you're the number one show in America."

"Because of my idea to work in the 'cops' angle. That's when the numbers started trending up. Sorry, Officer Boyle. Your boss Ceepak had more to do with making this show a hit than my boss Marty."

"So what about his Friday-night trips down to A.C.?"

"What can I tell you, the man likes to gamble. Me? I prefer a sure thing."

"Are there any?"

"Sure: sex and violence. They sell. Always have. It's why all those buff gladiators back in Rome wore skirts but no shirts. It's why the motorcycle episode was huge. Sexy college kids. Violent dudes on motorbikes. Works every time."

"You know, Layla, you and me—"

"Met cute. Dated a couple times. It was fun, now it's done."

"But—"

"What? You think I owe you something because you saved my life back at the Rolling Thunder? Fine. Here's the dealio: no way Marty Mandrake did or engineered to have done what you and Ceepak think he did or had done. He's not that clever. Lacks imagination. Now, if you'll excuse me. I have to find a puppy dog."

"What?"

"Don't tell anybody, it's a secret till we go live, but America voted for Mike Tomasino."

Of course they did. Vinnie with Barry Manilow and Jenny with that lousy lounge lizard never had a snowball's chance in Miami.

"Now Mike and his dad have pulled a fast one," says Layla. "While Soozy plays for the All American Tanning Team, they have Mike playing for some kind of Save The Starving Puppies charity. Gotta run."

And she does.

So, with nothing to show for my efforts, I head back to where we've set up a police command center under a bright blue tent we borrowed from Mrs. Ceepak's catering company. We don't have a craft services table. Just a box of doughnuts and a cardboard jug of coffee.

I hope none of the doughnuts start rolling.

37

BY 1 P.M., WE'RE ALL SET UP. NO ONE CAN GET ON OR OFF the boardwalk without passing through a metal detector and I.D. check, and then they have to be on the magic ticket list if they want to gain access to Pier Two.

Prickly Pear Productions has provided us with the names of pre-screened studio audience members and charity representatives who will start shuffling through security around four—five hours before the live show starts. We have a battery-powered TV set up in our command tent and keep it tuned to the *Fun House* network, just so we can keep up with any late-breaking developments.

Instead, all I hear is hype about the show: *"Will the gang-bangers make good on their death threat and take Soozy K out of the competition for good? Tune in tonight at nine, eight Central, for television's most exciting, death-defying season finale ever!"*

"Danny?" This from Ceepak as he comes up the ramp from where Joey T parked the last of the sand-filled dump trucks.

"Yeah?"

"It appears Mr. Gabe Hess has arrived." He head gestures toward the All American Snack Shack, which is directly across from the Fun House, on the other side of the Pier Two boardwalk, which, in this section, is about the width of a four-lane highway.

"Why is he insisting on not shutting down for the day?" I ask. "He won't have any customers, except maybe a couple crew members who get tired of all the free food at the craft services table."

"I assume," says Ceepak, "that, for Mr. Hess, who is something of a libertarian, it is the principle of the thing. He refuses to shut down his business simply because someone in authority told him he had to. In fact, given his recent loss, due in no small part to the presence of the TV show here in Sea Haven, he is probably even more defiant than usual."

I nod. It sort of makes sense. He's mad as hell and he's not going to close down his fried Oreo stand anymore.

"I'm going to ask him if he has heard anything from The Creed," says Ceepak.

"Are they still suspects?"

"We need to cover all bases."

I nod, even though I still think Ceepak's hunch about Mandrake is correct but it seems that part of my partner's penance for tipping our hand to the primary suspect will be to doggedly pursue a few dead ends.

"What would you like me to do?" I ask.

Another head bob from Ceepak. This time it's something behind me.

"Talk to Rebecca."

I turn around. Here comes Becca Adkinson, in high heels, a bright orange bikini, and a gauzy floral cover-up that barely does. If I'm not mistaken, Becca has been basting herself in coconut oil and lying out on the Mussel Beach Motel sun deck something fierce. Either that, or she dipped herself in a chocolate swimming pool—like the peanut M&M guy used to do. Her tan is darker than that orange-faced congressman from Ohio; the one who looks like he's related to The Great Pumpkin.

"Hey," I say to Becca as Ceepak hikes across the boards to the candy-bar booth.

"Geeze-o, man, Danny—am I gonna get shot?"

"What?"

"All this security. Metal detectors? What's with those trucks blocking the steps? I had to walk around them and almost snapped off a heel. Is this because of the death threat?"

"Yeah."

Now I notice that Becca has a green All Access Pass dangling on a chain around her neck, nestling right where her cover-up plunges down to show the world that Becca Adkinson could model swimsuits for Victoria's Secret without an assist from any of their underwire architecture.

Becca sees me staring at her chest, something I've been known to do ever since sixth grade. She was an early bloomer. I was an early gawker.

"My eyes are up here, Danny."

"Yeah. Sorry."

Then she kind of adjusts her chest to fluff everything up. "I look hot, though, right?"

"Yeah. So, why are you here?"

"I'm Soozy's charity."

"What?"

She shoulder-slugs me. The way my sister would if, you know, I had one.

"Pay attention, Danny Boy. I told you: I'm president of the local SPF chapter. The Skin Cancer Prevention Fund? Soozy's playing for us tonight. I'm supposed to be like her partner in the mad dash through the Fun House. I'm gonna be on TV!"

"Oh. Cool."

"So?"

"What?"

"Is it safe?"

"What? Oh, you mean all this?" I casually wave at the battalion of cops and barricades and metal detectors and trucks filled with sand.

"Uh, yeah," says Becca, adding a look that says "duh, Danny."

"Don't worry," I say. "It's all for show."

"You're kidding. What about the death threat?"

"The TV people did it themselves. To boost ratings."

"Get! Out!"

I shrug. "It's TV."

"Oh. Okay. You're sure I'm safe?"

"Totally."

Becca beams. "Excellent. I have to go check in. Catch you later, Danny boy." She bops off to enjoy her fifteen minutes of fame.

"Hey, kid?"

I turn around. Marty Mandrake. It looks like he wants to exit the boardwalk but Vic Daniel, one of the SHPD cops Ceepak has stationed at the metal detectors, won't let him out. It also looks like Mr. Mandrake isn't used to people telling him what he can't do.

I amble over.

"I don't have all day," snaps Mandrake. I grin because, basically, thanks to him, *I* do.

"What's up?"

"This meathead won't let me leave my own set."

"First of all," I say, "this is Officer Vic Daniel. And, trust me, he wouldn't be allowed on the force if his head was made out of meat. We have to take this physical—"

"Cute, kid. Cute. Look, I know your partner Cheepak has some cockamamie theory about me," he flaps his hand toward the Fried Oreo Stand where Ceepak and Gabe Hess are locked in some kind of intense conversation. "But I only gave the crew one hour for lunch and the catering company decides they're gonna grill everybody a burger."

I sniff the air. The scents of sizzling beef and charcoal do, indeed, waft on the breeze.

"Smells good," I say.

"I don't eat red meat, kid. I need to head over to this veggie place I found. Eat something that won't clog my arteries and kill me."

Ah, yes. Marty Mandrake—Veggin' On The Beach's best customer.

"We're trying to keep this area secure," I explain. "Limit access in and out."

"I told you, kid: there's nothing to worry about. The threat is bogus."

"You seem so sure about that."

"What? You think I'm running out to check in with my hired killers? This is the finale. Even if I did what your partner claims, why would I need to keep on doing it? After tonight, the show's over."

"Maybe you're cooking up a cliff-hanger. Like they did on *Lost*. Suck everybody back for another season of fun in the sun."

"You've been spending too much time with Ms. Shapiro."

No, I want to say, I haven't. Not for a couple weeks, anyway.

"Come on, kid. Now I only have fifty-five minutes till we're back."

I relent.

"Let him out, Vic," I say. "But screen him again when he comes back. And, Mr. Mandrake, you need to check in before six. That's when the boardwalk becomes a frozen zone."

"What?"

"Hey, we're taking this death threat seriously."

"See me when you get back," adds Vic.

"Yeah, yeah." Mandrake starts muttering as he scoots through the metal detector and hustles across the parking lot to his Mercedes convertible. "Just like fucking Nixon. . . ."

Vic Daniel turns to me. "Who's Nixon?"

I shrug. "I think he was president. Before Ford."

"The car company?"

"Yeah," I say because it's easier.

Mandrake climbs into his sporty little ragtop, which is somewhat difficult, given his paunch and general lack of elasticity. He's powering down the German-engineered roof when Ceepak joins us at the metal detectors.

"Where is Mr. Mandrake headed?" he asks.

"Veggin' On The Beach. Catering's serving burgers for lunch today. He's having a cow about it."

"Very well. You and I need to leave as well."

"What's up?"

"A gentleman by the name of Axel would like to talk to us over on Pier One."

"Axel?"

"He is one of Mr. Hess's other brothers."

"The Creed?"

Ceepak nods. "He's waiting for us at Pasquale's Pizza."

38

Axel looks like a balder Hulk Hogan in a backward baseball cap.

Ceepak and I stroll into Pasquale's Pizza (the best slices on the boardwalk, btw) and see this guy with a white handlebar mustache, Ray-Bans, five tiny golden earrings, and a serious 'tude sitting in a booth by himself. He's wearing a tomato-red tank top so we can admire the various tattoos displayed on his bulging arm muscles. I particularly enjoy the flaming skull and crossbones on his right biceps. However, the Jesus in the Confederate soldier cap on his left forearm just confuses me.

"You Ceepak?" Axel says to Ceepak. I'm guessing Gabe Hess gave him a description that included the adjective "muscular," so he knows it's not me.

"Yes, sir. This is my partner, Officer Boyle."

We both flash our badges. Seeing how we're not wearing uniforms, it's the least we can do.

We slide into the booth. Axel has a crushed Pepsi can and a grease-stained paper plate sitting in front of him. Guess he already ordered.

"Either of you wearing a wire?" he asks.

"Negative," says Ceepak.

"You packing?"

"Are you asking if we are armed?"

"Yeah."

"Of course. We're on duty."

Axel raises both arms off the table a couple inches. "I'm clean."

Ceepak nods.

"But I got six brothers covering my back."

I glance around the pizza parlor. All I see are guys in white aprons tossing dough in the air, tourists lined up three-deep at the counter, and my friend from high school, Sarah Pierce, grabbing drinks for customers out of the cold box.

"Don't worry," says Axel, taking off his sunglasses. "They can see you."

"Gabe informs me that you wish to exonerate your motorcycle club from involvement in the death of his brother, as well as that of Paul Braciole."

I can't believe Ceepak just called an outlaw biker gang a "motorcycle club." Then again, Axel, who looks like he taste-tests every batch of steroids they ship out so he can pump up like Popeye, might have gone ballistic and ripped our heads off if we'd called his "club" something more sinister-sounding.

"Yeah," says Axel. "We didn't do any of this shit."

"What about the stunt at Morgan's Surf and Turf?" I say.

"Well, yeah, obviously we did that shit, but none of this other. That shit at the restaurant wasn't the shit I was talking about."

"You were in no way involved in the death of Paul Braciole?" says Ceepak.

"Nope. Sure, most of the brothers thought he was a douchebag. But being a douche isn't sufficient grounds for termination."

Good to know the Creed has rules for this kind of stuff.

"And Skeletor?" says Ceepak.

"No way."

"And we are expected to take your word for all this?"

Axel grins. At the edges of his Pringle-man mustache, the guy has dimples. "No."

Now he reaches under the table and pulls out an interoffice envelope somebody in his motorcycle "club" probably stole from their day job.

"This is what we call a good-faith offering." Axel untwirls the string clasp and slides out a stack of eight-by-ten photographs.

Ceepak flicks the first one over.

It's a photograph of a Lincoln Town Car parked in a crappy section of some equally crappy city. In some state. Somewhere.

"What exactly are we looking at here?" Ceepak asks.

Axel leans across the table, taps the photograph with a finger. I see he wears the "88" tattoos on his knuckles.

"You see the guy behind the wheel?"

"Yes."

"That's Georgio Accardi, driver for Bobby Lombardo."

"How do you know this?" asks Ceepak, even though it's probably a dumb question.

Axel smiles. "Let's just say the Lombardos are friends of friends. You don't believe me, check it out with the Feds."

"We will run this by the FBI, have them confirm the identity of the driver."

"You do that." He head-nudges for Ceepak to check out photograph number two.

Ceepak flips over the second eight-by-ten.

"Holy shit," I say out loud.

"Indeed," says Ceepak, without reprimanding me for my poor choice of words. He's too shocked.

Because in photo number two, we see a certain young lady, wearing sunglasses and a conservative business suit, toting a boxy attache case and walking up to Georgio Accardi's Lincoln; a certain young lady who bears a striking resemblance to one Layla Shapiro.

"You know the chick, am I right?"

"From the distance this photograph was taken," says Ceepak, "it's hard to be one hundred percent certain."

"Try the next one. We zoomed in for you."

Ceepak flips over the third picture. It's a little grainy, a little blurry, but crystal-clear.

It's Layla.

"We started tailing these production people as soon as the TV started saying we were the ones who bumped off Paulie Braciole, because we knew we didn't have nothing to do with that. We figured they did."

"The TV people?" says Ceepak, not letting on that he had recently reached a similar conclusion.

"Yeah," says Axel, leaning back in his chair. "You make that big of a stink about something, it's like a fart, you know what I mean?"

Ceepak looks confused.

So I lend a hand: "He who smelt it, dealt it?"

"That's right, kid. He who denied it, supplied it."

"What is in the briefcase?" asks Ceepak.

"Cash," says Axel.

"How can you be sure?"

"The driver, Georgio, he is like a brother to me, you know what I mean?"

"He is a member of your organization?"

"I ain't saying he is, I ain't saying he ain't. Be that as it may, Mr. Accardi did not like seeing The Creed Brotherhood being maligned on TV. He witnessed the transfer of certain funds from this chicky who works for Mandrake, the big-shot producer who, not for nothin', needs to take remedial gambling lessons before he heads back to A.C."

"Perhaps Ms. Shapiro was simply acting as a courier to pay off her boss's gambling debts," says Ceepak, back in his let's-not-jump-to-conclusions mode.

"Maybe," says Axel. "Only, Georgio says as soon as little miss hot body is out of his Lincoln, his boss gets on this secure satellite phone he keeps in the back seat, makes a call."

"This is all hearsay," says Ceepak. "Where is Mr. Accardi? Perhaps we should talk to him."

"Sorry. That ain't gonna happen. And, if you send that black FBI bastard down to A.C. to knock on Georgio's door, we're done. I will swear up and down we never even had this conversation we're having here."

Guess the Creed has been tailing us, too. They know about Special Agent Christopher Miller's involvement in our investigation.

Ceepak sighs. "Very well. What was the nature of Mr. Lombardo's conversation, as reported to you via Mr. Accardi?"

"The meet took place a day or two after you boys found Braciole strung up with the stuffed animals. The money was for a hit. And, get this." Axel leans in. Looks both ways before talking. "It was, and I quote, a hit for a repeat customer."

"Come again?"

"Bobby Lombardo tells his contact that this job is being ordered by the same guy who ordered the last one, the one that got all the TV attention."

"You mean Paulie Braciole?" I say.

Up go his shoulders. "Mr. Lombardo don't come right out and say it, he don't name names. He just calls it the 'other one. From TV.'"

Wow. Ceepak was one hundred percent correct. Mandrake set up both hits. He had his chief lackey, Layla, deliver the down payments, because, I gotta figure, you don't pay everything up front when you order a hit, in case the contractor doesn't complete the job. It's sort of like putting in a swimming pool. You pay the guy up front, the only pool you're gonna see is where your backyard floods after a good rain.

"Why are you telling us all this?" asks Ceepak. "Why would your friend Georgio endanger his own life to pass along the confidential conversations of a reputed mob boss?"

"I told you: none of us like seeing our name dragged through the mud like this. Saying we took out Skeletor, a brother? That's shit-canning everything the Brotherhood stands for, man."

"But you realize, none of this is actionable. As I already stated, it's all hearsay—"

"Hell, you can at least start looking at somebody besides us for doing Skeletor like that. The Paulie punk, too."

"Trust me, sir, we are. However—"

"Sorry, fellas. I can't give you nothing else," says Axel. "Georgio wasn't wearing a wire or nothing, not when he's chauffeuring Bobby Lombardo around town. He did that, he'd be a dead man."

"Well," I say, "maybe your friend Georgio can help us I.D. the contract killer."

Axel is shaking his head before I finish.

"No way. First, he would never do that unless, like I said, he wanted to send his wife over to the funeral home so she could start picking out what color casket to bury him in. Second, he wouldn't know who the killer is. Neither would Bobby Lombardo."

"But Lombardo *called* the hit man."

"That's not how it works. Bobby reaches out to someone who reaches out to someone else who talks to people who talk to people. At the end of the day, nobody knows who the hired gun is. Everybody can deny everything. Money moves around in a screwy circle can't nobody follow, but everybody gets to dip their beak and take a cut. It's why these things take time to set up and are impossible to cancel, once you give the green light."

"There's no 'off' switch?" I say.

"No. Not in the last 24 hours or whatever. The doer goes dark. Executes his mission."

"May we keep these photographs?" asks Ceepak.

"Sure," says Axel, slipping his sunglasses back on. "I went with the double prints instead of the free roll of film."

I think he's making a joke.

Ceepak isn't smiling. He slides the three pictures back into their envelope. "Here is my business card. If you hear anything else, please call. Any time. Day or night. Danny?"

We head out the doorway and hit the boardwalk.

"So," I say, when I'm sure the biker boy can no longer hear us, "we need to go back to the Fun House and talk to Layla, right?"

"Roger that. We can certainly ask her why she was getting into a Lincoln Town Car with reputed members of the mob."

Yeah. Didn't her parents teach her about getting into a car with strange mobsters?

We're headed down the steps to the parking lot when our radios start squawking at us.

"This is base for Ceepak. Base for Ceepak."

Ceepak yanks the small handy-talkie off his civilian belt.

"This is Ceepak. Go."

"We have a Code 13."

Geeze-o, man! That's a shooting.

"What's the 10-28?"

"Hickory Street and Shore Drive. He was at the stop sign."

"Who?"

"The guy who almost got shot," says Mrs. Rence, her voice panicked—like mine would be if I were the one back at the house making this radio call.

"Dorian?" says Ceepak, rock-solid as always. "Slow down. Please I.D. the victim."

"Martin Mandrake."

Geeze-o, man.

"Some guy wearing a motorcycle helmet tried to shoot him!"

39

MANDRAKE WASN'T WOUNDED, JUST STUNNED.

Apparently, after the shooter missed, Marty stomped on his hot little Mercedes's accelerator and tore up Shore Drive from the Hickory Street intersection at like sixty miles an hour, completely ignoring all those cute 15 MPH speed-limit signs, the ones that say "Yes, You Can Drive That Slow."

When he hit Dogwood Street, Officers Ken Green and Kent Peterman, who were on patrol in that residential area—and not used to seeing sporty convertibles drag-racing up the road everybody else uses for bike riding, jogging, and pushing their grandkids' strollers—flipped on their lights and siren and initiated pursuit.

One block north of Dogwood is the Cherry Street parking lot for police headquarters.

When Mandrake saw the cop car chasing him plus all the cop cars lined up in tidy rows in the lot, he screeched into a hard left turn, pulled up to the curb in front of the station house, hopped out of his convertible (with the engine still running), and ran in the front door of the SHPD "screaming like he was having a heart attack," according to Officers Green and Peterman, even though I think, technically, screaming is sort of impossible when you're having a heart attack, what with the chest pains and difficulty breathing.

Anyway, Ceepak and I are currently headed down to the house to have a word or two with Mr. Mandrake.

Ceepak radioed Mrs. Rence to have her pull the file we have going on Paulie Braciole's killer. He wants Marty Mandrake to look at those security-camera still frames, see if his motorcycle dude looked like the one hauling Paulie's body over to the Knock 'Em Down.

We issued an APB for an assailant in a helmet and racing suit on a motorcycle, but both Ceepak and I are pretty certain that, as soon as the hit went bad, the shooter was out of his costume faster than that quick-change couple on *America's Got Talent.* He also, more than likely, ditched his motorcycle somewhere on one of the side streets. We have people looking for it too.

"If he even rode his motorcycle today," says Ceepak as we cruise south on Beach Lane.

"He was wearing the helmet and leather racing gear," I say.

"But I doubt he had plans to transport Mr. Mandrake's body away from the kill zone as he did with Paul Braciole. Also, he struck in broad daylight. He may have worn the racing gear simply to mask his identity."

"You think it's the same shooter who did Paulie Braciole, right?"

"Affirmative. It fits with Detective Wilson's description of the execution technique."

Right. The hit man walks up to your car while you're waiting at a stoplight, or, in this case, a stop sign. They whip out their pistol, and bam.

"But if this guy's a pro, how could he miss?" I ask.

"I suspect, Danny, that Mr. Mandrake is one of those drivers who does not come to a full and complete stop when they encounter a stop sign."

Ah, yes. We see a lot of those. Usually people from New York or Philly, always in a rush, think stop signs are a government plot to ruin their vacation. Typically, a "rolling stop" will earn you a warning, maybe a ticket if you do it on Shore Drive, which is jammed with kids riding bikes with training wheels. Today, a rolling stop may have saved Martin Mandrake's life.

I'm wondering if Ceepak will write him up for it anyhow, when his business cell starts chirruping.

"This is Ceepak. Go."

Behind the wheel, I tilt my head sideways. Try to make out who's calling. I get nothing.

"I see," says Ceepak, sounding extremely disappointed. "And is your decision final?"

Uh-oh. I'm figuring it's Ohio. Maybe they're taking away that job offer. Maybe they don't like seeing their future chief of detectives on TV so much anymore.

"But sir, as you know, we are in the middle of a very knotty investigation."

I shake my head. As much as I don't want Ceepak to leave, I want it to be his choice, not some Buckeye sheriff's.

"Have you informed Mayor Sinclair of your decision?"

Oh. Okay. Time out. This has more to do with Sea Haven than Cincinnati, the only city besides Cleveland I know in Ohio.

Ceepak pinches the top of his nose. Closes his eyes. "What would you like me to do, Buzz?"

Buzz is Chief Baines. And Buzz is really his name; it's not a nickname for something dorky like Arnold or Elmer. I saw it on the Florida State college diploma he has hanging on his office wall. I think the chief's parents didn't want to set unrealistic expectations for him, so they named him after the *second* guy to walk on the moon.

"Very well. Yes, sir. I understand. Enjoy the rest of your weekend."

I'm pulling into the municipal parking lot behind police headquarters. Ceepak is folding up his cell phone.

"That was Chief Baines," he says, when I shut down the engine.

"Huh," I say as if I couldn't tell.

"He has been offered a private-sector job as security chief for a major insurance corporation in Florida. Their headquarters is very close to where he grew up. It is, and I quote, 'his dream job.'"

"So he's quitting his job here?"

"Roger that. He has already telephoned Mayor Sinclair and tendered his two-week notice to the city council."

"Geeze-o, man," I mumble. "First you're leaving, now the chief. . . ."

Ceepak yanks up on his door handle. "I may need to reconsider my options. We can't all go home again, Danny."

I smile weakly. "Well, I never actually left."

"Perhaps your choice was the wisest. Let's go."

We head inside to talk to Marty "I Don't Brake For Small Animals Or Children" Mandrake.

40

MARTIN MANDRAKE IS WAITING FOR US IN THE INTERVIEW ROOM.

His choice. He requested a room "without any windows," according to Sergeant Broadwater, who's got the desk duty this afternoon.

"I think he's spooked," the sergeant says to Ceepak.

"Understandable. Have you been able to reach Detective Botzong from the State Police Major Crimes Unit?"

"Yeah. He said to tell you . . ." He reaches for a pink While You Were Out message pad. "That a 'Detective Jeanne Wilson is at the municipal garage where we impounded the vehicle and was able to remove a slug from the Mercedes in just about the same spot where we found the hole in the Mustang.' That make any sense to you guys?"

"Indeed it does," says Ceepak. "Thank you for taking such a detailed message, Sergeant."

Broadwater shrugs. "It's the job. Oh, here."

He hands Ceepak an envelope.

"From Mrs. Rence?" Ceepak asks.

"Yeah," says Broadwater. "Some kind of printout you wanted."

"Thank you."

We head up the hallway, past the empty Chief's office. Guess it will stay empty until the town fathers get around to hiring a replacement. I hope, this time, Ceepak puts his name in the hat. Or tosses his hat into the ring. Or that a hat in the ring has his name in it. One of those.

The last time the job became vacant, right after our first case together, Ceepak declined all offers to take over the top cop slot. But that was a few years ago. He had only been in Sea Haven a couple months. Now, there's nobody better.

We push open the door to the interview room. It looks a lot like a conference room but with crappy furniture, a box of old Christmas decorations in one corner, some files and magazines in another, and a humongous wall mirror that's actually a one-way window. Mandrake is on his phone, pacing at the far end of the long table.

"Ask Layla." He waves at us to "come in, come in," like our SHPD Interview Room is suddenly his new production trailer. "Ask Layla. Look, I am temporarily indisposed. If anybody has any questions, send them to Layla. I don't give a shit. I almost died. This is the second time a man has pulled a gun on me. The first was back in 'Nam. Some Viet Cong asshole didn't like the way I was looking at his girlfriend in a bar. This was worse. This asshole fired." He puts his free hand up to his free ear. "You ever hear a bullet whizz by, inches from your brain? I was like Lincoln, sitting at that stop sign."

Except, of course, Abraham Lincoln was president, freed the slaves, and won the Civil War. Martin Mandrake? He makes cheesy TV shows about kids playing Skee-Ball, hopping into each other's beds, and puking up beer.

"I gotta go. Some more cops want to talk to me. Talk to Layla. No. No! Don't even think like that. We cannot cancel the finale. The show must go on." He punches the OFF button on his iPhone.

"Where the hell were you two?" he snaps at us.

"Excuse me?" says Ceepak.

"You're in charge of security! How come you didn't stop this nutjob?"

"You chose to leave the secure location," says Ceepak. "To venture outside the Green Zone."

"Because I needed a Vegan Philly Cheese Steak."

Ceepak gestures toward a chair. "Please, have a seat."

"Did you catch this creep?"

"Not yet," says Ceepak.

"Who would do such a thing?"

"We suspect the same person who transported Paul Braciole's body to the boardwalk."

"Skeletor? No way. He's dead."

Yeah, I think, *because you paid Bobby Lombardo to whack him.*

"Mr. Braciole was not murdered by Thomas Hess, a.k.a. Skeletor."

"Oh, right. You think I did it."

"No, sir. I never said you were the triggerman. However, I suspect that, through various intermediaries, you hired this man to do your killing for you."

Ceepak pulls a black-and-white printout from the envelope Mrs. Rence has left for us at the front desk. It shows two guys on a motorcycle. The one in front wears a sleek racing helmet and a leather jumpsuit.

"Who is this?"

"On the back of the seat is the corpse of Paul Braciole. The motorcycle operator is, we hypothesize, one half of the professional hit team that Bobby Lombardo contracted on your behalf to murder Mr. Braciole."

Mandrake is staring hard at the picture.

"We figure someone else shot Paulie," I say. "Came up alongside his vehicle while he was parked at a stoplight, whipped up his pistol, and boom."

"Only," says Ceepak, "Mr. Braciole had come to a full and complete stop. Therefore, the bullet did not 'whizz past his ear,' as you just described. It coursed through both hemispheres of his brain."

Mandrake is still frozen. Everything except his hands. They're starting to rattle the picture he's staring at.

"Next time," I say, "he'll know that you roll through stop signs, so he'll compensate for the moving target. Next time, he won't miss."

"Jesus," Mandrake mumbles. "The helmet, with the lightning bolts. The flames on the jacket shoulders. It's the same fucking guy?"

"You tell us," says Ceepak.

"It's the same fucking guy! This is the maniac who came at me, put a gun to my head. . . ."

He puts the paper down on the table and reaches for a bottle of water. Liquid sloshes out of his lips. The man's hands are quaking because he's finally put two and two together and come up with five, maybe six.

The tables have been turned.

The great Martin Mandrake has been double-crossed.

The killer he contracted to kill Paul Braciole and Thomas "Skeletor" Hess has a new target: Martin Mandrake.

"Mr. Mandrake?" says Ceepak, "the time for deceit and prevarication is over. If you want us to protect you, then you must start telling us the truth. Immediately."

"This wasn't part of the deal," he mumbles. "This wasn't part of the fucking deal!"

41

AT APPROXIMATELY 3:15 P.M., BARELY THIRTY SECONDS after mumbling his semi-confession, Marty Mandrake totally clams up.

"I need to call my lawyer," he says. "I have the right to consult with an attorney and have that attorney present during questioning."

The guy has been in TV so long, he has the *Law & Order* version of the Miranda warning memorized.

"That, of course, is your right," says Ceepak. "However—"

"Don't try to strongarm me! I need to consult with an attorney."

"Would you like some privacy for your phone call?"

"What? You think I have a death wish? Suppose you two leave and this crazed killer bursts through that door to finish what he started? I'm unarmed here!"

He's also extremely paranoid, but I guess Abraham Lincoln would've been paranoid too, if John Wilkes Booth had missed. So we babysit him while he calls his lawyer.

Ceepak and I both cringe when we hear his lawyer's name: Louis "I Never Lose" Rambowski, the same creep hired by the O'Malleys earlier this summer when we were working the Rolling Thunder case. Every cop in the SHPD (and most of New Jersey) knows and despises Rambowski, ever since he helped a thug up in Newark waltz out the door by convincing the jury that it was a dead cop's own fault he got shot in the back of his head.

Today, it turns out, Rambowski is working out of his New York City office and needs to finish up "a few things." He'll have his driver whisk him down to Sea Haven ASAP, probably around four. At the start of rush hour. When the Lincoln and Holland tunnels are so clogged with cars, they need Drāno.

This means we don't expect to hear any more from Martin Mandrake until 7, maybe 7:30 P.M.

We leave him in the interview room. He asks for an armed guard. Ceepak promises he will lock the door and "take personal responsibility for the key." That means he's going to slip it into one of his cargo pants pockets.

"Is he talking?" this from Special Agent Christopher Miller, FBI, who's hovering in the corridor outside the Interview Room. So are about six other serious-looking individuals—male and female—dressed in suits, sunglasses, and Secret Service-style earpieces with wires resembling see-through pigtails. All six plus Miller are sporting suspicious bulges beneath the breast pockets of their natty jackets.

They've all got sidearms in shoulder holsters.

"He wants his lawyer," says Ceepak.

Miller nods. "Probably wants to cut a deal."

"If he gives up Bobby Lombardo, he might just get one," says a woman with a severe haircut (like she does it herself with a pair of orange-handled knitting scissors) and a serious scowl.

"John, Danny," says Miller, "this is Lisa Bonner. Works with the New Jersey State Police Organized Crime Unit. These other folks are with me. And we're expecting more guests any minute."

"Such as?" asks Ceepak.

"Some friends of mine from our Organized Crime Task Force, as well as a few folks from the U.S. Attorney's Office. Everybody wants Bobby Lombardo to go away, big-time."

And I thought all these nice people in suits were here to help us catch the hired killer on his motor scooter.

"I suggest you all make yourselves as comfortable as possible," says Ceepak. "Coffee and soft drinks are available in the break room. We do not expect Mr. Mandrake's lawyer to arrive for another three hours. Check back with me at 1900 hours for an update."

Ceepak makes like he's ready to leave. Ms. Bonner raises a hand.

"Maybe we could just go in there and have a friendly chat with Mr. Mandrake?" she says, cracking what I think she thinks is a smile.

"No, ma'am," says Ceepak. "That's not going to happen."

"Officer, we suspect that Mr. Mandrake can directly link Bobby Lombardo to your two homicides. We need to talk to him. Sooner, not later."

"I understand your frustration," says Ceepak. "However, Mr. Mandrake has requested that an attorney be present during questioning. We must respect his rights."

"Says who?"

"Let's go grab a cup of that coffee," says Special Agent Miller, putting his big hand at the small of Ms. Bonner's back to guide her down the hall. "It still as bad as I remember, Boyle?"

"Worse," I say. "Now we're burning hazelnut-flavored beans."

Miller chuckles a little and leads the disappointed suits away from the Interview Room.

Ceepak head-gestures to the left. We take a side door that opens into the parking lot.

"Let's head over to the municipal garage," says Ceepak, "check in with Bill Botzong and the CSI team."

"They're going to cut Mandrake a deal, aren't they?"

"Perhaps, Danny. However, that does not give us permission to abandon our investigation before we have gathered all the evidence we can."

And the MCU people have some for us.

Ceepak and I leave the sunshine for the darkness of the municipal garage where, once my eyes adjust, I see Marty Mandrake's sporty convertible parked next to the Sanitation Department's sand sweeper. Bill Botzong is with Detective Wilson over at a workbench, where they look like lab partners huddled around a microscope.

"What have we learned, Bill?" asks Ceepak.

"Plenty. Jeanne?"

The ballistics expert looks up from the microscope's eyepiece. The rubber ring at the top of the tube has given her a red circle around her eye.

"We found a casing in the street and pulled a .45 ACP slug out of the interior panel," she says, "right above the door handle, suggesting, as we said earlier, that our shooter took approximately the same downward firing angle as that used to take out your first victim, Mr. Braciole."

"But wait," says Botzong, in his best late-night TV voice, "there's more."

Detective Wilson nods toward her laptop. "I did a preliminary match with our ballistic fingerprinting database. Now, I can't give you the serial number of the weapon we're looking for . . ."

"But?" I say.

". . . but it looks pretty consistent with what we've seen on ammunition fired from the Heckler & Koch USP Compact Tactical."

Suddenly, Ceepak looks kind of green around the gills.

42

"As you know," Botzong says to Ceepak, "H&K developed the Universale Selbstlade Pistole, or 'universal self-loading pistol,' as a semi-automatic sidearm for the U.S. Special Operations Command's Offensive Handgun Weapon System program."

Ceepak nods. "The hired hit man may be former military."

"Yeah," says Botzong. "Special Forces. Navy SEALS. Delta Force. Green Berets."

Great. We're up against every character ever played by Steven Seagal.

"Plus," says Botzong, "the Compact Tactical gives the shooter the features of the full-size USP USP45."

"Such as the mechanical recoil reduction system," adds Wilson. "But in a smaller, more concealable package."

"Facilitating the assassination technique you described to us earlier," Ceepak says to Wilson.

"Yeah. Your bad guy could hide this thing in a zippered pocket of his racing suit."

At four, Gus Davis and the SHPD officers running security up on Pier Two start letting lucky locals pass through the metal detectors to be the "live audience" for tonight's "Fun House Finale."

Around six-thirty, we pick up another piece of evidence.

Gladys has found a motorcycle parked behind her restaurant when she dragged a bushel of rotting bok choy out the back door: a Harley, up on its kickstand and blocking the sliding door to her compost bin.

When nobody in her dining room claimed the motorcycle, Gladys called 9-1-1 so we'd come tow it away. Bill Botzong and his CSI crew borrowed a flatbed wrecker from my buddy George Hansen over at Undertow Towing and hauled the hog back to the municipal garage.

Every VIN (Vehicle Identification Number) on it has been filed down, even the hidden ones.

"We are dealing with dedicated professionals," says Ceepak. "They, obviously, tracked Mr. Mandrake's movements. Knew he frequented Veggin' On The Beach. It would not surprise me if the shooter—tipped off by his accomplice surveilling activity up at the boardwalk—knew that Mandrake had exited the Green Zone. The gunman then parked behind the restaurant. While Mandrake was inside eating, the shooter strolled over to Shore Drive and took up his position at the intersection with the stop sign."

"He went for a walk in his helmet and flight suit?" I say.

"Doubtful. However, I suspect, if we search the homes near the intersection, several will have backyard shower stalls."

"No," I say. "A Port-A-Potty."

"Come again?"

"All summer they've been doing major renovations at that mansion on Shore Drive between Hickory and Gardenia. But they must've had problems with the permits, because I haven't seen any workers there for weeks. Just their Port-A-Potty in the carport."

"Which our shooter borrowed and used as a changing booth. Well done, Danny."

Hey, if your routine patrol includes cruising up and down that street at 15 MPH after guzzling a gallon of coffee, you're always looking for a potential pit stop.

At 7:30, the lawyer finally arrives.

"I need a minute with my client," Rambowski brusquely announces. Ceepak and I usher him and his three-thousand-dollar suit into the interview room.

"We'll be back in fifteen," Ceepak announces before relocking the door.

We head into the chief's office. Hey, it's close and it's empty. The rest of the station is crawling with Fibbies and U.S. Attorneys and who knows who else.

"Nice office," I say, and gesture at the chief's very comfy, very padded, high-back rolling chair. "Nice chair."

"You can take it, Danny. I prefer to stand."

"Nah. Come on. You could lean back, prop your feet up on the desk—"

Ceepak's personal cell phone interrupts me. I recognize the ringtone.

"Hello? No, Mom. We are not watching TV."

Hey, the chief has a flat-screen TV in his bookcase. It's tucked between a few Kiwanis Club plaques and a Hummel figurine of a cop shadowed by a guardian angel, the two of them helping a schoolkid cross a street. I snap on the TV. It's tuned to the network that runs *Fun House.* At 7:30, they run some kind of Entertainment News show.

"Danny has found the program," Ceepak says to his mom. "Yes, that's Sea Haven. Our beach."

The show is running a feature about "Brave Soozy K." They show her strolling along the pristine sandy beach at daybreak, looking very thoughtful in her dove-gray tracksuit as a pink dawn breaks in the east and foamy waves crash hypnotically behind her.

"I know there's a target on my back," Soozy says, *"but I won't back down. I've come too far on this journey. . . ."*

"Are you sure?" Ceepak says. "No, Mom, it's just that Rita and I—"

His mom talks some more.

"Well, then, it's all good. I'll tell Rita. She'll be thrilled to hear your decision. Don't worry, Mom. We will. Love you, too."

He folds up his phone.

"What's up?" I ask.

"My mother tells me she is tired of eating walleye and shoveling snow." He indicates the TV screen. "She has been watching the show ever since a few of her church friends told her I was the star."

Now I'm grinning.

"Anyway, having seen Sea Haven in all its 'sunny, funderful' glory, she wants to move here. Provided, of course, I remain on the police force. She doesn't like all the killings that seem to happen here."

"She's moving here? You're kidding!"

He holds his hand up like he's taking an oath. "Scout's honor."

"Awesome."

"My mother also instructed me not to let anything bad happen to that nice young girl tonight."

"Soozy?"

"Roger that. According to Mom, Ms. Kemppainen is, and I quote, 'quite a pistol.'"

Christopher Miller pokes his head in the door.

"What's up?" I say.

"Mandrake. The lawyer says they're ready to talk."

43

WE SHOULD HAVE SOLD TICKETS TO THIS INTERVIEW.

Every chair at the long table is filled: Ceepak, me, Chris Miller, Lisa Bonner, some guy from Washington who never takes off his sunglasses, three other extremely serious scowlers. Martin Mandrake sits at the head of the table. Ceepak is on his left; attorney Louis Rambowski is on his right.

The overflow crowd is in the observation room, watching us through the one-way mirror. Marty, the producer, is beaming, basking in his newfound role as The Government's Star Witness.

Ceepak depresses a button on our digital recorder.

"This is Officer John Ceepak. It is Friday, August 27th, 20-hundred hours."

Mandrake looks up at the ceiling, does the math in his head.

"It's eight?"

"Affirmative," says Ceepak.

"Jesus. I need to make a phone call."

"Excuse me?"

"The show. It goes live in an hour. I need to talk to my associates. Make some last-minute adjustments."

Ceepak purses his lips. "Mr. Mandrake, we have been quite accommodating—"

"No. All you've done is grant me my constitutional rights. But now I really *do* need a favor. It's for the good of the show, which means it's for the good of Sea Haven. I was supposed to do this bit at the open and close tonight. Show off the fifty-thousand-dollar cardboard check when Chip does the opening; hand the money to the winner's charity in wrap-up at the end. Now somebody else has to go on camera in my place. They've only got an hour for hair and makeup. Help me out here, fellas, or do I need to call Mayor Sinclair? I have his cell number."

The lawyer touches Mandrake on the sleeve. That's how lawyers tell clients to shut up.

"My client intends to be extremely cooperative with all of you this evening," says Rambowski, "should we, of course, come to terms on a quid pro quo agreement for his testimony against Roberto Lombardo, including a witness protection plan that might allow him to continue his creative efforts in the entertainment industry. We, therefore, request that you extend us the courtesy of making one last phone call before initiating our deliberations and discussion."

Ceepak glances over at Christopher Miller. Miller gives him the slow "go ahead, we've got all night" nod.

"Very well," says Ceepak. "Make your call, Mr. Mandrake, and please make it quick."

"I have to!" Mandrake says, stabbing his stubby finger into a poor defenseless cell phone button. "We go live in just over fifty minutes. . . ."

While he waits for somebody to answer, it hits me: Martin Mandrake could walk away from this whole deal with a free pass and a cabin in Utah. I check out the law enforcement agents seated around the table. Most of them could care less about Mandrake orchestrating the murders of Paul Braciole and Thomas Hess. They want the big walleye: mob boss Roberto Lombardo. Ceepak and me, the two local-yokel beat cops, are the only ones who care about avenging the deaths of those caught up in Mandrake's sick scheme to boost his show's ratings.

And maybe Chris Miller. He's seated across from me, eyes closed so he can massage them the way Ceepak massages his when life isn't quite as good as the T-shirts proclaim.

"Grace? Get me Layla. I don't care. I need to talk to her. Now. Find her." He covers up the mouthpiece on his phone. Tries to charm us with his twinkling eyes and elfin dimples. Of course, his sinister goatee and coal-black eyes sort of undercut all that. "Layla, where are you? Well, get your ass over to the makeup truck. You need to go on. The bit with the big check at the top and bottom. Work it out with Chip. After he announces the finalists, you come on with the moola boola. And don't ham it up too much, kid. Just look dignified. Put on a business suit. Leave a couple buttons undone up top. Smile. Millions of people are going to be watching.

"You're welcome. You earned it, hon. And, don't worry, I'll be back in the saddle soon. Me? I'm fine. The guy was a lousy shot. No, babe. I don't know why he wanted to shoot me. Look, sweetheart, I gotta run. Some people want to ask me a couple questions about this thing this afternoon. Go make yourself look prettier than you already do. Ciao."

He thumbs off the phone.

"For the record," he says, "that was Ms. Layla Shapiro, one of my associates on the set. And, yes, I call every lady under the age of thirty who works for me 'hon,' 'babe,' and 'sweetheart.' Sue me."

One of the FBI guys actually chuckles.

Half an hour later, Louis Rambowski is finally satisfied with the deal being offered to his client.

If, and only if, the information he provides leads to the "arrest and conviction" of reputed crime boss Roberto Lombardo, the county prosecutor's office will grant Martin Mandrake a full and unconditional pardon on all charges related to the murders of Paul Braciole and Thomas Hess.

"After all," the shyster argued, "Mr. Mandrake did not pull the trigger in either homicide." Then he waved his sparkling cuff-linked arm in Ceepak's general direction. "These officers are the ones you should be angry with, not my client. The police, in this instance, have not done their job; they have not apprehended the actual killers!"

"Louis?" said Miller, his voice calm, cool, and scary deep.

"Yeah?"

"Save it for the courtroom."

Rambowski held up his hands, pouted out his lips, gave us the classic tough-guy "I'm-just-saying" gesture.

Anyway, that slowed us down for like five minutes.

Now it's 8:50 P.M. and Martin Mandrake finally has the floor.

44

"SORRY THAT TOOK SO LONG," HE SAYS. "I WAS HOPING WE could wrap this up and watch the show when it goes out live."

Everybody glares at him. Nobody responds.

So I pipe up: "My cable box has a DVR. I'll catch it later."

"Okay," says Christopher Miller in his role as big daddy mediator, "the Sea Haven P.D. gets first crack at the witness because, as Mr. Rambowski indicated earlier, they're still trying to track down a killer."

"Killers," says Ceepak.

Mandrake and Rambowski arch up surprised eyebrows.

"The evidence we have gathered so far in our investigation leads us to believe that at least two hitmen were involved in both killings."

"I didn't ask for two," says Mandrake. "I swear. Bobby didn't charge for two, either. At least he didn't tell me I was paying double—"

"So you freely admit that you, Martin Mandrake, did contact the Lombardo crime family and knowingly engage their services for the murders of Paul Braciole and Thomas Hess?"

"Yeah, but, well—that's not how it works. Let me begin at the beginning, okay? I like to shoot craps. Is that a sin? Maybe. I'll ask a priest next time I go to confession. Anyway, the Lombardos lent me some money so I could keep playing down in A.C. Unfortunately, I kept losing and they kept wanting their money back—plus interest at a rate even Goldman Sachs couldn't get away with. But I had this bonus clause in my contract on *Fun House.* If I hit a certain ratings number, there'd be this unbelievably huge payday. Of course the target was set sky-high, so no way was I ever gonna cash in on it." He smiles at Ceepak. "Then you showed up."

"You're referring to my inadvertent entrance into your reality television program when you were videotaping me without my permission during my off-duty hours at the Skee-Ball arcade?"

Oooh. Sounds like Ceepak might hire Rambowski next so he can sue Prickly Pear Productions for invasion of privacy.

"Yeah," says Mandrake. "But we had signs posted saying by entering the Skee-Ball arcade, you waived your right to privacy."

"I did not see those."

Mandrake shrugs. "We post 'em every time we shoot in a public space. Cuts down the lawsuits. Anyway, that bit with Paulie where he threw the ball at your head and you arrested him? That was beautiful. We hype it all week long, it turns into must-see TV. All of a sudden, I am the Phoenix rising up from the ashes. I showed those fat bastards at the network. They said I was done. Marty The Old Farty is what they called me behind my back. I heard about it. I got ears all over the place!"

"So you decided to add more 'crime story' elements to your program?" says Ceepak, trying to get Mandrake back on track.

"Yeah. Actually, she doesn't know it, but that kid I was just talking to, Layla Shapiro, she gave me the idea when she was kidding around, pitching ideas like 'It's *Cops* meets *The Jersey Shore* meets *Survivor.*' But you see, Layla's just starting out, doesn't really know how to spin a high-concept notion like that and turn it into

TV gold. I do. I'm not saying anything against the kid. Give her time. She'll learn. But this was all me."

Geeze-o, man. Now that he has the potential of immunity from murder charges, Martin Mandrake is giving us a seminar on how to create a surefire hit on TV: hire a hit man!

Ceepak places the photographs we obtained from Axel the biker on the table.

"Is this Ms. Shapiro?"

"Yeah. I'd recognize that ass anywhere."

Icy silence.

Mandrake clears his throat. "That's her. Ms. Shapiro. She's making the drop."

"She is taking money to the Lombardo family?"

"Yeah. That's Atlantic City. Not too far from the bus depot."

"And you sent her down there twice?"

"Yeah. Once for Paul, once for the other guy. The druggy. Skeleton Man."

"His name was Thomas Hess. His street name was Skeletor."

"Skeleton, Skeletor. Same diff."

I glance at my watch. 9:02. In homes all across America, couch potatoes and Ceepak's mom have heard that Mike and Soozy are the finalists. Now they're probably watching the lovely Layla Shapiro holding up one of those gigantic cardboard checks like the Publishers Clearing House people tote around town in their prize van.

"Was Ms. Shapiro aware of your true reason for sending her down to Atlantic City twice with briefcases full of cash?" asks Ceepak.

"You mean, was she an accessory to the crime? That's what you guys call it, right?"

Ceepak just nods.

"No way. I kept her in the dark. This was just between Bobby and me. Layla thought she was just paying off my gambling debts."

"And did Mr. Lombardo give you any information as to the hired killer's identity?"

"Nope. The way it works, he won't even know who the final vendor is. They have a very elaborate system. This guy calls that guy who knows these guys and so on. Nobody with a vested interest can be implicated in the hit. And, once the ball gets rolling, you can't change your mind. Twenty-four hours before the hit, the shooters go dark. There is no way to abort the mission."

"So you gave Mr. Lombardo the 'go' signal one day prior to the actual murders?"

"No. I just didn't call him up and say 'I've changed my mind.'"

"You paid Mr. Lombardo in full?"

"Yeah."

"You repaid your gambling debts?"

"I'm free and clear. They even sent me a voucher for a suite upgrade should I want to, you know, visit one of their casino partners again, which, trust me, I'm not doing anytime soon, not after ratting Bobby out like this."

"Do you know of any reason why Mr. Lombardo now wants you dead? Why he sent the same hired hit man after you?"

"No. And when you guys nab the bastard, I want five minutes alone with him." He turns to his lawyer. "Can we work that into the deal, Lou?"

"You don't really want that, Martin," says Rambowski, crinkling up his face like his client is giving him gas.

All of a sudden, I hear a cell phone vibrating.

It's Ceepak's, the business line.

He checks his belt.

His eyes are glued to the caller screen.

"I need to take this," he says as the phone keeps grunting and groaning. "Danny?"

And we head out into the hall.

45

"It's Axel," says Ceepak, when we're both out in the corridor.

We duck into the chief's empty office. Close the door.

It's 9:07.

"This is Ceepak. Yes. I see. How firm is your intel? He's certain? Roger that. We're heading to the boardwalk now. Appreciate your following through like this."

Ceepak closes up his cell. Talks fast.

"Danny, we have a situation. We need to speak with Ms. Layla Shapiro, ASAP."

I just nod and tap the Glock at my hip to make sure it's still there.

Ceepak shoves open the door to the Interview Room. Doesn't actually enter. I hang behind him in the hall.

"Mr. Mandrake?"

"Yeah?"

"Where is Ms. Shapiro currently located?"

"Layla?" Mandrake checks his Rolex. "She should be back in the production trailer outside the Fun House. The bit with the big check was on the rundown for 9:02 to 9:03."

"Chris?" he says to Special Agent Miller.

"Yeah?"

"Danny and I need to be on the boardwalk. Pier Two. Now. I'll fill you in later."

"Copy that."

Ceepak turns to me. "Danny?"

We hustle up the hall, smash through that parking lot exit, run to our car.

"Siren and lights?" I ask as I crank the ignition.

"Roger that. Kill them once we initiate our final approach to boardwalk parking."

I squeal wheels and burn rubber. Every light on our roofbar is swirling like crazy. The siren is wailing.

"What's up?" I ask.

"Axel received a phone call from his mob contact, the driver, Mr. Accardi."

"And?"

"Certain members of the Lombardo crime family had gathered at their social club this evening to watch the *Fun House* finale."

Figures. They were, more or less, technical advisers for the show.

"Apparently, Mr. Accardi does not drive Mr. Lombardo on Mondays or Tuesdays. Another driver fills in for him. That driver was also at the social club tonight. When he saw Ms. Shapiro holding the charity check, he said it was 'the same chick who made the money drop' on Monday. Made the big deal with Bobby."

"So she went down there three times?"

"Right. Apparently, the third visit was as an independent agent."

"To take out a hit on her boss?"

"Such is my supposition."

"Why?"

"Perhaps to ensure that, in Mr. Mandrake's absence, she would take over as executive producer of the program when it is renewed for another year. I suspect Ms. Shapiro knew full well why Mr. Mandrake was sending her to Atlantic City. By terminating Mr. Mandrake, she assumed she would also terminate our investigation, ending our potential threat to the *Fun House* brand image and its viability as a network money-maker."

Geeze-o, man. I always heard that television was a cutthroat business, but this is ridiculous. Layla isn't clawing her way to the top; she's hiring mobsters to whack her way up the corporate ladder.

We make pretty good time to Pier Two. It's 9:22. We hop out of our cruiser and sprint through our own security blockade.

"Lock down this access point, Gus," Ceepak barks as we dash past security.

Up ahead, I can see lights illuminating the bright red clown lips at the Fun House entrance. They have the TV show sound pumping through speakers so the live audience gathered on the boardwalk can hear everything as they watch the show on six giant-screen TVs set up for their viewing pleasure.

I can hear the final guitar chords of "The '59 Sound," this rocking song by an amazing Jersey group that sounds a lot like the new Bruce Springsteen.

"All right, let's give it up for The Gaslight Anthem," booms Chip Dale, the show's host.

Great choice of bands, I think. "The '59 Sound" is all about "which song they're gonna play" when you die.

We're jogging toward a trailer parked right in front of Gabe Hess's All American Snack Shack, where all the chaser lights are still blinking. We head for the attached staircase at the back. One of those generic young crew guys in shorts, tool belt, and headset holds up a hand.

"Sorry. This is a restricted area—"

"Sea Haven P.D.," says Ceepak, flashing his badge and flipping up the holster strap over his Glock. I do the same. "Step aside, son."

The young dude does as he is told.

We charge up the steel steps.

Slam open another door.

The trailer is dark except where it's illuminated by red and green buttons or the jittery glow of TV monitors—the feeds from all the remote camera crews. Guys wearing headsets are sliding knobs, toggling switches, saying stuff like "Go to two" and "Three, tighten up" into their headsets. In the middle of the chaos, I see the director, Rutger Reinhertz. He's waving his hands like he's an orchestra conductor.

"And take three. Cue Chip."

On the screens I see Chip Dale with Mike Tomasino. Mike's going into the Fun House first with a representative from his charity, a guy holding on to a dog leash attached to a very noble-looking German shepherd.

"Can we take Rex the rescue dog with us?" asks Mike as the puppy cradled in his arms licks his face. The crowd on the boardwalk oohs and aaahs.

"Sorry, Mike. The dog stays out here. It's just you and Dave against the clock. Soozy and Becca will tackle the obstacle course immediately after you. Now, the team with the best time. . . ."

While Chip explains the rules of the mad dash through the Fun House, I hear Layla before I see her.

"Unit three? Unit three? Where's my fucking smoke, Jimbo?"

Jimbo's voice leaks out of a tinny speaker set into the slanted panel in front of Layla. She's dressed in a tight-fitting suit that hugs all her curves and still has the three top buttons open on her blouse so everybody can get a peek at Victoria's secret.

"Jimbo? Where the fuck is my smoke?"

"Where's my fucking grip?" Jimbo slams back. *"I got lights, sound, no special effects."*

"I gave you a fucking grip!"

"You gave me a fucking P.A. and he's fucking A.W.O.L.!"

I nudge Ceepak. Point out Layla.

"We need smoke in the black-light mirror maze or it just looks like a bad Jimi Hendrix poster," she screams. "Someone find that fucking grip. Which one is it, Jimbo?"

"That doofus Sean. Wears a fucking ski cap in the middle of summer, doesn't know his ass from a half-apple. . . ."

"Sharon?" This from Layla.

"Yeah?" says Layla's underling/producer-wannabe.

"Find Sean. Send him in the back door with his smoke box. And remind me to fire his union ass after we wrap."

"On it," shouts Sharon as she bolts out the trailer door.

Ceepak and I are standing right behind Layla now. Ceepak taps her on the shoulder.

Layla spins around. "What?" Now she sees who we are. "What the . . . how the hell . . . this is a closed set. . . ."

"Outside," says Ceepak. "Now."

"You're kidding, right?"

"No. Now." He takes hold of her arm.

She pulls back. "Don't you fucking touch me!"

People are staring now. I glance up at the main monitor.

They're running commercials. Of course they wouldn't send Mike into the Fun House without teasing it first and saying he's going in—*right after the break*. Everybody in the control room has two or three free minutes to rubberneck the excitement in the back of the trailer.

"Fine," says Ceepak, "we'll do this here." He spies a gooseneck lamp attached to the top of the slanted console in front of Layla. He snaps it on. Aims it at Layla, who recoils under the harsh light.

Before she has a chance to speak, Ceepak unloads on her.

"We know you went to Atlantic City on Monday and made your own side deal with the Lombardo family."

Layla should never play poker. She has a tell—a little facial tic that gives away her whole hand. It's small, but it's there: a nervous twitch in her left cheek.

"That's bullshit."

"We suspect you are the one who engineered today's attempted hit on Martin Mandrake."

"Bullshit."

"That you, somehow, amassed enough funds to hire the same killers Mandrake hired to murder Paul Braciole and Thomas Hess."

Layla glances around the control room. Everybody is staring at her. Listening to Ceepak.

"People?" she pronounces. "Focus. We're back in sixty seconds."

Some of the eyes swing back to their blinking buttons. A lot don't.

"Officers," she says, "perhaps we *should* step outside. Let my crew do their jobs?"

Ceepak practically yanks her up out the chair. People move faster when propelled by Ceepakian fury.

We head out the door. Gus Davis, Alex Smitten, and a couple SHPD troops are waiting for us at the bottom of the staircase.

"Everything okay, Chief?" Gus asks.

"We need a secure location," says Ceepak. "Two armed guards."

Gus gestures toward the All American Snack Shack. "The owner finally went home when the hippies started in with the rock and roll."

Ceepak hustles Layla into the booth.

Officers Forbus and Bonanni follow after us. Both have their service weapons out of their holsters.

"Sit," says Ceepak, indicating a batter-splattered stool.

"Okay, Mike, Dave," we hear Chip Dale boom over the loudspeakers because it's after the break. *"On your mark, get set, go! The first obstacle is the maze of mirrors. . . ."*

Layla squirms on her stool. "I really need to be—"

"Would you like an attorney?" says Ceepak.

"What? Why would I want an attorney?"

"Because, Ms. Shapiro, as I stated previously, you are a suspect in a murder for hire."

"And why would I want to kill Marty The Old Farty?"

"That's a good question," I answer because I don't like her smirk. "Especially since Mandrake gave you partial credit for coming up with the True Crime angle for the show."

Now both cheeks quiver into a sickly smile.

"Partial?" she says, sounding like I just insulted her.

"Yeah. He says you saying 'it's *Cops* meets *Jersey Shore* meets *Snuff Movie*' gave him the idea to spice things up with a couple murders."

"I can't believe this shit." Now her whole face is one twingey, twitchy tell. Her nostrils rabbit open and shut like crazy. Her pupils dilate. "How is Martin The Hack Mandrake even alive, let alone spreading fucking lies like that? Does he have a TV in the cave where he's hiding from Bobby Lombardo?"

"Yeah," I say.

"Wonderful," says Layla with a self-satisfied smile. "Tell him to stay tuned for my big finish. Maybe he can try to pretend *that* was his fucking idea, too."

"And what, exactly, are you planning for the finish, Ms. Shapiro?" asks Ceepak.

"Something biblical," she says, her eyes bugging out of her skull. "The slaughter of an innocent!"

46

When I first met Layla Shapiro, back in June at the Rolling Thunder, I thought she was ballsy and brave.

She kicked a psycho killer's shotgun across the floor to me so I could take the bad guy down.

Now I realize she wasn't being brave.

She's just crazy. Whacked. Insane. All of the above.

She looks extremely ghoulish, lit up by the blinking red, white, and blue tracer lights trimming the deep-fried candy stand. They dance across her twisted features like a hundred flickering ghost-story flashlights.

"Is someone else going to be killed tonight?" asks Ceepak.

"Of course," says Layla with a grade school giggle. "But not until the very last minute. You have to draw out the suspense, never take your audience where they want to go right away, and always give yourself just enough time for a tidy denouement that will leave them breathlessly anticipating next year's show. This is what I promised my new business partners."

"The Lombardo family?"

Another grade school giggle. "You don't think I could actually scrape together one million dollars to take out Marty, do you, Officer Ceepak? So I made Mr. Lombardo a very sweet deal. A sixty-forty split. He gets the sixty, I get the forty and full producer credits, of course. I take over Prickly Pear . . . we're talking about a whole slate of new shows. . . ."

"Danny, we need to shut this down."

"No," says Layla. "Don't be an idiot, Officer Ceepak. If you in any way interfere with my storyline, a lot of people will die. I gave very specific instructions. If there is any deviation from the script, the shooters are to use their weapons and explosives and whatever else they brought with them to take out as many civilians as they can to give me my thrilling conclusion without getting caught, because these sorts of people never get caught."

"All right," I hear Chip Dale's voice over the outdoor speakers.

"If you tamper with my narrative," says Layla, "trust me: they will retaliate."

"Mike and Dave are upstairs in the second mirror maze, battling the baffling black lights."

"But no fucking smoke," mumbles Layla, more interested in her upside-down, hall-of-mirrors reality than what's happening out here in real reality.

"The tumbling tunnel slowed them down a little. . . ."

"Who are your shooters?" asks Ceepak.

Layla shrugs. "I don't know. Nobody knows. Not even Bobby Lombardo. It's all very hush-hush."

Ceepak glances at his watch.

"When is the big finish?"

"Ha! Even I don't know that, which makes it even more exciting, don't you think? It'll be raw and real. A total surprise. Sort of like when Jack Ruby shot Lee Harvey Oswald. Talk about a historic live-TV moment. Nobody saw that one coming."

"So, ladies, think you can beat Mike and Dave's time? You ready to rock, Soozy?"

"You bet!"

"I just asked for a death between nine fifty and nine fifty-five. Before we cut to the final commercial pod. I have a feeling the network will stay live when we hit ten. Push back the rest of their lineup. This is going to be so fucking huge, they'd be idiots if they just tossed to the local news. . . ."

I glance at my watch. It's nine-freaking-forty.

"I wish I could be more specific about the timing, but I wanted to build in some flexibility. After all, the two players are artists. They can't be boxed in."

Ceepak shoots me a glance. Holds up two fingers.

Layla has confirmed our suspicions and narrowed down our list of targets.

"Becca? You ready to win some money for SPF?"

"Let's do it, Chip!"

"Okay. You two are going in . . . right after the break!"

"Who do you intend to kill next?"

"Who do you think?" says Layla with a perverted playfulness.

"Soozy?" I say.

Layla laughs. "And that's why you'll never be anything but a flatfoot cop in cargo shorts, Officer Boyle. Do you know how hard it is to get a job in television or any of the glamour professions? How impossible it is for someone in their *twenties* to become an *executive producer* on the number one hit show in the country? I had to be smarter and hungrier than every other wolf in the pack. I don't have the luxury of being a slow-witted idiot like you. No, Danny. We do not kill Soozy. We *need* Soozy. Next season. Her character arc is vital to. . . ."

Geeze-o, man.

It's Becca.

47

"BOSS?" I SAY TO CEEPAK BECAUSE I'LL BE DAMNED IF I'M going to spend the last ten minutes of Becca's life listening to this cuckoo bird bragging about how freaking smart she is.

"Forbus? Bonanni?" Ceepak barks to our backups. "Run her in."

"What?" Layla protests. "If you think I'm leaving before—"

I may not have mentioned it, but Officer Nikki Bonanni won this New Jersey state female bodybuilding championship last winter. She deadlifts Layla off that stool with one hand while Forbus works on the FlexiCuffs. They have Layla hogtied in like five seconds.

"You try to stop me, you'll start a bloodbath!"

Fortunately, the commercials blasting through the outdoor speakers are so loud, they drown her out. Forbus and Bonanni hoist Layla Shapiro between them and start jogging toward the dump-truck end of the pier. Layla's kicking and screaming the whole way, but no one can hear her over the Coors beer song.

"I worked inside the Fun House one summer," I say to Ceepak. "There's an employee's entrance around back."

"Can we access it without crossing a camera's field of vision?"

"Yeah."

Ceepak slips his Glock out of its holster. I do the same.

He gives me the hand-chop "go" signal.

Hunkered down, we trot around the production trailer, move swiftly but quietly behind the cheering crowd.

"All right, Soozy and Becca," I hear Chip Dale. *"Give me a new clock. On your mark, get set . . . go!"*

More cheers.

Becca is following Soozy into the killing zone.

Ceepak and I head into the shadows offered by the line of shuttered arcades across from the brightly lit Fun House. I do a hand chop to the left and we loop around the slide exit just as Mike and his partner Dave zoom down to the finish line. The halogen lamp illuminating them is so blazingly bright, it keeps us hidden in the darkness fifteen feet away.

"Okay, that's the time to beat. . . ."

I push open a gate to a service road, a strip of potholed asphalt just wide enough for a delivery truck to squeeze through. I have my gun up now in both hands as we dash past dumpsters and abandoned golf carts and storage tanks and all the functional crap amusement parks keep hidden from public view. The "employees only" entrance to the Fun House is dead ahead.

"Danny?" This from Ceepak, behind me. "Down."

I duck behind a dumpster.

Ceepak points to his eyes with two fingers, swings them around to face the door we were running toward.

Now I see the guy Ceepak already saw. The man turns around and his face is illuminated by the soft glow of a handheld device of some sort. Maybe an iPod. Maybe the world's tiniest TV. He's clearly watching the *Fun House* telecast, keeping an eye out for any trouble.

My eyes adjust to the darkness.

I can see that the guy is wearing a wet suit and flippers. At his feet is a duffel bag and two scuba tanks. On his hip, that H&K USP .45.

"That's most likely the Mandrake shooter," whispers Ceepak.

I nod. It makes sense. When the hit went bad, he ran back to his Port-A-Potty and changed into his wet suit. A lot of surfers wear them. Then he scuba-dived up to the boardwalk, swam a mile and more under water so he could gain access to the pier with a bag full of weapons. He knew we'd have metal detectors and heavy security out front, so he climbed the pilings with his gear slung over his shoulder, came in via the water route.

"I could take him," I say because, yes, I am that good with my Glock.

"Negative," says Ceepak. Now he taps his ear and I look back to the scuba commando, who maybe used to be a Navy S.E.A.L. He's wearing a military communications device. Earpiece. Microphone rigged up to his mouth. He taps his chest to activate it.

"Seven minutes," we hear him whisper. "Roger that. Execute and extricate."

I turn to Ceepak. His eyes are narrow slits. Mine are about to explode with panic.

Seven minutes till they kill Becca?

"Do you still know your way through the Fun House?" Ceepak asks.

"Yeah."

"Then you need to be the one to go in."

I nod. He's right.

"Grab some camera gear if you can. Act like you're a crew member."

That'll work. I'm already dressed like one.

"I'll cover this shooter and take him out the instant you take down the player inside."

Again I nod. If he shoots this bad guy before I nail the one inside, Becca dies when scuba man stops communicating the countdown.

"Six minutes thirty seconds," we hear the guy say with ice in his voice.

Ceepak gives me the sharpest hand chop he has ever given me.

I'm up.

Moving on tiptoe. Fast.

Back up the alley. To the gate. Around to the front of the Fun House.

I see bundles of cable piled in a rolling bin. Grab one.

I move even faster, make for the big clown-mouth entrance. And—BOOM!—it hits me.

The guy inside is Sean, the grip in the knit cap who didn't know what a half-apple was. It has to be. Like Layla said, TV production jobs are hard to come by. You don't get on a union crew without knowing basic crap like what the hell a half-apple is—unless maybe the people who really hired you have ways of pulling strings to get you into any place you need to be.

It's how Sean made it past security tonight: he had a bright orange crew badge. And his teammate out back stowed his weapons for him in a prearranged drop zone, or maybe they met up out in the alley. That would explain why Jimbo didn't have his smoke machine upstairs in the second maze. Why Sean, his P.A., was A.W.O.L.

Sean would also have been with Jimbo's crew at Big Kahuna's when Paulie left with Mandy. He could have alerted his partner, the outside guy, the man on the motorcycle. Sean didn't stick with Jimbo's crew when they tailed Mandy and Paulie. He peeled off, met up with his partner.

Together, they did Paulie in Mandy's Mustang.

Now he's going to kill Becca.

48

I RUN INTO THE FIRST MAZE AND SEE A DOZEN ME'S REFLECTED back in brightly lit silver-framed mirrors.

The passageways are tight.

I drop the stupid coil of wire.

I'm in. Nobody cares who I am or what I'm doing, because the live TV feed is coming from further up ahead, the two camera crews attached to Soozy and Becca, maybe the one with Mike and Dave, breathlessly waiting to see how quickly their competitors complete the course.

Fortunately, when we worked here, Jess and I used to play "mice in the maze." First guy to reach the end didn't win a chunk of cheese, just an after-work beer at the Frosty Mug.

Up ahead, I hear laughter and squeals. The happy kind. Soozy and Becca. They might be on the second floor already. Maybe in the area called The Side Show. Audio-animatronic mannequins in a bathtub crack corny jokes as you wander past them in the dark. A clown dummy cackles at you.

I enter a black-lit hallway decorated with glowing clown faces and whirling swirls. Next comes a rolling tunnel, The Barrel Of Laughs. It's like walking through a psychedelic toilet-paper tube with a spinning clown face at the far end to make you queasy.

"Fuck me. Another maze?" I hear Soozy shout.

Becca giggles. "Come on, girl. We can win this thing!"

I step out of the rolling corridor and onto the oscillating floor where we used to blast air up pretty girls' skirts.

Next I'm in the hall of mirrors. The frames are clown faces. Their wide-open mouths distort my reflection. First I'm fat, then I'm stretched thin, now I've got a huge head and very little body, next my chest balloons up to the size of an elephant's.

I don't bother checking my watch.

I'm sure there's less than two minutes left.

I need to keep moving forward.

I climb the undulating stairs. They're split down the middle. One side rocks up while the other rocks down. It's like a spastic escalator.

Now I'm in the side show with the dummies cracking corny jokes. I move past them fast and step onto a spinning disc that'll make you all kinds of dizzy because you see a dozen reflections bouncing back at you.

I've reached the entrance to the second maze of mirrors.

The frames up here are painted colors that radiate bright pinks, purples, and greens under the influence of ultraviolet light.

My reflection moves forward.

No. Wait. That's not me.

I'm not wearing a knit cap.

49

Knit cap has his compact semi-automatic up in a two-handed grip.

I do the same with my Glock.

Sixteen images of him creep forward.

I don't know which one is really him, which ones are his reflection.

I inch ahead, match him step for step.

Now the killer repeats to infinity. His reflection is reflected back so many times, it looks like a receding mineshaft full of shooters. I notice he has a communicator headset, the same as the backdoor lookout's, strapped on underneath his ski cap.

A new image flickers off a mirror.

A blazingly bright light.

From the camera crew. It swings into a full-filament burn and bounces off the mirrors all around me. I am momentarily blinded.

I blink. Try to clear the floating sunspots singed into my retina.

Becca and Soozy jitter into view on half of the endless array of glass panels surrounding me. The shooter is still in the other half. He's aiming left and right and straight at me. The girls keep moving, bumping into mirrored walls, feeling their way in the dark.

Knit cap keeps following them, moving stealthily. He is a killer cat. A never-ending column of death.

The effervescent mirror frames glow under the black light.

So do the killer's teeth. Bright white. He's smiling like a shark.

And I don't dare take the shot because I have no idea which image is real, which is a reflection. I'm trapped inside a crazy kaleidoscope of killers.

Now the shooter's white teeth move. I read his lips: *Roger that.*

He pivots to take his shot.

His orange I.D. badge glows under the ultraviolet lights.

Big block letters all around me spell out: **W Ǝ Я Ɔ**

And in one flat space: **C R E W.**

That's the panel I target.

I don't have time to try something cute, like shooting the weapon out of his hands.

I aim for his chest. The floating I.D. badge.

My Glock explodes. The cramped maze reverberates. Glass shatters as the bullet rips through knit cap's chest and cracks open the mirror behind him.

The impact spins him around. He drops to one knee.

Becca and Soozy are screaming. Their camera crew is panicking. They drop their handheld light. The tungsten filament sizzles and sputters out. I hear stampeding feet as the hit man raises his weapon.

He sees me. Maybe my reflection.

His chest wound oozing DayGlo red, he squeezes off a round. A mirror to my right explodes.

I fire again.

He won't be able to.

He flies backward into a sheet of silver glass that crackles into a spider web of slivers.

He is dead.

I glance at my watch.

It's 9:54:30.

I just gave Layla Shapiro her big ending.

50

Turns out that the instant Ceepak heard me fire that first round, he took down the backdoor dude with a single bullet to his left kneecap.

"I had several minutes to line up the shot," he tells me. "You, Danny, did not."

They haul scuba man to the hospital.

I tremble.

I've killed yet another human being. Make that two indelible ink spots on my immortal soul. My chances of skating into heaven grow slimmer and slimmer the longer I stay on the job. Pretty soon I'll be a camel facing the eye of a needle, and not because I'm rich.

Of course Becca Adkinson hugged me and kissed me when she found out I was the one who had taken down the bad guy who'd had his sights set on her.

Then Soozy K bopped over and made a big show of planting wet sloppy kisses all over my face because Jimbo and his crew had found a fresh camera light and were shooting us live for the network and local news feeds.

I thanked Soozy and went back to Becca, who needed a blanket. She was shivering in her bikini, never the best costume to be wearing when you have that much adrenaline coursing through your veins.

"When did you become this awesome?" Becca asked me, realizing, maybe for the first time, that I'm no longer the kid who used to swing with her upside down on the monkey bars back at Holy Innocents Elementary. "You totally saved my life, Danny Boy."

I tried to shrug off the compliment. "We're pals. You would have done the same thing for me."

"Nuh-unh. I hate guns. They're so freaking loud!"

On Monday morning, after my big weekend of fame and doing TV interviews, I went to work and discovered I had a brand-new boss.

Because this time, when they offered him the full-time police chief job, Ceepak took it.

Seems he needs the pay bump so he and Rita can buy a house with what they call a mother-in-law apartment. Mrs. Ceepak—my partner's mom, not Rita—is moving to Sea Haven "right after Halloween." Guess she wants to see the Ohio trick-or-treaters one last time. Drop a big ol' slab of walleye candy in their bags.

Roberto Lombardo goes to trial next spring. He is currently being held without bail in a jail somewhere with lots of barbed wire and guards.

Layla Shapiro is undergoing psychiatric evaluation to see if she is mentally fit to stand trial. If not, they'll just keep her locked up in a hospital ward for the rest of her life. She'll be able to watch TV all day, every day.

Martin Mandrake has disappeared into the Federal Witness Protection Program. But if you start hearing about plans for a reality

TV Series based in, say, Wyoming, Utah, North Dakota, chances are it'll be another Marty The Old Farty production.

Oh, and here's the best news about the coming off-season down the shore: Becca's dad is officially running for mayor. After the shootout in the Fun House, when his daughter nearly died because of the grubby deal Hugh Sinclair made with even grubbier TV people, Mr. A. pulled out that clipboard and got double the number of signatures he needed.

Come the first Tuesday in November, Mayor Hugh Sinclair will be just like the star of that other reality TV series: *America's Biggest Loser.*

Which is a good thing.

We need to clean this place up.

Throw out the trash.

Air out our dirty laundry.

Quit sweeping stuff under the rug.

Because, like I said, Ceepak's mom is coming to town.

Thank You

First, to Tory Brady and Sherri Bunting who, in 2010, both sent me e-mails about the real Officer Daniel R. Boyle. Here is what Ms. Bunting wrote:

"A friend wanted me to contact you about your Ceepak mysteries. Seems you use the name Danny Boyle as one of the police and her brother was an officer with Philadelphia police department until his untimely death in 1991. Her mother just picked up the first two books and has ordered a few more. Seeing just his name in print brings a kind of joy to their hearts. To see them this happy over such an odd coincidence is beyond words. I just wanted to thank you for the stroke of karma that made you choose his name. Also, our Danny Boyle attended Holy Innocents School. Weird. Sending a link for you to the fallen officers page. Again thanks for putting a smile on their faces!"

If you visit his Fallen Officer page (http://www.odmp.org/officer/176-police-officer-daniel-r.-boyle), you'll learn that the real Officer Boyle, age 21, succumbed to a gunshot wound sustained after stopping a stolen car. Officer Boyle had served with the Philadelphia Police Department for one year. His "End of Watch" was February 6, 1991.

I'd also like to thank Chief Michael Bradley of the Long Beach Island, New Jersey Police Department, who not only serves his community so well but also acts as my police procedure technical adviser.

As always, I'd like to thank my wife, J.J. Myers, who has been the first reader of every book I have ever written and is the world's best (not to mention best-looking) editor.

To my agent Eric, Claiborne & Jessica at Pegasus Books, and all the readers who have faithfully followed Danny and Ceepak since they first climbed aboard the *Tilt A Whirl* seven books ago, back in 2005.

Thanks!